Winning Lana

A NOVEL

Winning Lana

A NOVEL

JANICE WILLIAMS

Primix Publishing
11620 Wilshire Blvd
Suite 900, West Wilshire Center, Los Angeles, CA, 90025
www.primixpublishing.com
Phone: 1-800-538-5788

Published by Primix Publishing   02/10/2022

ISBN: 978-1-955177-82-5(sc)
ISBN: 978-1-955177-83-2(e)

Library of Congress Control Number: 2021925802

Contents

Chapter One

Running upstairs to her bedroom closet, Lana could feel her heart racing. Glancing at her watch, she panicked. There wasn't much time to gather her belongings. Frantically ripping her clothes from their hangers, she threw her sparse wardrobe into a suitcase. Blake would be home in less than an hour, giving her just the time she needed to make her escape. Staring at her swollen, black eye in the mirror, it reflected the abusive relationship she had endured for the past two years. Lana's gorgeous profile now revealed scars that were both physical and mental. However, today was the day. She was finally leaving Blake and the sprawling beach house.

Grabbing the keys to her vintage Volkswagen Beetle, Lana decided to leave the new Mercedes convertible Blake had given her on her twenty-first birthday in the garage. She wanted no attachment to him.

Menacing dark clouds swirled overhead as Lana sprinted up the long, narrow drive toward her parked car. Quickly tossing her only piece of luggage inside, she looked back for the last time. Watching seagulls soar freely and unafraid above the angry waves seemed cathartic. She was, at last, after two long years of being trapped in a cruel, intolerable relationship, leaving her hometown, Newport, Oregon. But, more importantly, she was escaping the grasp of an unstable man.

Reaching for her cell phone, Lana called the only person to understand her reasons for leaving. Megan answered on the first ring.

"Hey, Honey, how are you?"

"Megan, I've finally left Blake. I was wondering if I could stay with you for a while."

"Yes. Of course. It's about time. Blake doesn't deserve you. I'll leave a key under the doormat if I'm not home. Oh, and Caesars Palace is hiring cocktail servers, so don't worry about finding a job. With your looks, you won't have a problem."

"Thanks. We'll talk when I arrive. I've just entered Highway 101, and I plan to drive straight through the night. It'll help clear my head and give me time to consider my options."

"I'm not sure that's a smart idea, but drink lots of coffee. Drive safe. See you tomorrow."

Lana and Megan were best friends. They had known each other since grade school. Megan was two years older than Lana, and after graduating from high school, she had moved to Las Vegas with her boyfriend. After their short relationship ended and against her parents' advice, Megan decided to stay in Vegas and not return to Newport. She'd quickly fallen in love with the unique excitement and glitz that Vegas offered. Megan easily made enough money to support herself by taking a job as a showgirl at the Luxor Hotel. Aware of the abusive relationship that Lana tolerated with Blake, Megan had begged Lana for more than a year to leave and move to Vegas. Finally, it appeared Megan would, at last, get her wish.

After graduating from Newport High in June 2011, Lana Harris was doomed to the fate of taking the first job available. There were no provisions for her continued education. Lana was young and naive, applying for a secretarial position at Boswell Realty, Newport's largest real estate agency. Her stunning, sculpted profile quickly caught the owner's attention. Blake Boswell hired her without prior experience. It was apparent her tall, curvy figure, long auburn curls, and azure blue eyes were the only qualifications needed. Lana was immediately employed to fill the position when a young woman quit without notice.

Blake Boswell, at their first meeting, appeared distinguished and debonair. His steel-blue eyes, jet black hair, and athletic physique gave him a demanding presence. In his early thirties, Blake graduated from the prestigious Harvard Business School and came from a family of significant wealth. Lana remembered their first meeting in his office and felt drawn to him like a magnet. He exuded an air of confidence and masculinity. Charmed by his appearance and intellect, Lana quickly found herself falling in love with Blake, and at his insistence, she agreed to move in with him. Unfortunately, she could never have known Blake's degree of control and manipulation over those around him. The past two years of her life had been a living nightmare.

Entering Highway 101, Lana looked back in her rear-view mirror. She gave no thought to leaving her family or informing them of her plans. She had never felt close to her parents, and being the middle child of ten, she assumed she would never be missed. Her childhood had been difficult. Her father, Roger Harris, operated a small fleet of fishing boats. Out at sea for long periods, he could usually be found drinking at the local tavern when he was home. Her mother, Nancy Harris, had spent her entire life busily raising her large family and working part-time as a hotel maid. Nancy's gorgeous profile reflected the appearance of someone whose life had been difficult and stressful. After years of constant worry, her once flawless complexion was now inundated with wrinkles. Fortunately, Lana inherited her mother's elegant, much younger appearance. It was the only visible connection to her family.

Driving through the night, Lana turned up the volume on the radio and rolled down her car window. Hopefully, the invigorating fresh air would keep her awake. Suddenly, a blanket of dense fog rolled over Highway 101, obstructing her view. Even though it was the middle of September, the weather often changed quickly along the scenic coastal highway. Reaching San Francisco, Lana decided to move inland and over to Interstate 5, where the driving conditions would be more favorable.

Driving across the Golden Gate Bridge, Lana admired the beauty of the City by the Bay at night.

Lana felt free singing along with the lyrics of *Since You've Been Gone* by Kelly Clarkson, which blared from her car radio. However, she couldn't escape the haunting memories of abuse. Why had it taken her so long to gather up the courage to leave Blake and their violent relationship? Quickly dismissing the ugly thoughts from her mind, it no longer mattered. She was finally out of his grasps and free, or so she thought.

After hours of driving, stopping for gas and snacks, Lana reached Los Angeles. The next exit, Interstate 15, was the last stretch of desolate highway remaining before she arrived at her final destination, Las Vegas. Deciding to continue her grueling journey, she pushed on. Lana wanted to put as much distance as possible between herself and Blake.

As Lana crossed the Nevada state line, the sun's early morning rays peeped over the horizon, painting the sky in bright hues of orange and pink. Finally, her long, arduous trip was almost over. Making a quick stop for coffee, Lana wanted to be fully awake when she arrived at Megan's apartment. Then, there would be time for sleep later.

Slowly sipping hot coffee, Lana once again entered the freeway. Thoughts regarding a new life excited her. Once more adjusting the volume on her car radio, Lana felt the exhilaration of starting over.

Finally, after twelve hours of relentless driving, the sprawling Vegas skyline came into view. Lana held her breath. The sun glistened off the giant neon sign, *Welcome to Fabulous Las Vegas, Nevada.*

Chapter Two

McGrath, Alaska, a small village near the Kuskokwim River, was now home to Eric Kolbeck. McGrath seemed the ideal place to relocate and start a small business with a population of less than five hundred. Recently retired after twenty years as a U.S. Marine, which included three tours in the Middle East, Eric found the idea of moving to Alaska intriguing. Now in his early forties, single and unattached, there was nothing to stop the young retired officer from pursuing his dream of becoming a Bush pilot. Flying AH-1W Super Cobra's during his service in the Marines, Eric loved flying. He obtained his FAA Certified Flight Instructor Certification on fixed-wing aircraft at Emory Riddle University. Being adventurous and an avid hunter, Alaska was the ideal place for Eric to retire and continue his love of flying.

Taking his life savings, Eric purchased a small, dilapidated cabin close to the Kuskokwim River and financed a used Aviat Husky A-1C Aircraft. Even though the plane needed minor repairs, it was considered an excellent aircraft for the rugged terrains of Alaska. Eric knew that he could easily have it in the air and provide an income within a short time. Needing transportation, Eric purchased a used four-wheel-drive jeep from a local tavern owner, Bill Tillman. Eric's quick transition to Alaska appeared to be going smoothly.

Turning his attention to the cabin, Eric noted that it would require some much-needed repairs before the harsh winter arrived. Two broken windows and leaks in the roof needed his immediate attention. But, considering himself to be a jack of all trades, Eric knew his proficient skills would quickly get the job done. Purchasing the small one-bedroom cabin for only fifty-thousand dollars, Eric figured the inconvenience of the repairs was indeed worth the cost he had paid for the property.

Dressed in a light blue plaid shirt, denim jeans, and boots, Eric grabbed the keys to his jeep. In his early forties, Eric looked young. His physique effortlessly portrayed the image of a former Marine. Tall, muscular, with tapered brown hair and piercing blue eyes, his handsome, rugged appearance seemed fitting for someone choosing to live in the harsh topography of Alaska. Driving into McGrath, Eric decided to replace the broken windows and pick up roofing materials. After stopping by the local hardware store, he felt the need for a cold beer. Making a pit stop by Tillmans Tavern, Eric walked inside, taking a seat at the bar.

"What can I get you?" the stout bartender asked.

"I'll have a Coors Light."

"Aren't you the guy who bought Bill's Jeep?"

"Yes. It looks like news travels fast around here. I just bought the small cabin near the river from the Browns. I guess Alaska and the cold winters finally got to them. By the way, I'm Eric Kolbeck. Nice to meet you."

"Well, Eric, nice to make your acquaintance. I'm Norman Price, a friend of Bill's. We've been running this bar for longer than I care to remember. Yeah, you would be right about McGrath. It's a small place. I think our tough winters were a little too extreme for the Browns, even though they were really nice people. Usually, the only new faces we see around these parts are tourists who fly up to bag some game," Bill remarked as he continued drying pint glasses.

"Speaking of tourists, that reminds me, would you happen to know anyone in the local area who has an FAA Airframe and Powerplant License to repair aircraft? I just bought an Aviat Husky. I'm starting a new venture, and I don't need any down days."

"I think the guy you could be looking for is Gunner Gaffey. He's well known around these parts for keeping Bush pilots in the air. However, he stays pretty busy, and I must warn you his reputation precedes him. Don't get me wrong. No one knows aircraft better than Gunner. He's definitely the best aircraft mechanic in McGrath, but he's not sober half the time, and he has a beast of a temper. He's cleared more tables in this bar than I have if you catch my drift. Gunnar certainly doesn't back down from a fight. However, I think he's your man if you can tolerate his bad habits."

"Well, he does sound a bit intimidating, but if he knows aircraft as well as you say, then I think he's just the man I'm looking for. Here's my number; tell him to give me a call."

After downing a few beers, Eric called it a night and drove back to the cabin. Tomorrow, he would get started on the repairs. It was early September giving him a short reprieve to fix the window and roof before the severe winter set in.

Waking to the sound of his phone the following morning, Eric was surprised to see the incoming call was from Gunner. It appeared news traveled fast around these parts. After a brief conversation, Gunner agreed to meet Eric at the airport. Perhaps, Gunner would be willing to take on the extra maintenance.

Quickly getting dressed, Eric put on a pair of worn denim jeans and a warm cable knit sweater. After brewing a pot of coffee, he fried several pieces of bacon and scrambled a few eggs. Pouring himself a cup of coffee, he sat down at the small kitchen table. The intoxicating aroma of fried bacon filled the tiny, primitive kitchen. Cooking on a wood stove presented no problems for the retired Marine. Eric's survival skills and training had undoubtedly prepared him for the meager existence of living in a cramped, rural cabin. Glancing down at his watch, he realized that he had just enough time to clean up.

Driving out to the airport, Eric questioned his decision of even meeting with Gunner. His reputation didn't seem conducive to a skilled aircraft mechanic. Nonetheless, he was desperate and time was money. He couldn't afford downtime due to maintenance problems. Maybe there was more to the man than his reputation. Norman had vouched for his experiences and valuable knowledge of aircraft. McGrath was a small outpost, and it was evident the town lacked certified A & P mechanics. Beggars couldn't be choosers, he thought. Maybe after meeting Gunner, his opinions would be more favorable.

Arriving at the airport, Eric parked his jeep. Noticing a tall, burly man with red hair and a long scruffy beard walking around the wings of his plane, he wondered if the older gentleman was possibly Gunner. Wearing a pair of worn denim overalls, the old guy didn't portray someone who might have extensive knowledge of aircraft. However, Eric knew looks could be deceiving, and he was desperate.

"Hey. Is she yours?" the old guy yelled as Eric walked towards him.

"Yes. You must be Gunner. I'm Eric. Nice to meet you."

"She's a beauty. I knew that I didn't recognize her when I drove up. I'm pretty familiar with most of the aircraft around these parts. She seems to be in great condition. Norman said you were looking for an aircraft mechanic."

"Yes, that's right. Norman said you were the most experienced mechanic in McGrath. He also mentioned the fact you have an A & P license."

"Yep. Norm would be right about that. I've worked on most of the planes which fly in and out of McGrath. Jim Warren, who used to live here, was the only licensed mechanic other than myself, and he's long since moved away. So, if you're looking for a certified mechanic, I guess I'm your man."

"Great, then I suppose you're just the person I'm looking to hire. That is if you're available?"

"Well, I normally get about thirty-five dollars an hour. If that fits your wallet, then I suppose you've got yourself a mechanic," Gunner chuckled.

"Seems reasonable enough to me. Why don't we drive over to Tillmans, and I'll buy you a cup of coffee? Then, we can go over my plans."

"Sounds good. I'll follow you."

Arriving at Tillman's, it appeared there was ample parking on Main Street. Walking inside the dimly lit tavern, it was somewhat empty. Noticing Norman working behind the counter replacing a beer kegerator, they stepped up to the bar.

"Well, it looks as if you two have finally met. Gunner knows more about planes than anyone around these parts. What can I get you?" Norman grinned.

"I'll have a cup of coffee. It's too early in the day for anything stronger," Eric replied, pulling up a bar stool.

"I'll have my usual, a Duck Fart. Oh, and make that a double since my new friend, Eric, is paying. No such thing as too early in the day," Gunner countered.

"What the hell is a Duck Fart?"

"Oh, it's only the best drink in Alaska. It's a layered shot of Kahlua, Bailey's Irish Cream, and Crown Royal."

"I guess I'll have to take your word on that. It sounds nasty. Why don't we take our drinks over to that small table in the corner," Eric suggested noticing a group of noisy tourists walk in.

"Don't knock it until you've tried it! I promise you; the flavors mesh great together. So, what brought you to McGrath?" Gunner inquired, tossing back his entire double shot in one long, continuous gulp.

"I've always had this dream of moving up to Alaska and starting my own business. After retiring from the Marines, the timing just felt right. I flew Cobras for almost twenty years. However, I'm also a certified FAA flight instructor on smaller, fixed-wing aircraft. I find the idea of flying for a living fascinating. I've always loved the outdoors, and the two just seemed the perfect mix.

"Well, I must say you've picked the right place if you don't mind the weather. So, where do you call home? Are you married?"

"No. I've always been married to my career. Years of deployments aren't conducive to a good marriage. I saw too many divorces during my time in the Marines. I was born and raised in Carson City, Nevada. My dad, Roy Kolbeck, was a well-known poker player. Sadly, he passed three years ago. How about you? Are you married?"

"Oh, hell no, that ended years ago. I was married. My wife, Mary, left after two short years. Guess the depressing cold weather finally got to her. I'm perfectly happy being single. No one puts demands on this old fart. I'm way too old and set in my ways. Now, getting back to your need for a mechanic. I definitely won't turn down the work. However, I must warn you the weather around here can wreak havoc on aircraft. It can be harsh and unrelenting. I hope you have a backup plan for your little venture. Do you have a partner or another plane to put in the air?"

"No. Guess you could say I'm flying solo. If things work out and business is good, then I'll check into adding another plane and possibly a business partner."

"Hey, I hate to cut this short, but I've got some work to do this morning on another aircraft. So, if you can afford thirty-five dollars an hour, you've got yourself a mechanic." Gunner agreed, slowly pushing his chair back from the table. "Thanks for the drink. You've got my phone number. We'll be in touch.

"Thanks. I look forward to working with you."

On the drive back to the cabin, Eric wondered if he had made the right decision to hire Gunner. Faced with no other choice, he needed to get his plane in the air and earn an income. However, thoughts regarding a backup plan were a little daunting. All that remained of his initial start-up money was a little less than six-thousand dollars. Hopefully, with a bit of luck and good weather, he would be able to get his new business off to a great start. Eric had already booked his first clients. He was scheduled to fly two businessmen up to the Innoko Wildlife Refuge to hunt moose. Kolbeck Air was about to experience its first day in business.

Waking early the following day, Eric made coffee. Then, hurriedly eating breakfast, which consisted of fried eggs and bacon, he put on heavy thermal underwear, a pair of camouflaged pants, and a jacket. Then, grabbing his dependable rifle and a few rounds of ammo, he rushed out the door.

Racing to the small airport, Eric arrived just as his first clients were stepping out of a rugged four-wheel-drive Yukon. They appeared relatively young. The fact they had just flown in from San Jose, California, led him to believe they were likely internet geeks who worked in Silicon Valley. On the other hand, perhaps, they were inexperienced hunters just looking for a new type of fun. Laughing to himself, he realized it didn't matter. He would fly them up to the hunting lodge near the wildlife refuge, and with any luck, they would bag a moose over the next few days.

"Good morning, I'm Eric Kolbeck. Are you ready to get in a little moose hunting this morning? The weather looks great!" Eric smiled, continuing his inspection of the aircraft as he walked around the wing of the plane.

"Awesome. I'm Brian Brinsfield, and this is my buddy, Jeff Moore."

"Glad to meet you. I'll take your bags and throw them in the back. We should be in the air soon. Is this your first visit to McGrath?"

"Yes. We've heard the flights out of McGrath offer the best hunting experience."

"Well, you'd be right on that," Eric grinned, stowing their gear.

It appeared his new business venture was off to a great start. Hopefully, over the next few days, his recent clients would eagerly recount their first moose hunting expedition as one of their most memorable experiences. And, with a little bit of luck, they would highly recommend Kolbeck Air to their friends and family.

Landing on a rough, narrow strip of dirt near the lodge, Eric dropped off his clients and picked up three returning passengers to McGrath. His first day in business was going even better than expected. Later that evening, as he returned to his small primitive cabin, he smiled, reflecting on his extraordinary day. His new venture had quickly become satisfying.

However, it wasn't going to last. Over the next three weeks, Eric unexpectedly punctured two tires while landing on the weathered terrain and encountered several down days due to inclement weather. As a result, he lost several precious work days. Apparently, Gunner was right. He did need a backup plan, and now he was caught with his proverbial pants down. He needed a cash infusion to stay afloat, and immediately he knew of his next plan of action. Taking the last of his savings, Eric decided to book a flight to Las Vegas. Playing poker seemed the most likely way to make some quick cash. After all, his skills as a poker player had always been a resourceful way of earning extra money. As a young boy, he had learned from the best, his father. In fact, during his time in the Marines, he felt this advantage was the sole reason he always walked away from every card game with money in his pocket. So, without giving it a second thought, Eric booked a flight to Vegas.

Chapter Three

Eric arrived in Las Vegas the following weekend. There was no better way to spend a few days. His father was a legend in Vegas, and his name was synonymous with poker. He checked into his regular hangout, Caesars's Palace, and took the elevator to the twelfth floor. Opening the door, he set his one bag on the credenza and walked over to draw back the drapes. Running his fingers through his sandy, brown hair, Eric stopped for a moment to enjoy the brilliant views. Staring at the numerous neon signs reminded him of Reno and home. Glancing at his watch, he realized it was already 8:00 p.m. Feeling the rumblings of an empty stomach, he groaned. He was starving.

Craving a hearty steak and potatoes meal, Eric locked the door and walked towards the elevator. He needed a good night's rest, and there was no better way to go to sleep than after consuming a huge, starch-filled meal. Tomorrow Eric had to be at his finest, fully awake and ready to take on the sharpest poker players in Vegas. He knew Vegas never lacked professional card sharks. Even though he never cheated, Eric knew that he had to be ready to take on the skills of everyone seated at the table to win the money he needed for his business

Exiting the elevator, Eric made his way across the gaming floor. The sound emitting from numerous slot machines gave the large casino an air of excitement and energetic ambiance. Resisting the urge to take a seat in front of an open slot, he continued to stroll through the smoked filled room. About an hour later, after devouring a large New York Strip steak smothered in onions with steak fries, he began to feel tired. Mission accomplished, he thought. The only thing Eric was lacking included a soft pillow and a good night's sleep. He returned to his room, immediately took off his shoes, and stripped down to his boxers. Jumping into bed, he sighed. Tomorrow would come soon enough. Hopefully, by the end of the day and with a bit of luck, his poker winnings would provide him enough money to return to McGrath and continue his charter service.

Too soon, the morning sun crept in through the sheer curtains, bathing the room in a soft glow. Eric sat up sleepily, rubbing his eyes. Then, reaching for his cigarettes and lighter, thoughts of a winning poker hand consumed him. He knew his innate skills at the game could easily rival the best players.

Putting out his cigarette, he headed for the shower. Standing under the warm water, he lathered shampoo through his chestnut hair. Relaxing for a few moments as the soothing water gently flowed over him, he finally reached for a towel. Tying it around his waist, he stepped out of the shower. Pausing briefly, he flexed his biceps and smiled. Eric took pride in the fact that he maintained his muscular, athletic body. Even though he wasn't adept in any particular sport, his years in the Marines had required him to keep in shape.

Running his fingers through his day's growth of dark stubble, Eric decided against shaving. Splashing on his favorite cologne, he dressed for his mission. Pulling his favorite blue flannel shirt and pair of jeans out of his bag, he dressed casually. His next plan of action included coffee, lots of coffee. Picking up the phone, he ordered room service. After all, there was no better way to start the day than eating a hearty breakfast. He was desperately craving blueberry pancakes covered in maple syrup with bacon.

A soft knock at the door announced the arrival of breakfast. The concierge brought in a large silver tray laden with food. Suddenly, the entire room was infused with the delicious aroma of fried bacon. Eric quickly tipped the young attendant, who nodded and made a quiet exit. Lifting the top of the silver chafing dishes, he promptly filled his plate with a ridiculous stack of blueberry pancakes. Eric ate so fast that he almost felt sick. Pouring himself another cup of coffee, he lounged back in his chair, groaning as he attempted to let his enormous breakfast settle.

Reaching for his pack of smokes, Eric lit a cigarette. Putting out his second cigarette of the morning, he looked down at his watch. It was almost 10:00 a.m. Pulling a small envelope from his overnight bag, he counted the contents. The envelope contained his entire life savings of six-thousand dollars. Transferring the money into his wallet, he slipped it into the hip pocket of his blue jeans. Grabbing his lighter and cigarettes, he was finally ready. Almost forgetting his lucky rabbit's foot, he hurriedly put it in his other pocket. Not that he honestly felt the need for it. His poker skills were quite sufficient. But today was vitally important, and he couldn't chance to leave it behind. Locking the door, he walked over to the elevator.

As the doors opened onto the casino floor, the loud sounds from the slot machines seemed hypnotic. Slowly walking towards the back of the sprawling casino, Eric felt drawn to a row of dollar slots. Deciding to try his luck, he sat down. Reaching into his wallet, he took out a twenty-dollar bill and fed it into a Wheel of Fortune machine. Slowly pulling the handle, Eric watched anxiously as the giant spinning wheel gradually came to a stop. Not winning after several attempts, it became apparent that he wasn't sitting in front of a paying machine. Deciding to play the dollar slot at the end of the row, Eric reached inside his wallet for another twenty. Taking a seat, he inserted the money, hoping his luck would change. Within moments, Eric won a bonus round. With the next spin, he won five hundred dollars. Cursing that he hadn't played the max amount, which would have instantly paid double, he eagerly pulled the winning ticket from the machine. It wasn't a bad start. However, he wasn't there to play the slots. Continuing to make his way through the labyrinth of machines, he slowly sauntered towards the back of the casino to cash in his winning ticket and purchase chips.

Eric had not gone far when he felt the presence of someone rushing up behind him. Turning around, he suddenly found himself staring into the azure blue eyes of a curvaceous cocktail server. She was gorgeous, wearing a low-cut shimmering blouse, miniskirt, and black fishnet tights. Unexpectedly, Eric found himself mesmerized by the natural beauty of the young girl.

"Excuse me, this fell out of your pocket," she smiled, handing him his wallet.

Shocked to see her holding his entire life savings and his sole reason for coming to Vegas in her hand, he was speechless. How could he have been so careless?

"Thank you." Those two little words seemed hardly sufficient. "So," he stammered. "What's your name?"

"Lana."

"Well, Lana, nice to meet you. I'm Eric."

Returning her smile, Eric was sure she had no idea of the importance of what she had found. However, as unfortunate as it was that his wallet had fallen out of his pocket, he felt fortunate for it to have been found by someone so honest. Captivated by her exquisite charm and striking appearance, he felt the need to repay her act of kindness.

"Please, let me buy you dinner this evening. It's the least I can do." Eric wasn't about to let her out of his sight so quickly. He had an unnatural desire to know more about her, a perfect stranger.

"Thanks. But it isn't necessary. However, if you insist, I get off work around 7:00 p.m."

"Do you like Italian food?"

"Of course. What girl doesn't'?" she laughed nervously.

"Great. I'll make reservations for dinner at the Bellagio. Why don't we say about 8:00 p.m.? I'll meet you in front of the fountains."

"Sounds good. See you then," Lana smiled demurely.

Watching as she walked away, their brief encounter almost made him forget his primary reason for being in Vegas. Returning his wallet to the safety of his hip pocket, he rambled through the numerous rows of slots. Cashing in his winnings and converting his savings into chips, he began surveying the busy poker tables. As he walked past a table near the middle of the casino floor, he finally spotted an open seat. Gauging the faces of the two older gentlemen sitting at the table, he felt confident in his abilities. The gentlemen appeared by their expressions to be more involved with the pleasure of smoking exquisite cigars than winning at the table. The other player seemed to be young and probably the most conscientious. Apparently, the older gents had more money than God and were merely there for their amusement. Taking a seat next to the young man, Eric studied his expressionless face and mannerisms. Pushing his chips towards the center of the table, Eric smiled. He was now in the game.

Over the next hour, Eric watched his winnings slowly rise and fall. It was excruciating, and his heart began to race. His palms were clammy, and he quickly wiped beads of sweat from his brow.

Hearing a familiar voice, he looked up. Once again, his eyes met those of the gorgeous young woman whose kindness was the only reason he was still seated at the table.

"Would you care for a drink?" Lana inquired with a smile.

"Yes. I'll take a Jack Daniels and Coke."

Returning her smile with a wink, he couldn't believe her sudden, unexpected appearance. Reaching for his lighter, he lit a cigarette. As the dealer dealt out the next round of cards, Eric surprisingly picked up a straight-flush, five cards of the same suit in consecutive order. He held the ace, king, queen, jack, and ten of spades, and a broad smile broke out across his face. Undoubtedly, Lana's unexpected appearance at the table had brought him a stroke of luck. Eric was now more than ever infatuated with her. Taking a quick look at his watch, he could hardly wait until 8:00 p.m.

Putting his focus back on the game in front of him, it appeared over the next six hours that he would easily walk away with more than he had ever hoped to win. Later that evening, he flashed a huge smile to the young woman sitting behind the cashier's cage. Eric cashed in trays of chips worth over eighty-thousand dollars. Looking up at the ceiling, he smiled. "Thanks, Dad."

Walking toward the elevator, he quickly glanced down at his watch. It was almost 6:00 p.m. Unlocking the door to his room, he first made a dinner reservation for two at the prestigious Lago Restaurant. The restaurant overlooked the beautiful fountains at the Bellagio and was well-known for its exquisite Italian cuisine. Next, he called room service and ordered a bottle of Blanton's Bourbon to help him relax. Removing his shoes, he lounged back on the bed and lit a cigarette. Within a short time, a knock at the door announced the arrival of his bourbon and ice.

Pouring himself a smooth shot of the single barrel bourbon, he took his drink and once again walked over to the large window. Eric never tired of the fantastic views which Vegas offered. It was indeed a city of neon lights. Then taking a slow sip of his drink, he savored its vanilla and caramel notes. Reflecting on his unbelievable day, he smiled. Never in his wildest dreams had he imagined that he would walk away from the table with eighty-thousand dollars.

But even stranger than his winnings was his encounter with the gorgeous girl he was about to meet downstairs later in the evening. Lighting another cigarette, he sat down, pouring himself another drink. It seemed he never needed his lucky rabbit's foot. Unbelievably, Lana had dropped into his game, and then simultaneously, he was surprisingly dealt a straight flush. Lana had brought him more unforeseen luck than he ever expected.

Later that evening, Eric took a quick shower and rummaged through his overnight bag. The occasion called for the perfect attire. Wanting to look fashionably dressed without being too presumptuous, he chose a light blue dress shirt, gray tie, and dark dress pants. Realizing it was the end of September and that nights could often be somewhat chilly in Vegas, Eric decided to bring along a matching sports coat.

Anxiously glancing at his watch for the third time, he realized that it was almost 7:30 p.m. Picking up his jacket, he was just about to grab his room key when he heard a soft knock at the door. Walking over to answer it, he was surprised to find a concierge from the hotel waiting patiently at the door.

"Sir, we would like to comp you with an upgrade. It's our pleasure to offer you two additional nights in one of our luxury suites. Would you prefer smoking or non-smoking? Your father, Roy Kolbeck, was a frequent guest before he passed."

"Smoking, please. You knew my father?" Eric questioned.

"No, not personally. However, Mr. Kolbeck was well-known by our staff. I believe the word *Legend* comes to mind. I would be happy to transfer your luggage to your new accommodations."

"Thanks. But I only have an overnight bag."

"Not a problem. I would be happy to take care of that. Here is your new room key. We sincerely hope that you enjoy your stay. If there is anything further I can do to make your visit more pleasurable, please give me a call.

We look forward to seeing you again soon," the young man smiled, handing Eric his business card.

"Thank you."

It was indeed his lucky day. Walking to the elevator, he pushed the button to the main floor; he couldn't wait to spend the evening with Lana.

Leaving Caesars Palace, Eric decided to walk the short distance to the Bellagio. Watching the famous illuminated fountains, he had been there a short time when he caught sight of Lana walking toward him. She was a vision of beauty wearing a sequined black halter dress with heels. Her long auburn curls were swept back and held in place with a rhinestone clasp. She was gorgeous, carrying a black lace shawl along with an evening clutch.

"I hope I'm not overdressed," she smiled

"You're stunning. I've made dinner reservations at the Lago. It overlooks the fountains, and I hope it meets with your approval."

"Yes. Of course. I've heard amazing things about the Lago."

Reaching down, Eric took her hand, leading her over to the edge of the famous illuminated fountains.

"I just happen to have a couple of coins. Do you believe in making wishes?" Eric questioned.

"Yes. Do you?"

"Absolutely," he winked, unable to take his eyes off her.

"Well, why don't you go first?" she suggested.

"Thanks, but ladies first."

Taking the quarter from him, she held it tightly in her hand. Pausing for a brief moment, she smiled, closing her eyes as she tossed it into the fountains.

"Your turn," Lana smiled.

"Okay."

Holding the coin snug in his hand, Eric hesitated for a second. Then, staring into her captivating blue eyes, he hurled it into the fountain. He would never know what she wished. However, his wish included the beautiful young woman standing next to him.

"I don't suppose you're going to tell me your wish," Eric teased.

"No. You can never divulge a wish."

Taking her hand, he lovingly led her towards the grand entrance of the Bellagio. Entering the impressive lobby, they followed the right-hand path into the casino. Walking past Hermes, the breathtaking Lago Restaurant was on the right, just past the famous Hyde Nightclub. Taking in the ambiance of the magnificent hotel and casino, its décor was spectacular. It offered the very best. The Bellagio's standards were beyond that of a AAA Five-Diamond Resort. Reaching the elegant eatery, Eric approached the maître d'. Inquiring about their reservation, they were quickly ushered to a table for two, which sat in full view of the enormous fountains.

"Wow, this is incredible," Lana smiled as Eric pulled out her chair.

"I'm glad you approve. I owe you for returning my wallet. You have no idea how much that meant. Later, I'll explain," Eric winked, placing the napkin on his lap. Then, taking the menu from the waiter, he carefully viewed their choices for dinner.

"So, what have you decided to order?" Lana questioned, looking up from her menu.

"Well, if I could be so bold to suggest, I think we should try the truffle mushroom risotto and lobster gnocchi."

"I can't say that I've ever tasted either of those," Lana hesitantly explained.

"Trust me. I think you'll love it. Remember the old saying, *When in Rome, Do as the Romans Do?*"

Inquisitively surveying the other patrons and their main courses, Lana laughed.

"Well, I can't say everyone around us appears to be eating truffle mushroom risotto or lobster gnocchi, but I'll trust you," she smiled.

When the waiter returned, Eric asked to speak with one of their knowledgeable wine sommeliers. Within minutes a young man approached their table.

"Good evening, I'm Alan. May I help you with your choice of wine?" he questioned

"Yes. Thank you. We would like your recommendation for a nice red to go with our choice of truffle mushroom risotto and lobster gnocchi."

"Certainly, I would highly recommend a bottle of pinot noir. Specifically Wedell Cellars 2010 Pinot Noir. I think you will be pleased."

"Thank you. We greatly appreciate your recommendation," Eric acknowledged. "I'm sure we will enjoy it."

Returning with the pinot noir, Alan uncorked the bottle and poured a small sampling for Eric to taste.

Swirling the wine in his glass, its fragrance hinted of light plum, dark strawberry, rhubarb, and lavender. Taking a sip, the elegant floral taste was delightful.

"Wonderful, I certainly agree," Eric stated as the sommelier poured them each a glass, leaving the open bottle on the table.

"Geez, you're certainly a big spender tonight." Lana teased, placing her napkin on her lap.

"Sweetheart, you've more than earned it. Honestly, I could never thank you enough," Eric winked.

"Well, I guess there must have been something important in the wallet I returned to you earlier today in the casino."

"Just my entire life's savings," Eric remarked, taking a sip of wine.

"Oh my God! I had no idea." Lana dropped her fork in surprise.

"Sweetheart, don't get so excited," Eric smiled. "It wasn't that much. I'm afraid it was only six thousand dollars. However, I had purposely brought it to Vegas to purchase chips at a high-stakes poker table. To make a long story short, I hoped to win enough money to save my business back in Alaska."

"Well, did your plan work? Did you win a lot of money?" she curiously questioned.

"Yes. I walked away with eighty-thousand dollars. So I guess you could safely say that I managed to keep my business in the air."

"Wow, that's quite a story. I'm glad that I could help."

Finding herself intrigued by the handsome man sitting across from her, Lana wanted to know more about him. His story fascinated her. How on earth could anyone have the boldness to risk their life savings in a poker game, especially someone hoping to save a business venture? Surprisingly Lana felt drawn to his sheer tenacity. She had never met a man with such confidence, and now she sensed a warm, mutual attraction developing between them.

At that moment, the waiter placed piping hot plates in front of them. Eric's choice of dinner entrees looked delicious. Tasting the risotto with truffles and mushrooms, Lana sighed. It was delicious. Pouring them another glass of wine, Eric smiled, raising his glass.

"Let's toast to a wonderful evening."

"Yes, to a wonderful evening," Lana remarked, lifting her glass.

"Now that you know my story, at least some of it, what brought you to Vegas?" Eric inquired.

Staring deep into her eyes, Eric found himself infatuated with her. He wanted to know everything about her.

"Well, I'm afraid my story isn't as adventurous as yours. There's not much to tell. I just left an abusive relationship which lasted far too long." Taking a bite of her lobster gnocchi, Lana seemed embarrassed to look up at him

"Sweetheart, how in the world does a gorgeous young woman like yourself wind up in an abusive relationship?"

Rubbing his fingers through his five o'clock shadow, Eric could feel his blood boiling at the very thought of anyone mistreating her.

"All too easy, I'm afraid. However, if you don't mind, I don't care to discuss it. We are having such a wonderful evening; let's just keep our conversation light-hearted and fun. That part of my life is simply too depressing," Lana frowned.

"Not a problem. It's quite understandable."

Watching as Lana quickly downed the remaining wine in her glass, he poured her a refill. Noting her reaction, he had evidently hit a nerve. He felt terrible for inquiring. Over the next hour, they leisurely enjoyed dinner and managed to drink the entire bottle of pinot noir.

Unexpectedly, Lana's cell phone began buzzing.

"I'm sorry. It's Megan, my roommate. I should take the call." Lana fumbled through her clutch to find her phone.

"Not a problem," Eric smiled. However, he couldn't help overhearing their conversation.

"Hey, Megan, what's up?"

"Lana, Blake just called the apartment. It appears your mother gave him my number. He's in Vegas, and he is looking for you. I don't think you should come back to the apartment tonight. He would recognize your car, and he sounded angry and upset. Is there another place you could stay for the night?"

"Well, I'm not sure, but don't worry. I'm definitely not coming back, at least not tonight. I cannot believe my mother gave him your number!"

"It doesn't matter. I'm sure Blake would have suspected that you came to Vegas. He knows that I have been trying to get you to leave him for months. I'm terrified that he will find you. Please, whatever you do, don't come back this evening."

"Thanks for the warning. Don't worry about me. I'll come up with something. I'll call you later. Love you." With trembling hands, Lana hung up the phone.

Concerned at overhearing Lana's conversation, her expression reflected shock and fear. Eric frowned. He was worried for her safety.

"Sweetheart, I'm sorry, but I overheard your phone call. Is everything alright?" Eric questioned.

"Remember our earlier conversation and the fact that I didn't want to ruin our lovely evening by discussing my past? Well, my past just showed up in Vegas." Lana frowned. "I'm afraid he isn't happy. My roommate, Megan, was calling to warn me. She said it wouldn't be safe to come home tonight. He would recognize my car, and I'm pretty certain he is watching the apartment. I'm afraid he can be unpredictable and mean. I'm sorry. I didn't mean to burden you with my problems this evening." Lana reached for her evening bag and grabbed a tissue to wipe her eyes.

"Oh, my God, Sweetheart, I'm so sorry. Please don't cry," Eric mentioned reaching across the table gently taking her hand. "I've got this. Please don't worry. As unimaginable as this may seem, I was comped two nights at Caesars. You're staying with me, no questions asked."

Lana hinted a faint smile staring into his captivating blue eyes. He would never know the relief she felt hearing his gracious offer.

"Eric, I don't want to be an inconvenience."

"Sweetheart, trust me, you're not an inconvenience. Would it help if I told you that I'm a retired Marine? Babe, I'm more than capable of taking care of you tonight," he grinned.

"You're kidding, right?" Lana laughed. "Seriously, you're a retired Marine?"

"Lana, you have nothing to worry about. I would never let anything happen to you. I would love to have an encounter with this monster in a dark alley, and yes, as a matter of fact, I'm seriously a Marine," he winked.

Paying for dinner, Eric left a generous tip. Then, pulling back Lana's chair, he reached down, taking her hand.

"Let's go check out this new suite, shall we?"

Walking out of the magnificent hotel, Eric waved for a cab to drive them the short distance to Caesars Palace. Leaving the Bellagio, their evening appeared to be getting even better, despite Lana's unexpected phone call.

Arriving back at Caesars, Eric noted the new room number 1104. Once again, taking her by the hand, he led her over to the elevators and up to the suite. Entering the room, it was exquisite. Undoubtedly, there must have been a mistake. It showcased two floors of sheer luxury and spacious floor-to-ceiling windows beautifully enhanced the back of the room. A stunning glass-enclosed staircase led up to the second level, the main suite. Outside, the massive sliding glass door of the bedroom was a uniquely designed Grecian terrace containing a jacuzzi. The view of the neon lights was amazing. Tall oversized urns elegantly surrounded the entire balcony. Looking around, Eric smiled.

"Thanks, Dad."

His dad had died penniless, except for the family ranch, which remained self-sustaining. However, it appeared his reputation was still very much alive and well. Eric had not been born with a silver spoon in his mouth. He had worked hard all his life, even though he loved every minute of his time as a Marine. His dad had always taught him to never depend on anyone other than himself. The only thing he inherited from his father was his extraordinary skills at playing poker. Eric knew his abilities at any card table could easily rival the best of players.

"Wow, do you always stay in such extravagant places?" Lana questioned, looking around the spacious suite. "Are you rich?"

"Sorry, Doll, as I told you, I'm just a retired Marine. I flew helicopters for over twenty years."

Lana felt there was much more to his life's story than what he had told her. However, it didn't matter. Fate had somehow brought the two of them together for the evening, and she was beginning to have feelings for him. Feelings that made her tingle with excitement. Her heart raced at the mere sight of his tall, muscular frame. Eric was by far the most handsome man she had ever met. And just because she had found his wallet on the casino floor, she was about to spend the night in his suite. She could only hope that he shared her feelings.

"We have champagne, along with a fully stocked bar. So I'll pour us a drink."

Popping the cork on a bottle of Dom Perignon, he filled two glasses.

"Sweetheart, let's sit in front of the windows," Eric suggested, handing her a glass of sparkling beverage.

Following him over to the long sectional, Lana took off her heels and snuggled next to him.

"This place is amazing," she smiled, taking in the sophisticated elegance of the suite.

"You're right. It's pretty darn amazing," Eric winked, taking a sip of champagne.

"So," she hesitated, staring into his deep blue eyes. "What really brought you to Vegas?"

"Geez, Sweetheart, I thought I already covered that at dinner," Eric laughed.

"Well, why do I get the feeling there's more to you than what you've said?" Lana questioned, sipping her champagne.

"Oh, you mean the part about me being the son of a famous poker champion. Doll, I hate to break it to you, but he had lost everything except the ranch before he died. My mother, Kathie, still lives in Carson City, Nevada, with my younger sister, Karen."

"I'm sorry. I didn't mean to pry into your personal life."

Walking over to retrieve the bottle of champagne, Eric poured himself another drink and sat the bottle on the coffee table.

"Sweetheart, seriously, my life is an open book. So what do you want to know? Would you like a refill?"

"I suppose, but I must warn you, it doesn't take much to make me feel a little tipsy."

"Babe, we are in for the evening. Trust me. I don't see that as a problem," Eric grinned, pouring her a refill. "However, what I would like to know is how you managed to get hooked up with the wrong guy? I mean, you're so gorgeous. How could something like that happen?"

"It's pretty easy. Let's just say that I finished high school with no money to further my education. I was the middle child in a family of ten. My dad owned a fleet of deep-sea fishing boats, but he was never home. He spent most of his time in the local tavern. My mom worked hard cleaning for a nearby motel. Unfortunately, I met Blake when I interviewed for my first job at Boswell Real Estate. He owns the largest agency in Newport, Oregon, where I grew up," Lana paused, taking a sip of champagne. "He was rather handsome, refined, and wealthy. You could say that he had all the traits that my father didn't. After Blake hired me to work in his office, it didn't take long for us to fall in love, supposedly, or at least that's what I thought it was at the beginning. Shortly after that, we moved in together. He owns a stunning house on the beach," Lana explained. Nervously she finished her entire glass of champagne in one long, continuous gulp.

"Geez, Sweetheart! Slow down. You just downed your entire drink." Eric laughed.

"Well, you just said we had nowhere to go, and I guess reliving my past is making me a little nervous." Lana grimaced. "Eric, Blake has come to Las Vegas to force me to return with him to Newport. He's used to getting his way, and when he doesn't, he gets angry. You don't know him. He's the reason I moved to Vegas and came to live with my girlfriend, Megan. Now he's here, and I'm petrified," Lana continued quickly, looking away as her eyes filled with tears.

"Lana, please don't cry." Then, taking the back of his hand, he gently wiped the tears from her eyes. "You trust me, right?"

"Yes. I guess. No. I mean, I do trust you. I do," Lana sniffled.

Eric's heart broke for her as he got up to find some tissues. He wanted to kill Blake, and he'd never met him. Walking into the bathroom, he pulled some tissues from the dispenser. Returning to the sofa, it was apparent Lana was beginning to feel the effects of the alcohol. She was curled up on the couch with her eyes closed. Leaning over, Eric kissed her softly on the forehead.

"I'm sorry. I must have fallen asleep." Lana murmured.

"No worries. I'm sure it's a combination of the wine we drank at dinner and the champagne."

Sitting up, Lana panicked."Oh, my God, I feel nauseous!"

"Hang on, Sweetheart. I'll take you upstairs."

Hurriedly, scooping her up in his arms, he carried her upstairs to the primary bedroom. Laying her on the bed, he ran into the bathroom to warm a washcloth. While running the hot water, she came running in. He could only watch as nausea consumed her. Sitting on the cold marble floor next to her, she refused to leave the bathroom. Taking the warm cloth, he lovingly wiped her face.

"Sweetheart, what can I do?"

"Nothing, but don't leave me. Please," Lana begged.

"Okay, I'm not going anywhere. I feel terrible that you're not feeling well."

Continuing to wipe her face, Eric lovingly pulled back her long curls, which had fallen loose from her hair clasp. Then, once again warming the washcloth, he softly rubbed her face. Gently putting his arms around her, he already felt an attachment to the gorgeous and adorable sick girl.

Feeling a little better, she looked up at him with tears running down her cheeks.

"What am I going to do? I don't have a change of clothes."

"Don't cry. It's truly not the end of the world. I promise. Wait just a minute. I'll be right back."

Running downstairs, his heart was again breaking as he remembered the earlier phone call from Megan. He knew she was scared, and it no doubt was taking an emotional toll on her. Quickly grabbing his duffle bag, he ran back upstairs. Setting it on the bed, Eric rummaged through the contents. Undoubtedly, it contained something she could wear. Pulling out a soft gray flannel shirt, he walked into the bathroom.

"It's not much, and I'm sure it's way too large, but you can wear this," he suggested handing Lana the shirt.

Looking up, she smiled. "Thank you, but are you sure?"

"Sweetheart, I don't think you have a lot of options," he winked.

"Okay. Thanks. If you don't mind, I think a warm shower would feel heavenly."

"Great. Enjoy your shower. I'll be downstairs."

Slowly walking down the grand staircase, the day had honestly been one for the books. Losing the money was horrifying, yet miraculously, it had brought Lana into his life. He had never lost and surprisingly found so much at the same time. Maybe his wish was coming true.

Deciding a stiff drink was in order, Eric walked over to the bar. Pouring himself a bourbon with coke, he drew back the towering curtains which covered the vast wall of windows. The view of the strip at night was hypnotic. Reaching over, he dimmed the lights, allowing the kaleidoscope of neon lights to immerse the elegant room in a soft, colorful glow. Sitting on the leather sectional, he removed his shoes. Just as he was about to enjoy another sip of bourbon, he looked up, utterly mesmerized. Lana was slowly descending the long staircase wearing only his flannel shirt. Her long auburn curls shimmered under the soft lights. She took his breath away. Coming closer, she exuded a radiance. How lucky could one guy get?

"My God, Doll, you're gorgeous."

Pulling her close, he began kissing her with such passion it sent shivers of excitement throughout her entire body. Giving into the moment, Lana completely melted into his arms.

"Sweetheart, you take my breath away," he whispered. "Where have you been all my life?"

"Eric, before tonight, I'm not sure I knew how a real man was supposed to treat a lady. But, for the most part, the men in my life have not been loving or compassionate."

"Babe, that's truly sad. Just know that you're safe with me."

Holding tightly to him with every ounce of her being, she never wanted to let go.

Eric carried her up the stairs. For once in his life, nothing else mattered, only the beautiful girl in his arms. Turning out the lights, he gently laid her on the bed. Pulling back the duvet, he slowly began unbuttoning her shirt. Then, putting her under the warm covers, he removed his clothes, slipping into bed next to her. Feeling the warmth of her skin touch his, he had never felt such desire for another human being. The memories of their evening would stay with him forever.

Waking early the next morning, Eric wiped the sleep from his eyes. He was surprised to find Lana intently staring at him.

"Good morning, Sweetheart. I hope you haven't spent the entire night staring at me," he teased.

"Eric, last night was unbelievable. I just had to know that you're real."

"The last time I checked, I believe I was still breathing," he winked with a smile.

Gently taking her hand, he held it close to his heart.

"Well, does this convince you?" he smiled teasingly.

"You're silly, but I love you."

"Maybe this will help."

Pulling her into his arms, he kissed her. The intensity of his kiss invaded her body with a warmth of sheer ecstasy. She was beginning to sense a strong connection between them as he held her close. Every moment she spent with him, thoughts of Blake drifted further and further from her mind.

"Sweetheart, if this continues, I'm afraid we may never leave the room today," Eric smiled, staring into the depths of her gorgeous blue eyes. "I have a surprise. I want to take you to one of my favorite places on earth, and I haven't much time. I leave tomorrow evening. What do you think? Are you onboard?

"Well, your offer sounds fascinating. However, I have nothing to wear, and I'm not about to show up at Megan's apartment to change clothes. With my luck, Blake would be parked out front," Lana remarked.

Shocked to hear that he was leaving so soon, Lana bit her bottom lip. She was devastated. Desperately trying to prevent the myriad of tears welling in her eyes, she was losing any attempt at containing her emotions. Getting out of bed, she bolted for the bathroom. Following close behind her, Eric couldn't fathom a reason for her sudden actions. Then, it hit him. It was the mention of his leaving.

Opening the bathroom door, Lana was bitterly sobbing as she stood in front of the bathroom sink. Walking over, he lovingly pulled her against his chest. Holding her tight, he knew tomorrow was going to be difficult. But, they would deal with tomorrow when it came. However, his plan for today was meant to take her away from her problems and any thoughts of Blake.

"Sweetheart, please don't cry. Surely, you must know that my feelings toward you are real."

His heart was breaking as he kissed away her tears. He knew the stress she was under, and his plans were never meant to hurt her or leave her in a dangerous situation; The past twenty-four hours had been the best of his life. But, there had been no mention of taking their relationship further. Even though he knew his life would not be the same without her. Unexpectedly, he had fallen in love with her, and there was no way his leaving categorically meant leaving her. But, unfortunately, his return ticket to McGrath had previously been booked for tomorrow.

"Babe, do you trust me?"

"Yes."

"Lana, I've fallen in love with you. You have nothing to worry about. Sweetheart, let's take today, and the remaining time we have together and shut out the world. Trust me. Tomorrow will take care of itself. Everything is going to be fine. So, how about taking a little trip with me?" he asked, wiping her tear-stained face.

"Okay. But what about clothes? I only have my sequined halter dress and heels."

"Well, Sweetheart, as gorgeous as that dress is, I'm afraid it will not be appropriate. However, I'm sure we can find suitable attire at one of the boutiques."

"Wouldn't it help if I knew where we were going? Then, I could have a little input on my choice of wardrobe."

"Not a chance, silly girl. I'm afraid you're going to have to trust me once again. I will only inform you that it will require casual, warm clothes. Nothing more, so don't even try to get the location out of me, deal?"

"Alright, if you say so," Lana hesitated. "You have my word. No more questions."

"Good girl. Let's order breakfast. How do pancakes and sausage sound?"

"Fattening," Lana frowned. "Hey, I'm only teasing. It sounds delicious. However, could you please order orange juice?"

"Not a problem."

Later that morning, after breakfast, Eric took Lana shopping. After purchasing a pair of dark denim jeans, a beautiful beige cable knit sweater, and boots, Lana was at last appropriately dressed for the day. Pulling her hair back into a ponytail, she was elegant yet casually dressed for whatever the day might hold. Eric, as always, looked handsome wearing his trademark flannel shirt and denim jeans.

Taking a taxi out to the airport, Lana looked around, apparently confused.

"Eric, there was no mention of an airport. Are we leaving Vegas?"

"Maybe?" he winked mischievously.

Lana panicked as the taxi parked close to a sleek, silver ECO-Star helicopter.

"And there was no mention of a helicopter either," she worried. "Eric, I'm freaking out right now. I've never flown in a helicopter. So I'm not sure about this."

"Sweetheart, the helicopter belongs to a good buddy of mine. Brad owns an entire fleet. He's agreed to let us use it today. So you're worrying about nothing. Remember, I told you that I flew helicopters for over twenty years in the Marines. So you're in great hands. Trust me, I make my living flying the remote outbacks of Alaska," Eric explained, hoping to ease her fears.

Taking her hand, he carefully helped her inside.

"Now, don't panic," he teased, adjusting her seat belt.

Closing her door, Eric walked around to the other side.

Entering the helicopter, he tightened the grip on her seat belt.

"Eric, I'm scared. I might throw up."

"Sweetheart, you're going to be fine. However, just in case you need it, there is a barf bag next to your seat," he winked. "Just sit back and relax. I want you to enjoy the flight. We're going to fly over Lake Mead and Hoover Dam before reaching the Grand Canyon. So relax, I love you," Eric smiled.

Contacting the control tower, he handed her a headset and instructed her on its use. Within minutes, they lifted skyward. Looking at him, she smiled. Perhaps he was right, and she would try to enjoy the flight. Flying over the Vegas strip, Eric took pride in giving her the best views possible. Reaching Lake Mead, he pointed out the shimmering blue waters and the incredible vistas of Hoover Dam. Lana laughed. Eric was both a fantastic pilot and tour guide.

Thirty minutes later, Eric safely landed near the rim of the Grand Canyon. They were about thirty-five hundred feet above the canyon floor.

"Did you enjoy the flight?" Eric asked, helping her out of her seatbelt.

"It was amazing, not quite as scary as I thought. The brilliance of the topography is breathtaking. The fiery red and orange colors of the canyon walls are magnificent. It's spectacular," Lana exclaimed. "Oh, by the way, thanks for not crashing," she smiled.

"Sweetheart, you'll be happy to know, crashing was never on my agenda," Eric laughed, helping her down from her seat.

Reaching into the helicopter, he retrieved a wicker basket and large quilt which had been stowed for the trip. Taking Lana by the hand, he carried the basket and quilt in his other hand as he led her closer to a clearing near the rim. Then, spreading out the large quilt, he put the basket in the middle and gently pulled her down next to it.

"Well, let's see if Brad kept his promise. I asked him to fill the basket with everything we would need for a picnic."

Opening the basket, it contained champagne, bottled water, fruit, cheese, crackers, and an assortment of cold cuts along with a loaf of homemade French bread.

"It appears he kept his word," Eric smiled, popping the cork on the bottle of champagne. Pouring Lana a glass of the sparkling beverage, he grabbed a water bottle. Then, taking out a small platter, he piled it high with grapes, cheese, and cold cuts.

"What do you think of my favorite place?" he winked.

"Eric, it's incredible. How long have you been coming here?"

"Well, not as frequently after I joined the Marines. Most of my time was spent overseas. However, I came here often as a child. We were in Vegas a lot when my father played on the poker circuits. My mother loved coming here as well, so my dad always brought her to the Grand Canyon when we were in Vegas."

Suddenly, a rush of cold wind lifted the edge of the quilt, almost toppling the bottle of champagne. Luckily Eric managed to catch the champagne before it tipped over. Shivering from the unexpected drop in temperature, Lana huddled closer to him. Quickly putting his arms around her, she snuggled into the warmth of his embrace. Taking advantage of the moment, Eric tenderly caressed her face. Gently lifting her chin towards him, he kissed her with such intensity her entire body felt numb. Returning his passionate kisses, she could have stayed in his arms forever.

"I always came here when I needed to do some serious soul-searching. I always felt spending time here gave me clarity. So, Babe, that's why I've brought you here today."

"Is something wrong?"

"No. In fact, it's just the opposite. Sweetheart, I've fallen head over heels in love with you. Lana, you know that I'm leaving tomorrow evening and I want you to come with me to Alaska. I know this is sudden and unexpected, but there is no way that I can leave you tomorrow in the situation that you appear to be in with your ex-boyfriend. I would be worried. And being so far away, it would be impossible for me to help you from such a distance."

"Wow, Alaska, that's pretty far," Lana hesitated. "Eric, I do love you. I've never felt this way about anyone so soon after meeting them. Trust me. You have no idea how much I want to be with you, but Alaska?"

"Lana, it's just a location on a map. You're reading too much into this. I truly don't see how Alaska has anything to do with your decision. Do you love me? Sweetheart, I think that's the choice you have to make?"

"Eric, as crazy as it sounds, I do love you, but I've just started my job at Caesars. What would I do in Alaska?"

"Babe, you're beginning to make me nervous."

Reaching into his pocket for his cigarettes and lighter, he cupped his hands against the wind lighting his cigarette. Maybe, he had misinterpreted Lana's feelings.

"I guess," he paused, exhaling smoke from his cigarette. "If simply being with me isn't enough, then perhaps you've already made your decision."

"Eric," she hesitated. "I do have feelings for you, and you're right. Alaska is just a location. It's you that I can't live without. You have nothing to worry about."

Lana knew this whole scenario sounded more than crazy. They had just met, and already she was seriously considering the thought of following him to Alaska. Lana had known him less than twenty-four hours, yet, unexplainably it felt like a lifetime. However, she knew in the depths of her heart that she would follow him anywhere. So why was she trying to make everything so complicated? What was wrong with her? The timing was perfect. With Blake now in Vegas, she needed to escape. He would never look for her in Alaska.

"I need to give notice that I will be leaving my job. I'm not sure that I can get away as soon as tomorrow."

"Lana, with Blake in Vegas, I don't think you need to worry about giving your employer notice. If he is as ruthless as you say, he will not stop looking for you. Your life could be in danger. So I'm going to upgrade our tickets to first class. The flight leaves tomorrow evening at seven. Your ticket will be waiting for you at the check-in counter at Alaskan Air. I love you, and I can only pray that you make the right decision."

There was nothing more he could do to persuade her. Nervously lighting another cigarette, she would never know her effect on him.

"If you're game, let's take a short hike. I haven't been here for quite some time, and I want to show you some amazing sights."

Grabbing two water bottles, Eric pulled Lana up from the quilt.

"The views from the rim are spectacular. Hopefully, one day we can come back and hike the lower canyon. But, of course," he hesitated. "I guess that depends on your decision," he smiled, taking her hand.

After being alone for most of his life, he didn't see his future without her. He easily wore his feelings on his sleeves, and thoughts of returning to Alaska without her were making him extremely anxious.

Following a narrow path that led away from the clearing, Eric pointed out spectacular vistas of the vast, cavernous floor of the canyon and the Colorado River. The ever-changing colors were stunning as the sun and clouds moved overhead. Amazed at the geological wonders, Lana quickly understood why Eric claimed it was one of his favorite places to visit. Finally, after hiking for over an hour, a cool breeze let them know they should probably turn back.

"Wow. This place is incredible. I can't believe I've never been here," Lana explained, snuggling against him as they walked back towards the helicopter.

"Well, if you like incredible scenery, you will fall in love with Alaska," Eric winked. "I promise."

Later that evening, as their incoming flight brought them back to Vegas, Lana commented on the gorgeous neon lights which make it famous.

"Sweetheart, if you love the lights along the strip, I can't wait to show you the Northern Lights."

"Eric, you should have been a travel guide," she teased.

"My love of flying gives me a greater appreciation of the landscape below. I think it just happens naturally over time."

Arriving back at the hotel, Eric realized it might be their last night together. Craving every second of alone time, he ordered a delicious dinner consisting of steak and seafood, along with a bottle of champagne. Finishing their delectable meal, Eric playfully pulled Lana over to the sofa. Pouring them a glass of champagne, Lana snuggled against him. Never before had she loved anyone as much as Eric. However, she was still uncertain whether she would follow him to Alaska. Sensing her indecisiveness, Eric knew the importance of the evening. He only had a few precious hours to win her heart. Enjoying the spectacular views of the strip, their discussion quickly turned to their future and the possibility of them being together in Alaska. Sitting their champagne glasses down, Eric pulled her closer.

"Sweetheart, what can I do to convince you to come with me to Alaska?"

Staring intensely into her azure blue eyes, he waited pensively for her answer. Thoughts of returning without her were driving him crazy. However, he would do anything she wished.

"Eric, Sweetheart, I love you. The past few days have been the best days of my entire life. But, I need you to know whether or not I board the plane tomorrow evening has nothing to do with my love for you. Everything has happened so fast. A lot is going on in my life, and I need time to think. I just moved to Las Vegas, and I must say that I love living here. Meeting you was totally unexpected. Please, no more talk about Alaska. Let's just spend our last few hours together without any worries or pressure about what tomorrow holds. Tonight I just want to be with you," Lana whispered.

Eric knew the ball was in her court. There was nothing more he could say. However, actions spoke louder than words, and the night was still young. Reaching for the bottle of champagne and glasses, Eric lovingly scooped Lana up in his arms and carried her upstairs.

"Silly, hand me the champagne and glasses before we fall," Lana giggled as they ascended the stairs. She knew that he would make it extremely hard for her to let him go.

"I'll turn on the lights in the jacuzzi. Then, we can enjoy our drinks on the balcony."

Eric's only thoughts were of winning Lana's heart. The jacuzzi would be a great place to start their evening.

"Babe, once again, I have no clothes."

"Sweetheart, you're with me. Clothes are optional," he winked, handing her a fluffy white bathrobe.

Walking into the bathroom, Lana pulled back her long auburn curls with her hair clip. Looking down, she noticed his flannel shirt folded neatly on the vanity. Deciding to wear his soft flannel shirt again, Lana removed her clothes. Putting the bathrobe over his shirt, she looked into the mirror. It wasn't provocative clothing or lingerie, which generally would be worn for a romantic evening. However, she had to work with what she had at the moment.

Quickly stripping down to his briefs, Eric carried the champagne and glasses outside. Turning on the lights in the jacuzzi, he circulated the warm water. Then, stepping inside, Eric poured them each a glass of the sparkling beverage. Watching as Lana walked outside, he smiled, thinking she wasn't wearing anything under the luxurious robe. However, he laughed when she removed the bathrobe revealing his flannel shirt.

"Wow, doll, a flannel shirt. Aren't you a little overdressed?"

"Aren't you?" she teased, noting his black briefs.

"Okay, point taken."

Stepping into the warm, swirling water, she smiled, putting her arms around him.

Their romantic evening was off to a great start as he handed her a glass of the sparkling beverage.

"So, tell me all the things I don't already know about you?" Lana smiled.

"Sweetheart, I think we should start with you. After all, you're the one who's just moved to Vegas?"

Leaning over, Eric kissed her passionately. Setting their glasses down, it quickly became apparent that lengthy discussions regarding their pasts could wait for another time. Pulling her close, Eric began unbuttoning her wet flannel shirt. Zealously kissing the nape of her neck, Eric picked her up, carrying her inside to the bedroom. The remainder of the night was spent in a state of romantic bliss. Shutting out the world as only lovers would, Eric knew he had never loved anyone as much as Lana. As the morning sun made its appearance, it found them wrapped in each other's arms, not having slept.

Staring into Eric's gorgeous blue eyes, a brief moment of sadness washed over Lana. She knew this would be their last evening together unless she chose to give up her life in Vegas.

"Wow, Doll, what a night."

"Yes, Babe, you're right. It was quite a night."

Trying to hide her emotions, Lana wiped tears from her eyes. However, Eric quickly noticed her uneasiness.

"Sweetheart, what's wrong?"

Gently kissing away her tears, Eric knew she was undoubtedly having difficulty deciding whether to stay in Vegas or go with him to Alaska. However, he wasn't going to put added pressure on her. It was entirely up to her at this point. There was nothing more he could do. Holding her in his arms, he could only pray that she would make the right decision.

Later that morning, he felt his heart breaking as he walked Lana to the door. Holding her tight in his arms, he kissed her goodbye. Eric would never love anyone as much as he loved her.

"Well, Doll, I guess this is it. I'll be waiting."

"I love you," Lana smiled.

Arriving at the airport later that evening, Eric checked in for his return flight. Turning around as he stepped onto the escalator, he quickly surveyed the entire bottom floor of the airport, hoping desperately to catch a glimpse of her. But she was nowhere in sight. Apparently, she had decided to stay in Vegas. Taking a deep breath, he continued to the boarding gate.

He took a seat in the waiting area and nervously picked up a magazine. Perhaps it would take his mind off the fact that Lana might have decided to stay in Vegas. But, quickly flipping through its pages, clearly reading wasn't working as a distraction. Lana held a prominent place in his heart, and he would always love her. He anxiously searched for her as he waited for the gate attendant to make the final boarding announcement.

"At this time, we'd like to offer early boarding to all first-class passengers. Also, passengers traveling with small children, as well as those passengers who may need assistance, are welcome to board," the gate agent loudly announced.

Getting up from his seat, he again searched for any sight of Lana. Then, disappointed, he slowly walked down the jetway. He'd never felt more alone. Boarding the aircraft, he took his seat in first class. Lounging back, he decided a stiff drink was in order. Perhaps a glass of straight bourbon on the rocks would ease his worries.

His hands trembled, taking the glass of bourbon from the flight attendant. Downing a quick sip, he touched the smooth, grey leather of the empty seat next to him. His life would be perfect if he could only will her to appear. Reflecting over their incredible weekend, he began to worry if there had been anything he could have done to change her mind.

Starring at every person who slowly boarded the plane, there was no sign of Lana. Finishing his entire drink, Eric decided another shot of bourbon was needed. Stopping the flight attendant as she walked past, he hesitantly asked for another bourbon. With shaking hands, he took the glass and lifted it to his mouth. Undoubtedly, at this point, Lana probably considered him not worth the risk of another move. One which would take her even farther from home. However, nothing mattered to him. Only the fact that he was leaving Vegas without the love of his life.

"At this time, we would like to ask all passengers to take their scats. If you need help storing luggage in the overhead compartments, please inform one of our flight attendants. We will be pushing back from the gate momentarily," the young flight attendant announced.

Reluctantly sitting back in his seat, Eric took in the last views of Vegas. He had accomplished his mission of winning the money needed to keep his business afloat. However, Alaska was beginning to feel like a cold, lonely place. He took another sip of his drink and laid his head against his seat. Closing his eyes, he dreaded the flight home.

Suddenly, hearing a familiar voice, he bolted upright.

"Sir, I believe this seat belongs to me," Lana smiled.

"Oh, my God, Babe, you came." Eric grinned, pulling Lana into his arms for a passionate embrace.

Leaving Vegas, Eric knew he had won more than a poker game. He had unexpectedly won the girl of his dreams.

Chapter Four

"Welcome to McGrath, Alaska," the flight attendant announced. "The local time is 9:30 a.m. The weather this morning is currently clear with a balmy temperature of fifty-two degrees."

"Wow. Is it always this cold?"

"Sweetheart, that's warm for late September, and it's Alaska. I hope you packed some warm clothes. If not, I can share."

"Eric, I refuse to live in your flannel shirts," Lana giggled.

"I think you look sexy in flannel."

Lana glanced out her window and got her first glimpse of McGrath, Alaska. Noting her expression, Eric laughed.

"Geez, Eric, I know you said it was remote, but this is ridiculous. Where's the mall?

"Well, Sweetheart, would you be too disappointed if I told you McGrath doesn't have a mall?"

Reaching for his bag in the overhead compartment, Eric laughed. He knew McGrath offered none of the amenities she was used to in Vegas.

Driving to the small remote cabin, Lana began to have second thoughts about relocating to Alaska. The terrain appeared rugged and isolated. It was utterly foreign to her. Moreover, it offered none of the conveniences she enjoyed in Las Vegas.

"So, how far is your cabin from McGrath?"

Lana began to panic. It seemed as if they had been driving forever.

"You seem worried. It's only about twenty minutes out of McGrath. However, I must warn you it's quite primitive."

"Well, does this primitive cabin have a bed? I feel exhausted." The layover in Seattle had worn her out.

"Sweetheart, don't be silly. It most definitely has a bed. It's not exactly like camping. However, it does have a wood stove."

"Wood stove," Lana freaked. "Did you say wood stove?"

"Lana, it's actually great. But, don't worry, I've become proficient at cooking on it."

Arriving at the cabin, Lana laughed.

Staring at the primitive, weather-beaten structure, it appeared as if it had been standing since the beginning of time. Moss covered the decaying roof, which leaned dangerously. Two mottled windows near the front door seemed inadequate to keep out local wildlife.

"Well, it definitely lives up to your descriptions. Although I must say, it feels worlds removed from Vegas."

Once again, staring at the dilapidated shack, Lana was too tired to care about her new residence. Nevertheless, she was here and would have to make the best of it. There was no turning back.

Unlocking the door, Eric brought the luggage inside. Starting a roaring fire in the fireplace soon gave a soft glow to the log-timbered interior. The cabin began to feel warm and cozy. Even though the rustic decor lacked modern amenities, it felt inviting and relaxing.

"You'll be happy to know that we have a fully functional bathroom behind that door. I'll take your luggage to the bedroom. Are you ready for bed?"

"Are you kidding?" Lana yawned. "I feel drained. I know it's early morning, but if I could just get a few hours of sleep, I think I would feel a lot better."

Reaching for an oversized quilt in the closet, Eric spread it over the bed. Then, pulling back the soft cotton sheets, Lana took off her shoes and jumped into the squeaky bed without the thought of removing her clothes.

"Geez, Sweetheart, aren't you going to change clothes?" Eric laughed.

"I'm too tired," Lana yawned, pulling the covers over her head.

Removing his shoes, Eric stripped down to his briefs and slipped into bed next to her.

"Lana, I'm so glad you're here," Eric winked, giving her a quick kiss.

"Me too, I think?" Lana teased, snuggling against his warm body.

"Eric, do you think Blake would ever come to Alaska? I never told you, but I didn't return to the apartment after leaving the hotel. Megan packed what few things I had and brought them to the Luxor where she works. Blake was still watching her apartment, and she didn't think it was safe. What if he comes to McGrath? I'm worried."

"Please don't worry. No one knows you're here except for Megan, and she would never tell anyone, especially him. You're with me, and you're safe," Eric whispered, holding her tight in his arms. "Get some sleep."

"What the hell was that?" Lana screamed.

Instantly sitting up in bed, she trembled like a frightened child.

"Sweetheart, we're not in the city. You'll get used to the sounds of the local wildlife," Eric laughed.

Finally laying her head on his shoulder, Lana slowly drifted off to sleep. She was too tired to care. She was safe in the comfort of his arms, and that was all that mattered.

Waking up several hours later, Eric felt the rumblings of an empty stomach. Glancing at his watch, it was only five in the evening. However, not having restocked his pantry since leaving for Vegas, Eric knew eating would mean waking sleeping beauty and taking a short drive back to McGrath for supplies. So, leaning over, he gently kissed Lana awake.

"Sweetheart, I hate to wake you, but I fear we might starve unless we drive into town and shop for groceries," Eric teased, smothering her with kisses.

"Eric, I'm still tired. Aren't you supposed to go hunting and kill something? Isn't that how it works out here in the wilderness?" Lana laughed.

Her sense of humor amused him. It was vital to live under such harsh conditions, and it made him love her even more.

"Well, not today," he laughed, giving her a quick kiss. "Let's take a drive into McGrath. I want to take you to Tillman's and introduce you to Norman. And, I need to let Gunner know that I'm back. But, for now, I'll make coffee."

"Okay. If you insist." Rolling over, Lana pulled the covers over her head, trying to sneak in a few extra minutes of sleep.

Returning with a hot cup of coffee, Eric smiled, finding her buried under the warm blankets.

"Sweetheart, I've brought coffee."

Unable to resist the aroma of the hot beverage, Lana threw back the covers.

"Thanks, Babe. Hopefully, the caffeine will wake me from my stupor. I feel completely exhausted."

Finishing her cup of coffee, Lana reluctantly put on her shoes. Then, walking into the tiny makeshift kitchen, she quickly surveyed the pantry.

"Wow. You weren't kidding. There's nothing in here."

"I told you. We have to go shopping, but first, we're stopping at Tillmans Tavern."

Driving into town, Lana once again questioned if her move to Alaska was the right decision. It was disconnected from the lower forty-eight and would be a significant deterrent. Hopefully, Blake would never search for her in McGrath. Glancing at Eric as he maneuvered the Jeep over the rugged single-track road, she gently ran her fingers through his sandy brown hair. She knew he would do anything to keep her safe. It seemed as if fate had somehow mysteriously brought them together. Arriving at Tillmans, Eric parked next to an older Ford Bronco.

"Wow, I think Gunner is here. That's his Bronco," Eric mentioned.

Walking inside, Eric felt proud to show off his girl. Holding Lana's hand, they made their way up to the bar.

"Welcome home," Norman grinned. "Who's this pretty little thing with you?"

"Norman, this is Lana Harris. We met in Vegas, and I persuaded her to relocate to McGrath."

"Nice to meet you," Lana smiled.

"Oh, my God, you're back," Gunner yelled, catching sight of Eric. "I kinda figured you might not come back. McGrath isn't for everyone. But, wow, did you win her in the poker game?" Gunner added, staring impolitely at Lana. It always appeared his rude behavior got the best of him.

"Gunner, this is Lana Harris, and no, I didn't win her in a poker game. However, she did save my new business venture. It's a long story. I'll explain later."

"Well, Lana, any friend of Eric's is a friend of mine. Norman, pour them each a Duck Fart," Gunner remarked, unable to take his eyes off her.

"What's a Duck Fart?" Lana questioned, somewhat suspicious of Gunner's request.

"Oh, it's a layered shot of Crown Royal, Kahlua, and Bailey's Irish Cream. Trust me. It's Gunner's favorite," Eric interjected.

"So when did you get back?" Gunner inquired. "I sure hope that poker game paid off cause I sure would like to keep my job. I can use all the work I can get around here."

"Well, you're safe for now, thanks to this beautiful girl," Eric winked, giving Lana a quick kiss.

"Norman, give this gorgeous girl a bowl of that chili you made this morning. Norman makes the best chili you've ever eaten. Just don't ask what's in it," Gunner laughed. "It could be caribou, moose, or elk."

Nudging Eric, Lana's eyes silently showed she was completely freaked out.

"Babe, I don't think I can eat that," Lana whispered.

"Sweetheart, I'm sure he's just teasing. But, don't worry, Norman makes a great grilled cheese sandwich."

"Why don't you folks take that empty table? I'll bring everything over in a minute," Norman suggested. He knew Gunner was giving the young girl a hard time. His chili was always made with 100% lean beef. The best money could buy.

"Norman, I think Lana would love one of your famous grilled cheese sandwiches along with her bowl of chili," Eric laughed, playing along with Gunner's amusement.

Inconspicuously reaching under Eric's jacket, Lana suddenly gave him a painful pinch as she whispered in his ear.

"Eric, I don't want the chili. Didn't you hear me?"

"Lana, you don't have to eat it. Trust me, it's just a joke."

"I'll have the chili and grilled cheese out in a few minutes," Norman replied, setting their drinks on the table.

She wasn't sure about the Duck Fart either. However, it appeared more palatable than wild game.

"Well, Eric, let's toast to your return, specifically to this stunning beauty you brought with you," Gunner grinned, lifting his shot glass towards Lana. "Thanks for saving my job."

Sampling a small taste of the chili, Lana smiled. She was relieved to discover the dish appeared only to contain ground beef. However, she wasn't entirely convinced. Eric's friends seemed a bit bizarre but harmless. After catching up on the latest news regarding the local Bush Pilots and enjoying their drinks along with the chili, Eric suggested they call it a night.

"Gunner, thanks for the drinks and chili, but I think we better call it a night. I need to stop at the grocery store before heading back to the cabin. Then, I'm going to teach Lana how to cook on a wood stove."

"Well, good luck with that," Gunner laughed, pushing his chair back from the table. "Oh, Miss Lana, I'm sure you're a great cook. I meant good luck with that wood stove. They can be a bitch, uncontrollable like the temperament of a woman, either hot as a firecracker or cold as ice."

Shocked at Gunner's description of wood stoves, Lana wasn't quickly warming up to him or his rude personality. However, she was willing to give him the chance to redeem himself since he seemed to be such a good friend of Eric's.

Stopping by the local grocery mart, Eric purchased a small stockpile of fresh vegetables, meats, condiments, everything they needed for the next week. After adding a case of water and two bottles of wine, they were finally ready to leave McGrath. Driving out of town after dark, the jeep's headlights reflected the narrow, dirt road filled with potholes. Swerving to avoid the bumps, Lana felt it was like playing a game of dodgeball in the dark. Finally, rounding the next curve, the familiar sight of the dilapidated cabin came into view.

"Babe, we're home. It's certainly not Caesar's Palace," Eric laughed.

"You're right. It certainly isn't," Lana agreed.

For a brief moment, she again doubted her decision to relocate to McGrath. However, as Eric ran around to open her car door, she knew she would follow him anywhere with just one look at his handsome, muscular body. After all, he was a retired Marine, and she felt safe with him. Taking another glance at the derelict cabin, it was clear that it would definitely need a lot of improvements. Hopefully, the place was only temporary, but it would be home for tonight and the immediate future. After helping Eric bring in the groceries and putting them away in the pantry and small fridge, the fatigue from their earlier flight returned with a vengeance. She'd never felt more exhausted.

Quickly starting a roaring fire, the cabin felt warm and cozy once again. Opening a bottle of wine, Eric poured them each a drink.

"Sweetheart, it's so wonderful having you here. This old cabin can get lonely."

Pulling her over to his shabby, worn sofa, she removed her shoes, tucking her feet under her petite frame. Snuggled against Eric's muscular body, she felt safe and relaxed as she closed her eyes. The effects of the wine and the warmth of the fire consumed her. Suddenly, hearing a loud, ferocious howl, Lana opened her eyes. Bolting upwards, she cringed.

"Oh, my God, what was that?"

"Babe, it's just a wolf," Eric laughed. "You're completely safe. Finish your wine; it will help you relax."

Quickly downing her entire drink, Eric refilled her glass.

"I've never lived in the woods. How do you ever get used to hearing those weird, creepy sounds?" Lana asked frantically, guzzling her drink.

"Sweetheart, I think you should slow down on those. Remember, you tend to get nauseous when you drink. Those creepy sounds, as you call them, are simply the wildlife. We are, after all, in their territory. It's completely natural. You'll eventually get used to hearing them. I think we should turn in for the evening."

"Great idea. I feel exhausted, and I'm not sure that I like being awake after dark."

As Lana clung tightly to Eric, he gently pulled her towards the tiny bedroom. Her naivety made him smile. Evidently, she was out of her element being so isolated. However, he knew their isolation was a significant distance from Blake. Whom, he couldn't rule out trying to hurt her.

Waking to the early morning sun peeping in through the mottled window panes and the smell of coffee, Lana sat up, wiping the sleep from her eyes. Then, as her feet touched the cold wooden floors, she grabbed her slippers and robe. Hurriedly making her way out to the warmth of the fireplace, she found Eric stacking wooden splinters under the round, flat cast iron burners of the wood stove.

"How do eggs and bacon sound?" he asked, handing her a steaming cup of coffee.

"Great, I must have been tired. I didn't know you were up."

"I knew you were exhausted, so I decided to let you sleep. How do you prefer your eggs?"

"Scrambled."

"If you feel up to it, I thought I would fly you up to the wildlife refuge. I want to show you why I fell in love with Alaska."

"Sounds interesting. I know there has to be something other than this cabin keeping you here," Lana questioned.

"Sweetheart, I know our living conditions are rather harsh, but I promise it's not permanent. If you want, we can look for a place in town. The cabin was a quick decision when I arrived. I was alone, and it didn't take much to make me happy. I put most of my savings into purchasing my Aviat Husky."

"Actually, that would be an awesome idea. Why don't we look for a rental in McGrath, and you can keep the cabin."

"Great. I totally agree. Next week, we'll look for a rental. However, today I want to show you what I do for a living and why I chose Alaska. So finish your eggs, and I'll pack us a quick lunch."

After spending a fun-filled day with Eric flying over the spectacular outbacks of Alaska, Lana began to fall in love with its beauty. She wasn't even bothered by the flight. The unbelievable magnificence of the vistas and terrain below kept her glued to the window. It was easy to understand why Eric had chosen this part of the world to settle down and start a new business.

The cabin would temporarily provide them with an escape from town if Blake showed up. However, the next day found them back in McGrath and searching for a new residence.

Chapter Five

After an exhaustive search and finally settling into a spacious two-bedroom apartment above Willard's Hardware Store, they were home. It was completely furnished and conveniently located across the street from Tillmans Tavern. The location couldn't have been better. Its convenience allowed Eric to discuss business at a moment's notice with the locals and incoming tourists. Chatting with prospective clients over beer gave him the edge to enlarge his clientele. It also allowed Lana to go back to work. Eric convinced Norman that he lacked someone of the female persuasion to serve drinks. However, Lana's resume from Caesar's Hotel, along with her gorgeous profile, made her more than qualified to serve drinks and tend the bar at the local establishment. Norman consulted Bill, and without hesitation, Lana was hired on the spot, no questions asked.

Their new residence gave Lana a feeling of security. She no longer felt vulnerable and disconnected from town. Snuggling into the warmth of Eric's arms on their first night in the apartment, she felt safe. She was falling in love with Alaska, and more importantly, she had finally found someone who cherished her. Lana no longer questioned her move to Alaska.

Turning over in bed to face Eric, Lana smiled. "Thanks for renting the apartment. I absolutely love it," she whispered.

"Your wish is my command," Eric laughed, giving her a quick kiss.

"And, thanks for persuading Norman to hire me."

"Sweetheart, that was easy! You're overqualified. Tillmans isn't exactly Caesar's Palace. Bill and Norman are lucky to have you."

"Awe, thanks, Babe."

Playfully returning his kiss, Lana cuddled even closer.

"Eric, I received a text message from Megan yesterday. She said Blake finally left Las Vegas. However, he called and put a nasty message on her phone before he left. It appears Blake is going back to Newport, but he told Megan that he would never stop looking for me. Blake said I could run, but I could never hide. I'm worried. He is determined to keep searching for me. Do you think he will somehow find out that I'm in McGrath? I'm terrified."

"Didn't Megan promise to keep your location a secret? She's your best friend. I don't think she would betray your confidence."

"Yes, but you don't know Blake." Sitting up in bed, Lana's expression quickly reflected panic.

"Sweetheart, we're in Alaska, and McGrath isn't exactly a huge place. Don't worry." Pulling her back into his arms, Eric held her close.

"You're safe with me. Remember, I'm a retired Marine," he teased, flexing his biceps. "Doll, I think I'm more than capable of taking care of you. Let me show you," he winked wickedly.

Falling helplessly into his embrace, their heated, passionate kisses quickly melted away her remaining worries, for now.

The following day, Eric dressed quietly. Deciding to let her sleep in, he walked into their modern kitchen, which now contained a few luxuries, a gas stove, microwave, and a large fridge. Recalling the old wood stove left behind in the cabin, he smiled. Lana had been a good sport regarding its primitive amenities. Relocating from Las Vegas to the rugged outbacks of Alaska could not have been easy.

Nevertheless, he was determined to make life as comfortable as possible for her. So after brewing a pot of coffee, he reached into the fridge and gathered the ingredients to make omelets. Shopping for groceries the day before, it was completely stocked.

Slowly strolling into the kitchen, Lana rubbed the sleep from her eyes.

"Good morning, sleeping beauty. I hope I didn't wake you?"

"No. It was the invigorating aroma of freshly brewed coffee," Lana smiled, pulling her hair into a ponytail.

Reaching into the cabinets, Eric grabbed a cup. Then, giving her a quick kiss, he poured her a cup of the hot brew.

"I was going to wake you when breakfast was made, but since you're up, would you please hand me the skillet?"

"Not a problem."

Reaching for the skillet, Lana placed it on the burner.

"I have to say this stove is a huge improvement," she laughed.

She took a seat at the small dinette table. Gazing into the adjoining room, the morning sun brilliantly streamed through the tall, narrow windows. It immersed the living room in a soft glow. The apartment was more than she could have hoped for, considering they were in McGrath. The rooms were large and completely furnished. A beige leather sectional sat near the front windows, and light oak custom cabinets containing a small television lined the length of the interior wall.

"What are your plans for today?" Lana inquired, taking a sip of the hot liquid.

"I promised to meet Gunner at the airport. He wants to go over a couple of maintenance issues before the harsh winter sets in."

Placing a tasty omelet in front of her, Eric returned to the stove.

"Wow, this looks amazing. Aren't you going to eat?"

"Of course, I'm just adding a few pieces of chopped moose jerky to my omelet. I assumed you might not appreciate the local flavor."

"Well, you assumed right," Lana smiled, smothering her omelet in ketchup.

"Would you like to ride out to the airport after breakfast?" Eric questioned, pouring himself another cup of coffee.

"Thanks, but I promised Norman that I would come in this afternoon. He's expecting a large delivery from Anchorage, and I'm going to cover the bar for him while he stocks."

Taking a seat next to Lana, he cut into his delicious omelet.

"Sweetheart, about last night, I don't want you to worry about Blake. McGrath is a small town, and if he ever dared to travel this far north, the locals would notice. The people here are suspicious of newbies. Strangers showing up for anything other than a booked excursion are scrutinized and watched relentlessly. However, once the word got out regarding his reason for coming to McGrath, the natives would have no problem dealing with him. Trust me. You're completely safe."

"Thanks for trying to make me feel safe; however, like I said last night, you don't know him. That relationship cost me not only physical scars but emotional ones as well."

"Babe, you're with me now," Eric winked, reaching over to take her hand. Finish your breakfast, and don't worry."

Noticing the extreme anguish in her eyes, he wished Blake would make the fatal mistake of following her to McGrath. Eric felt as if he could effortlessly kill Blake without remorse. If he didn't beat him to the point of death, Eric would undoubtedly make him pay for the long months of abuse he inflicted on Lana.

Carrying their empty plates to the sink, Eric had an idea that would surely take her mind away from her worries.

"Tonight after you get off work, I have something special planned. I'll stop by Tillmans later this evening and pick you up."

"Well, aren't you going to give me a hint?"

"No, let's just say that if it all works out, I think you'll be impressed," Eric winked.

McGrath was a small place, remote, and lacking in amenities. Unless you were an avid hunter or adventurous, she could not think of a single thing that it offered which would remotely impress her. However, she was willing to play along with his silly ideas.

"Okay, I can't wait," Lana insisted, walking to the bedroom to dress for work.

Later that evening, the sun was setting as Eric parked in front of Tillmans. He couldn't wait to see Lana. The mere thoughts of taking her up to the summit of the Revelation Mountains excited him.

"Hey Norman, where's Lana?"

"Oh, she's in the stock room organizing the shelves. I don't know what I would do without her. She's the best thing that ever happened to this old bar and by far the best-looking young woman around these parts. You were fortunate to meet that gorgeous girl in Las Vegas. I'm surprised she wasn't already taken."

"You would certainly be right about that. Lana is definitely one of a kind and just crazy enough to follow this Marine back to Alaska."

Knowing Lana was in the backroom and unable to hear their conversation, Eric felt he should make Norman aware of the remote possibility that Blake might show up in McGrath. Even though the chance of Blake actually following Lana this far north seemed outrageous, he knew Tillmans would probably be the first place he might inquire regarding her whereabouts. The fact Lana worked at Tillmans put her in a dangerous situation. It seemed like a good idea to make Norman aware of the potential problem. At least he could give them a heads up if Blake decided to walk into the bar unexpectedly.

"Speaking of Lana, I'm sure she hasn't mentioned her connection to someone by the name of Blake Boswell. She was in a relationship with him before moving to Las Vegas. In fact, she relocated to Vegas to escape his abuse. From what I know about him, he appears to be potentially dangerous. However, he owns a Real Estate Business in Newport, Oregon, and comes from a wealthy family. Can you believe he followed her to Vegas? Now it appears he told her roommate that he would not stop searching until he found her. I know it sounds unbelievable that he would come all this way to try and find her, but Lana seems convinced that he would do just that. She's even having nightmares about him showing up in McGrath." Eric sighed. "If you happen to notice anyone that might seem suspicious or ask questions about her, I need you to call me right away. Don't mention that we had this discussion; I don't want her to feel overly concerned. I just want to err on the side of caution. I don't have a photo, but if anyone asks about her, call me immediately."

"Don't worry. I'm not going to let anyone know Lana is in McGrath. In fact, I kind of hope he shows up. If you catch my drift, this is a great place for someone to disappear. I'm not going to let anyone harm that gorgeous, sweet girl."

"Thanks, Norman."

"Hey, Babe," Lana smiled, walking out of the stock room. "I didn't know you were here. I was in the back room organizing the shelves. What a mess, but I finally got it all done. Are you ready to go?" Lana questioned, looking down at her watch. "I still have a half-hour before my shift ends."

"Norman, could you possibly let this beautiful girl leave work a few minutes early?"

"Of course, I think she's earned it; that stock room was a disaster. I'm not a very organized person, and it was long overdue. You two get out of here," Norman grinned, waving them towards the door with his bar towel.

"Thanks, Norman," Eric grinned, taking Lana's hand.

Hurriedly pulling Lana towards the exit, Gunner surprisingly walked into the bar.

"Where are you guys going in such a hurry?" he questioned.

"Oh, I promised to show Lana one of my favorite places in McGrath."

"Really? We have special places around here," Gunner teased. Then, scratching his long, scruffy beard, he wondered where on earth they were headed as he watched them run out the door.

"What can I get you?" Norman asked as Gunner approached the bar.

"My usual."

"Okay. One Duck Fart."

"They sure make a cute couple. I think Eric won more than a poker game while he was in Vegas," Gunner chuckled, throwing back his first drink. "They seem perfect for each other."

"Well, after what I just heard from Eric, I think she deserves a nice guy," Norman frowned, pouring Gunner another drink.

"Oh yeah, what did he tell you?"

Gunner wasn't about to let Norman off the hook without answers. After all, this was a tavern, and McGrath was a small town. There were no secrets in this remote outpost.

"Well, Eric is worried about someone from Lana's past following her to McGrath."

"What? Why in the world would someone follow her all the way up here? They would have to be crazy."

"I suppose you could say that he is crazy and abusive, at least according to Eric. He appeared to be somewhat worried. He wanted to make sure that I was put on notice to watch out for someone by the name of Blake Boswell. He didn't have a photo, but you and I both know this town like the back of our hands. We don't get a lot of strangers other than tourists. So it would be easy to spot anyone who doesn't appear to have a good reason to be here, especially if they are inquiring about Lana. Keep this bit of news just between the two of us for now—no need to involve Eric until we need to. Oh, one last thing, Eric mentioned this guy owns a Real Estate Company in Newport, Oregon, and comes from a family of significant wealth. That in itself would distinguish him from just about everyone around these parts," Norman smirked, pouring another Duck Fart.

"You just let me know if someone comes in asking questions. I ain't about to let anyone hurt that sweet girl. He'll have to answer to me first," Gunner growled, throwing back another shot. "You know it's easy to disappear around these parts."

Norman worried he had spoken out of place. Knowing Gunner as he did and the fact that Gunner had taken Eric under his wing, so to speak, he knew it might be all too easy for Gunner to handle the situation in his style. Norman was sure that Eric wasn't aware of Gunner's entire past or the fact he'd served time in Folsom Prison as an accomplice to murder. A lot of the people living in these parts had a criminal history. Like Gunner, it was usually the reason they had relocated from the lower forty-eight.

Reaching the jeep, Eric quickly started the engine to warm up the vehicle.

"It's only a short distance out of town but well worth the drive," Eric winked, leaning over to give her a quick kiss.

"You and your surprises," Lana smiled, holding her hands up to the warmth of the heater. "This better be worth the trip because I'm freezing."

"Babe, you worry too much. It will only take a few minutes for the car to get warm. I promise you won't freeze," he smiled.

Driving out of McGrath, it wasn't long before they reached the foothills of the Revelation Mountains. Winding up the rugged, narrow road towards the summit, darkness soon enveloped them. The cold, clear, starlit night was breathtaking. Hopefully, tonight they would catch a glimpse of the Northern Lights. There was no way to know for sure. It was always a guess as to whether they would be visible. However, it was the perfect location and his only reason for bringing her to such a remote site. He didn't have to wait long, as luck was on his side.

"Babe, did you see that?" Lana screamed. "I think I see the Northern Lights," she exclaimed. She was like a naive child experiencing the wonders of something so unexpected. Something which others hope to experience, but most never get the chance.

Rounding the next curve, they arrived at the summit. Parking the jeep, Eric grabbed the warm coats, a thermos of hot chocolate, and a heavy blanket.

"Sweetheart, I know you're partial to the lights of Vegas, but I wanted to show you our amazing lights. What do you think?" he asked, helping her into the warmth of the quilted jacket.

"Eric, it's unbelievable," she answered totally fascinated by the swirling, green lights which danced so brilliantly overhead in the night sky.

Taking Lana's hand, Eric led her over to a massive flat rock that jutted outward from the side of the mountain. Spreading out the blanket, he gently pulled her down next to him. Lovingly he drew her into the warmth of his embrace, kissing her passionately. It felt as if their bodies literally melted into the vastness of the universe. The coldness of the night quickly vanished with each kiss. Tingles of excitement raced throughout her small frame.

Eric squeezed her hand, suggesting they lay back on the flat, rock outcropping to enhance their view. Gazing upward into the immensity of the dark, starlit night, they watched the brilliance of the swirling, green, iridescent lights move transparently across the night sky. It felt as if they were the only two people on earth. The stars appeared close enough to touch. Closing her eyes for a moment, the night felt magical. The sensation of floating upward into the vastness of the night sky crept over her as she imagined herself encased in the dazzling, green mist. In the tranquility of the moment, Lana felt at one with the universe. Then, hearing Eric's soft voice, she opened her eyes.

"Sweetheart, you appear totally captivated. Thanks for sharing this incredible evening with me. I love you. I'll always love you," he whispered, leaning in for another kiss.

"Why are you whispering?" Lana laughed. "I believe we're the only ones here."

"I guess it's because each time that I come here, it feels like being in church. I can't explain it. Surrounded by such beauty, it exemplifies the fact that we are not alone."

"Wow, Babe, that's deep. I think it's time for a cup of hot cocoa," Lana suggested playfully, returning his kisses.

Getting up to pour the hot chocolate, Eric knew he would always be hopelessly in love with her. However, it so happened that fate had brought her into his life. Eric knew he never wanted to be without her.

Sipping their hot drinks under the magical influence of the Northern Lights was incredibly romantic. Looking over at Lana, he smiled with a wink.

"So, sweetheart, which lights do you prefer? Is it Vegas or Alaska?"

"Yours, of course, there's nothing magical about neon lights." Lana grinned.

Pouring the last of the hot chocolate, it was finally time to leave. Folding the blanket, Lana never imagined finding love so soon after leaving Blake. Perhaps she had been the lucky one finding Eric's wallet.

Chapter Six

Lana found herself falling more in love with Eric and the quaint town of McGrath. Life was good. Memories of Blake drifted further from her mind with each passing day. So she was startled and unexpectedly caught off guard when Eric walked into the living room late one evening with a perplexed expression.

"Sweetheart, we need to talk," Eric mentioned nonchalantly.

Not wanting to alarm her, he considered his tactics of breaking the news. However, it appeared she'd read his mind.

"What's going on? It's Blake, isn't it?" Lana grimaced, immediately laying her magazine on the coffee table. "Is he in McGrath?"

"I can't say for sure, but a man fitting his description came into Tillman's this evening. Norman said he showed your photo and was inquiring about you. Norman gave no indication of ever having seen you or the fact you're living in McGrath. Please don't worry. I'm sure he'll be gone in a few days. Maybe he's already left. However, just to be safe, Norman doesn't want you to come into work for a few days," Eric explained, giving her a quick kiss.

"Eric, I've told you more than once, you don't know him. Blake considers me his possession. He's unstable, and there's no way to know what he might do."

Standing up, Lana was visibly shaken as she walked over to close the living room drapes. "What are we going to do?"

"Well, for one thing, we're not going to panic. Trust me. There is no way that either Norman or I will ever let him find you. You do trust me, right?"

"Yes, I guess, but what are we going to do?" Lana reiterated, pacing the floor.

"Nothing at the moment, except for the fact you're going to take a few days off. Let's just see how long he stays."

Lana appeared extremely worried. It was evident that flashbacks of Blake's abuse still tormented her.

"Babe, sit down. I'm going to pour you a shot of bourbon. It'll calm your nerves."

Even though the situation concerned him, he would never allow Lana to know. The last thing he wanted was for her to worry. However, if Blake should make the brutal mistake of continuing his search for her in McGrath, Eric knew that he was more than capable of handling the situation. What he could have never known were the steps that Gunner would take to keep Lana's whereabouts a secret.

Hearing the sound of her cell phone, Lana shivered nervously and answered.

"Hello."

Answering the call, she feared it might be Blake. However, after changing her cell number, there was no way on earth he could have known. Hearing Megan's voice, she felt relieved.

"Lana, I'm sorry to call so late, but there's something you need to know. I'm afraid Blake might be on his way to McGrath," Megan warned.

"Thanks for the warning, but you're a little late. Blake is here. He came into the bar where I work, asking questions. Norman, my boss, said he even brought out my photo. So how in the world did he know I was in McGrath?"

"Well," Megan paused. "I'm sorry. I'm really sorry. I think your sister told him. I'm sure she wasn't aware of the consequences."

"Which sister? And, how in the hell did she know that I was in Alaska? Megan, you promised not to say anything. You promised! What happened?" Lana screamed.

"Lana, calm down. It was Beth. You know she always had a soft spot in her heart for Blake. His money always had a way of influencing her even though she was aware of his abusive nature."

"That just figures. Mom and Beth have always been close. If mom was as upset as you said, it only makes sense she might have mentioned something to her. Who else knows?" Lana demanded, walking over to take a quick peep out the window.

"No one as far as I know."

Megan, how could you let this happen? You're my best friend. I trusted you."

"Lana, please, you have to forgive me. Your mother called and insisted that I tell her where you were. Lana, she was upset. I had to tell her. She was worried. Hearing how distraught she was, I had no choice. I didn't broadcast the fact that you moved to Alaska. I love you. You know that I would never purposely do anything to harm you or get you upset. Trust me, no one could have ever wanted you to escape the bonds of that deranged man more than me," Megan explained, crying softly.

"Well, it doesn't matter how it happened. Blake is here now, and I have to find a way to deal with it. I'll call you later. I'm just too upset to talk right now."

"I'm sorry," Megan sobbed.

Hanging up the phone, Lana sat down on the couch. Curling up into a ball, she was visibly shaken.

"Please, take a few sips," Eric encouraged, handing her a small shot glass. "You need this."

Sitting down beside her, Eric held her in his arms.

"Babe, we're going to get through this. I'm a Marine. I've dealt with a lot worse things in my life. But, trust me, when I get finished with him, he'll regret he ever thought of following you to McGrath." Taking the back of his hand, he softly wiped the tears from her eyes. "I'll never allow him to harm you again. I promise. Now, finish your drink."

"Eric, I don't want you to hurt him. That's not what I want. Maybe you could just find a way to encourage him to go home."

"Oh, I'll encourage him, alright," Eric grinned.

Staring into his eyes, Lana smiled with tears gently rolling down her face. She knew Eric meant every word.

"Babe, what would I do without you? I feel so lucky to have you in my life."

"Sweetheart, I'm the lucky one. Let's go to bed. No more crying," Eric winked, picking her up.

Gently pulling back the soft duvet, it was apparent the strong drink had worked its magic to relax the beautiful girl he held in his arms. She just needed a good night's rest, and hopefully, tomorrow, things would be better. However, it was evident sleep wasn't the only thing on her mind. Playfully kissing him, Lana pulled him down beside her. Reaching over to turn out the light, Eric lovingly drew her into his arms. Feeling the warmth of his body, Lana's worries vanished with each passionate kiss.

Waking first the following morning, Eric stared at the gorgeous girl who still slept peacefully next to him. Hopefully, today would bring news that Blake had left McGrath.

"Good morning, Doll," Eric whispered as Lana opened her eyes. "Why don't you sleep in this morning? You don't have to be at work. I'm going to make coffee and start breakfast. Afterward, I'm going down to Tillmans. But, first, I need to talk to Norman."

"Wait, I'll come with you," Lana announced, sitting up.

"You're not going anywhere, young lady. You're going to remain here in the apartment with the doors locked until I get back," Eric insisted, kissing her gently on the forehead.

"I'm a big girl. I can take care of myself."

"That may be, but you're with me now, and I don't want you anywhere near Blake. He could be dangerous. His history of abuse makes him unpredictable, and I'm not taking any chances. So go back to sleep. I'll call you later."

"Oh, I'm making blueberry pancakes," Eric winked with a smile. "I'll put yours in the oven to keep warm. I love you."

Lana felt secure pulling the covers over her head, knowing she no longer had to fight her battles. Instead, she had a confident Marine, who just happened to be the love of her life.

Walking into Tillmans later that morning, Eric was surprised to find Gunner sitting at the bar conversing with Norman. However, it appeared their conversation quieted as he approached.

"So, what brings you here this early?" Norman questioned.

"What do you think?"

"Oh that, don't worry, Gunner and I have devised a little plan," Norman teased.

"Can I get you something to drink?"

"No thanks, too early in the morning."

"Ain't no such thing as too early," Gunner scoffed under his breath.

"Did you let Lana know to stay home today?" Norman inquired.

"Don't worry, she's sleeping safely at the apartment," Eric answered, taking a seat next to Gunner. "I'm almost too afraid to ask, but tell me more about this so-called little plan of yours."

"Oh, not much to tell, really. Gunner just offered to take him for a little ride."

"Why do I fear that has a deeper meaning?" Eric laughed. "On second thought, you can pour me a cup of coffee."

"Just made a fresh pot," Norman replied, reaching for a cup. He knew that Eric had no idea of Gunner's past or the fact that he had served time in Folsom Prison for manslaughter.

"We're not going to let anything happen to our beautiful girl," Gunner spoke up, tossing back a shot.

"That wasn't exactly my question."

Eric knew these old gruffs like the back of his hand. He also knew if they had a plan, they were not about to let him in on it.

"Oh, there ain't no plan," Gunner mentioned. "He wouldn't want to mess with an old goat like me, that's for sure."

"Why do I have a hard time believing you?" Eric grinned, finishing his coffee.

He didn't want to leave Lana alone for too long. But, knowing how easily she worried, he felt the need to stay close. He could never forgive himself if, God forbid, Blake somehow managed to find out about the apartment or something tragic happened.

"Well, gents, I'm heading back over to the apartment to check on Lana. If Blake happens to come back, I want to be called immediately. I have my suspicions that he's still in the area. Don't hesitate to call me. And, thanks for the coffee."

"Will do, and please tell Lana not to worry," Norman insisted.

"Yeah, we've got this," Gunner scoffed, stroking his thick, scruffy beard.

"That's what bothers me." Eric laughed, walking out of Tillmans. He knew the two old guys were up to something.

"Wow, I'm glad he's gone. He might be a Marine, but he ain't got nothing on this old fart. I might be older and a lot crustier, but when it comes to this neck of the woods, I'm a wise old owl," Gunner scowled. "Pour me another shot."

"You've got it," Norman replied, opening a new bottle of Crown Royal. "Seriously, Gunner, how far would you go to ensure Blake never comes back?" Norman questioned, unsure if he really wanted to know his answer.

"Far enough."

Hearing those two words fly out of Gunner's mouth sent chills down Norman's spine.

"Say, if you've got a few minutes, I could sure use some help in the back room before it gets too busy out here. Giving Lana the day off has left me short-handed."

"Sure."

Throwing back his entire drink, Gunner managed without staggering to get up from his barstool and follow Norman to the storage room.

Arriving back at the apartment, everything was quiet. It was apparent Lana was still asleep.

Walking into the bedroom, Eric began kissing her awake.

"Geez, Babe, what time is it?" Lana asked, rubbing her eyes. "I must have slept the entire morning."

"You needed the rest. You received some rather shocking news last night. While you were sleeping, I stopped by Tillmans for a few minutes," Eric smiled, slipping into bed next to her. "I believe Norman and Gunner are up to something. Their conversation got awfully quiet when I walked in."

"Oh, it's only your imagination running wild. What could those two possibly be up to at their age?"

"I'm not sure."

Eric laughed, thinking about the situation.

"You know those guys love you, and they would do anything for you. I guess that's what scares me."

"Well, they already seem like family. Norman didn't think twice about giving me a job, and Gunner has been a big help at the airport with your plane."

"I know. The people in McGrath are really nice. No sign of Blake. I'm sure he's left the area." Trying to keep Lana's emotions calm, Eric didn't believe a word he'd uttered.

"No harm in a little white lie," he thought to himself.

"I'm starving. Did you make pancakes?"

"Yes, ma'am. Are you ready to eat breakfast? Stay here. I'll be right back."

Running into the kitchen, Eric warmed the blueberry pancakes and maple syrup. Then, adding a couple of sausages to the plate, it looked scrumptious. Checking the coffee pot, it was still hot, so he poured Lana a cup of coffee and brought breakfast to her.

"Wow, I feel pampered. So, what am I supposed to do on my day off?" Lana inquired, shoveling pancakes into her mouth. "You don't really think you're going to keep me locked up in this apartment for the entire day, do you?"

"Well, I can think of a few things we can do," Eric teased wickedly.

"Babe, I'm serious."

"Oh, and I'm not?" Eric winked.

"Come closer. I want to thank you for breakfast."

"My kind of girl."

However, before Eric could even set the breakfast tray on the bedside table, his cell phone rang.

"Damn, talk about timing. This better be important."

Hearing only half of the conversation, Lana knew something was up. She suspected Blake had returned to Tillmans.

"It's Blake, isn't it? He's still here. He came back to Tillmans, didn't he?"

Shivering from thoughts of him not having left McGrath, Lana pulled the covers up to her chin.

"Yes. Sweetheart, don't worry. Norman said he left with Gunner."

"What the hell is that supposed to mean? Why would Blake leave Tillmans with Gunner? He doesn't even know him?"

"I'm not sure, and that's what scares me?"

"You don't think Gunner would hurt him, do you?"

"I don't think so, but Gunner definitely has anger issues. I certainly wouldn't want to get on his bad side, and he drinks like a fish. Unfortunately, there's not a lot we can do at this point. Norman said he would keep me in the loop. He's supposed to call when Gunner returns."

"Wow, Gunner," Lana grinned, sitting up in bed. "Maybe Blake has finally met his match. I just hope he doesn't kill him."

"Gunner might not be the smartest guy in town, but I seriously doubt he would kill anyone."

Eric knew Gunner had a bad temper, but he didn't want Lana to know those exact thoughts had crossed his mind.

"No, Gunner would never do anything like that," Eric lied, trying to convince himself. "He might make Blake squirm, but I'm sure he would never seriously harm anyone."

"Well, I'm getting dressed. I'm going down to Tillmans."

"No. You're staying right here. We're going to wait for Norman to call."

"Eric, I love you, but you're not going to tell me what I can or can't do. Got it."

"Alright," Eric reluctantly caved. "I'm coming with you. Marines never back down from a fight."

"Babe, it's not that I'm worried about Blake. I feel responsible. I don't want anyone to get hurt."

"Okay, but if Gunner and Blake return and things get ugly, I'm getting you out of there."

"Alright, let's go," Lana frowned, putting on a pair of jeans with a light gray sweater. Then, quickly pulling her long auburn hair into a ponytail, they walked out the door.

Eric didn't see Gunner's Ford Bronco parked out front. This wasn't good. Entering the dimly lit tavern, things were unusually quiet. In fact, the place was almost deserted.

"Wow. Where is everyone? It's almost noon, and you serve the best lunch in McGrath," Eric complimented, pulling out a bar stool for Lana.

"Lana, I'm not sure you should be here. I told you to take the day off," Norman admonished.

"It's okay. Eric told me not to come, but I feel responsible. If things get out of control between Gunner and Blake, I would feel bad if anything happened to Gunner. But, trust me, I'm not the least bit worried about Blake. That man deserves to be roughed up."

"Well, you certainly don't have to worry about Gunner. He can hold his own," Norman laughed, reaching behind the bar for coffee cups.

"Yeah, but there's a whole lot of wilderness out there. Someone could easily disappear," Eric blurted out. The words just flew out of his mouth without consideration of Lana's feelings.

"Oh, Sweetheart, I'm sorry. I didn't mean to imply that Gunner might actually kill Blake."

"Wow, where did that come from?" Norman questioned, pouring them each a cup of coffee.

He knew that Eric was unaware of Gunner's past. However, Norman knew that Eric's training and time spent in the Marines had undoubtedly given him proficient skills at reading people, and Gunner wasn't exactly hard to read. He readily gave his opinions on everything.

"How does a bowl of chili and grilled cheese sandwiches sound?" Norman asked, changing the subject.

"Actually, that sounds pretty good. How about you, babe?" Eric spoke up, looking at Lana. "Would you like a bowl of Norman's famous chili and a grilled cheese sandwich?"

"Oh, I'm good. I just had blueberry pancakes, remember?"

Lana had never forgotten her previous experience with Norman's chili. These guys were great at practical jokes. She could never be sure what type of meat Norman used in his famous dish. She wasn't so sure about his assurance that he always used only 100% ground beef, and she wasn't going to chance eating local, wild game of any description.

"Geez, Sweetheart, you should try it. It's delicious. You've tasted it before," Eric teased as Norman sat a large bowl in front of him.

"That's okay. You enjoy it. I've got other things on my mind."

"Lana, please don't worry," Norman smiled, reaching across the bar to take her hand. "Most girls who endured what you have at that man's hands would love the idea of Blake meeting up with someone like Gunner. Everything is going to be fine. It's been a long time since anyone was murdered in McGrath. I'm just teasing. There has never been a murder in McGrath, at least that I'm aware of," Norman laughed. "Lighten up. I'll make you something to calm your nerves."

Returning with a Duck Fart, Norman set the drink on the bar with a napkin.

"What is it about this drink that makes it so popular with you guys?"

"Oh, I don't know," Norman paused. "Maybe it's the name or the color, just down it. It isn't so bad. I'll fix you another."

"Geez, Babe, you're a big girl," Eric grinned. "I'm sure you can handle a few stiff drinks."

Looking up at the ornate cuckoo clock which hung on the back wall of the bar, it seemed as if time was standing still. Eric's eyes were instantly drawn to the rifle depicted in the hunting scene. Surely, Gunner wouldn't do something stupid. However, Eric could only imagine how the scenario might play out if he were alone with Blake. The possibility undoubtedly existed that he might also kill Blake.

An hour later, all eyes were on Gunner as he slowly strolled into the bar. He was alone. There was no sign of Blake. Giving him the once over, Norman was shocked that he didn't appear disheveled. The fact he was not breathing hard or seemed anxious was perplexing. Gunner just walked up to the bar, pulled out a barstool, and sat down.

"Pour me a stiff one," Gunner requested, running his fingers through his unkempt, frizzy hair.

"So, what happened? Where's Blake?" Eric quickly inquired.

"Let's just say that I called in a few favors from some of the locals. He's on a plane back to Newport. That's all that matters," Gunner answered with the hint of a smile. "You don't have to worry about him. He'll not be bothering you again," he grinned, looking at Lana.

Gunner was a man of few words, and he offered no further explanation.

"Thank you," Lana answered, totally confused and bewildered.

It wasn't relevant to her what had transpired between Gunner and Blake. Getting up from her barstool, she walked over to Gunner. Under no circumstances had she ever imagined that he would be the one to rid her life of Blake. Throwing her arms around the large, burly man, she gave him a big hug. Without being asked, he had somehow miraculously taken care of the man who haunted her dreams.

"I really owe you," Lana smiled, giving him a quick kiss on the cheek.

"Oh, you don't owe me," Gunner smiled. "Any man who would lay a hand on a pretty little thing like you deserved to be dealt with. It was my pleasure."

"That's it," Eric vented under his breath.

Walking over to Lana, he whispered into her ear, "Gunner isn't going to fill us in on what happened, is he? You're not going to press him for details, are you?"

"Does it really matter?" Lana mouthed inaudibly.

"Well, it does to me."

"Why? Are you feeling inferior because you're a Marine? I'd suggest you buy the man a round of drinks," Lana softly whispered.

"Norman, a round of drinks for our hero," Eric reluctantly grinned.

To some degree, Eric felt inadequate. He felt as if he had let Lana down. Some part of him wished that he could have been her knight in shining armor. And the funny part was, he'd been outdone by a crusty older man more than twice his age. He sighed. He was a Marine, for heaven's sake.

Setting a drink in front of Gunner, Norman knew he was a man of few words.

"Babe, let's go home," Eric grinned.

Eric decided that he would have to come to terms with the fact that he might never know what had transpired between Gunner and Blake. But, perhaps, Lana was right. Knowing Blake was on a plane back to Newport was all that mattered.

"I believe you were about to thank me for breakfast," Eric winked.

"Okay, you silly man. Let's go home," Lana smiled, taking his hand. "Who cares if you didn't slay any dragons for me? You're still my hero, my Marine, and you belong to me. I love you."

Leaving Tillmans, Lana felt elated. No more worries about Blake, all thanks to someone she hardly knew. Putting her arms around Eric, it had been the right decision to follow him to Alaska. Life was good.

Chapter Seven

After enduring their first harsh winter, spring finally arrived, bringing the realities of melting snow and ice. Walking inside with his boots covered in thick, oozing mud, their new apartment lacked for only one thing, a mudroom. Deciding it would be best to remove his shoes before going farther, Eric sat down on the small porch outside their front door. Just as he was about to begin the daunting task, his cell phone rang. Reaching into his pocket, he was surprised to see the incoming call was from his sister, Karen. The news wasn't good. Slipping back into his mud-soaked boots, he knew he needed to see Lana. Extremely worried, he ran down the stairs. Hurriedly dodging potholes created by the early spring rains, he walked across the street to Tillmans. Regrettably, he had to relay tragic news regarding his mother's health. Approaching the bar, he was still covered in mud and out of breath.

"Is everything alright? You look like you could use a drink." Norman questioned.

"Well, to be honest, Karen, my sister, just called. It seems my mother, Kathie, has been admitted to the hospital. She had a stroke earlier today, and she's in critical condition."

"I'm so sorry," Norman frowned, reaching for a bottle of bourbon. "Maybe this will help," he suggested pouring Eric a shot. "Lana is in the back room. I'll let her know that you're here."

"Oh, don't bother. I'm sure Lana will be out in a few minutes. Norman, I really hate to ask, but do you think you could spare Lana for a few days? I'm going to book a flight to Carson, City, Nevada, and I'm sure she will want to come," Eric explained, quickly tossing back the entire shot.

"Not a problem. Bill can pitch in while she's gone. Are you guys leaving tonight?" Norman asked, pouring Eric another stiff drink.

"No. Probably first thing in the morning."

Walking out of the stock room, Lana sensed something was wrong. Eric seldom walked over to meet her after work. The fact he was a few minutes early and appeared frazzled worried her. Noting the strong drink only added to her concerns.

"Hey Babe, you're early. Is everything alright?"Lana frowned as she wiped her hands on her apron.

"It's mom. Karen called, and mom had a stroke earlier today and is now in critical condition."

"Oh my God, is she going to be alright?"

"I certainly hope so, but I need to get down to Carson City. I'm worried. Karen is with her."

"Well, I'm going with you. How soon can we leave?"

"Tomorrow morning. I'm going to book us on the first flight out."

"Norman, do you think you could handle the bar without me?" Lana asked, unaware of Eric's prior conversation with him.

"No need to even ask. Eric and I have already talked. This old bar has been here long before you arrived. I'm sure it will survive a few days without you. Now, I'm not saying that I won't miss you and how organized you keep everything, but I completely understand. As I told Eric, I can get Bill to pitch in if needed. You guys get out of here. Don't worry about this old bar. Now go, get out of here," Norman reiterated, waving his hands and shooing them away

"Thanks, Norman," Lana smiled, taking Eric's hand as they headed towards the door. "I'll call later."

"Thanks, Norman," Eric added.

"Eric, I'm so sorry. But, please, don't worry. I'm sure everything will be fine."

Reaching the apartment, Eric made flight reservations for the following day.

"Lana, I hate to tell you, but we're leaving at 6:00 a.m. I know it's early. Can you be ready?"

"Eric, don't worry. It will not take me all night to pack a suitcase. How is your sister Karen holding up? I'm looking forward to finally meeting her and your mom."

"Okay, I guess. Sweetheart, they're going to fall in love with you."

Leaving McGrath, there were only two connections between Alaska and arriving in Reno the next morning. Taking a cab immediately to the hospital from the airport, Eric was a ball of nerves. However, it was a short drive to the Northern Nevada Medical Center. Karen was waiting for them near the entrance.

"Oh my God, Karen, how is mom?" Eric questioned frantically.

"Unbelievably, she's already been downgraded from the ICU Unit and appears to be doing much better. She's sitting up in bed chatting away as if nothing ever happened. Eric, what if she has another stroke and we lose her? She's complained of losing some of the feelings in her leg. What if she never walks again?" Karen sobbed.

"Karen, don't panic. You're acting irrational," Eric answered, giving her a tight hug. "Karen, this is Lana."

"Lana, it's nice to meet you. Mom and I have heard such sweet things about you from Eric. Giving Lana a huge hug, Karen looked over at Eric. "We better get upstairs. I don't want to leave mom alone. She might need me. The nurses are attentive, but I feel better when I'm with her."

"Okay," Eric smiled, taking Lana's hand.

"Karen, it's so nice to meet you too. I've looked forward to meeting you and your mom. Still, I hate it's under these circumstances," Lana replied sympathetically, following Eric inside the hospital and over to the elevator.

Karen resembled Eric. She was attractive and shared many of his features. Karen was surprisingly tall in her late thirties with long, sandy brown hair and striking blue eyes. Yet, amazingly, she was still single like Eric.

"Thanks for coming down with Eric. Mom can't wait to meet you. When she heard you were coming, I must say it put a smile on her face."

"Awe, thanks, Karen. I can't wait to meet her as well."

Pushing the button to the tenth floor, Karen stared at Eric.

"Geez, bro, I must say it's good to see you. Sometimes I feel you've abandoned us."

"Sis, I would never do that. Life gets busy. You know I just started a new business in Alaska."

"But, why in the world Alaska? You know mom always wanted you to follow in dad's footsteps."

"Well, maybe one day, but right now, I'm thrilled with my life, especially after winning this gorgeous girl's heart," Eric winked with a smile. Then, giving Lana a quick smooch as the elevator doors opened, he secretly hoped his mother would approve.

Following Karen down the long, dim hallway, Eric held tightly to Lana. Walking in, Kathie Kolbeck smiled, beckoning her only son towards her bedside.

"Eric, Sweetheart, it's so good to see you. This gorgeous girl must be Lana. It's so nice to meet you finally."

Taking his mother's hand, Eric leaned over her bed, giving her a gentle kiss. Her pale appearance gave him cause for worry. In her mid-sixties, Kathie was lovely. Her chiseled facial features and sapphire blue eyes were clearly reflected in Eric and Karen's profile. Sporting a short pixie cut, her blonde hair made her appear much younger than her actual age.

Trying to hold back tears, Eric knew he had to be strong. All of the women in the room were dependent on his strength. The guilt of not moving back home after his dad's passing wore heavily on his heart. Karen stood silently against the wall, next to her mom's bed. She had been left with the daily hands-on responsibilities of keeping the ranch in working order after his dad had passed.

"Mrs. Kolbeck, I must say it's nice to meet you too. Eric and I were concerned when Karen called. How are you feeling?"

"Well, I've certainly been better, but they're taking great care of me. Please, just call me Kathie, no need for formalities." Giving Lana a thorough glance, Kathie smiled. "I knew Eric would eventually find himself a wonderful young lady."

"Awe, thanks, Kathie, I feel as if I'm the lucky one to have met him," Lana smiled, looking up at Eric. "We met at Caesar's Palace in Vegas."

"Yes, I heard. Charlie, a friend of Roys, my late husband, works in management at Caesar's. He called to inform me that Eric had checked into the hotel. He also mentioned that they were going to comp Eric with an upgrade. Roy was well-known in Vegas. Eric's dad was a famous poker champion. I always hoped that Eric would follow in his dad's footsteps. He inherited Roy's unique strategies."

"I've heard all the stories surrounding his legendary career. I'm sure you were very proud of him. That's quite an accomplishment. But, I have no luck when it comes to playing cards. But, of course, this handsome guy certainly does," Lana beamed, staring into Eric's gorgeous blue eyes. "I guess you could say that poker brought us together," Lana smiled, squeezing Eric's hand.

"Mom, for heaven's sake, you're becoming a Chatty Cathy. You're trying to recover from a stroke. You need to relax and try to sleep," Karen insisted, walking over to her mom's bed.

"Mom, Karen is right. You need to rest. Sis, have you spoken to mom's doctor today?"

"No, but he should be making rounds later this evening."

"So, how are things at the ranch?"

"As good as can be without you," Karen frowned. "We had to sell off the remaining black Angus Cattle. Mom and I aren't getting any younger, and the work involved has become overwhelming. You're living in Alaska doesn't help either," Karen frowned. She never hesitated to make Eric aware that she had been left to care for their mom and the ranch. "Why don't you take Lana out to the Circle K? Oh, that's the family ranch," Karen smiled, looking up at Lana. "Mom needs to get some rest. I'll stay. I'm sure Lana would love to freshen up after the flight. Here are the keys to my car; it's the older, silver suburban in the hospital parking lot. Just use the key fob to locate the car. You can't miss it. Oh, the guest room is available, and Jake is still living at the ranch."

"Thanks, sis."

Leaning over his mom's bed, Eric gave her a quick kiss. "Mom, do as you're told. No giving the nurses a hard time," he teased. Eric needed to make a quick escape before arguing his reasons for leaving home with his sister. Karen always blamed him for not moving back to Carson City after their dad's death. He wasn't in the mood to revisit the subject, especially now. He already felt guilty for leaving the ranch and its heavy workload in the hands of his mom and Karen. Evidently, Karen also blamed him for their mother having a stroke, even though she hadn't verbalized it.

"Lana, why don't we take Karen up on her offer and drive out to the ranch? You can freshen up, and I'll give you a quick tour of the place."

"Sounds wonderful," Lana smiled, sensing Eric's need to make a quick escape. "Kathie, take care. We'll be back later this evening to relieve Karen," Lana added. Looking up at Eric, Lana sensed his inner conflict with his sister.

"So, what was going on back there?" Lana questioned as they entered the elevator.

"It's a long story. Let's just say that my sister has always held resentments against me for not moving back to run the ranch after dad died. She didn't understand the fact that I couldn't just throw the towel in on my military commitment. I was just a few short years away from retirement, and now, I'm sure she blames me for mom having a stroke."

"Eric, I didn't get that impression at all. On the contrary, she seemed happy to see you and naturally concerned about her mom's health. She even gave you the keys to her car."

"Lana, I didn't say that I vehemently hate her, but you didn't grow up with her. I know dad always wanted me to follow in his footsteps.

Maybe I should have after retiring from the Marines. At least I could have made enough money on the poker circuit to take care of mom financially after he passed. I don't want to talk about it. I already feel guilty." Eric held his head in his hands, clearly frustrated.

"Eric, I didn't mean to pry into your relationship with Karen, and you have no reason to regret pursuing your dream of moving to Alaska. I'm sure your mother doesn't blame you for not moving back after you retired. She seemed really happy to see you."

"I know. It's just sibling rivalry between Karen and me. Coming from a large family like yours, I would think you could easily relate."

"Oh, trust me, my mom always had her favorites. But, unfortunately, I wasn't one of them. Being the middle child in a family of ten siblings, it was like I didn't exist. No one ever seemed to notice me."

"Sweetheart, I'm sorry to hear that—no more talk about family. I want to take you out to the lake. Have you ever been to Lake Tahoe?"

"No. But I've heard it's gorgeous. I thought we were coming back to relieve Karen later this evening. So maybe we should save that for another day."

"Oh, it's not that far. We can do both. First, we can stop by the ranch. I'll show you around, and then I can introduce you to Jake. He's an old family friend, and the only reason I didn't feel it was mandatory to move back after I retired. He's been looking after the ranch since my dad passed."

"Okay, if you say so," Lana smiled, closing the car door.

It wasn't long before they entered the interstate driving south towards Carson City, located about thirty miles away. The distant snow-covered mountains revealed the natural beauty of Northern Nevada. Leaving the high desert behind, they soon turned onto Highway 50 towards the sprawling ranch.

"I must say this part of Nevada is gorgeous," Lana remarked.

"Yep, but it doesn't compare to the beauty of Alaska."

An impressive wrought iron gate encircled overhead with an enormous 'K' soon announced their arrival. It was remarkable and not easily missed. However, the narrow winding road leading through the gate gave no hint of the ranch house, only the vastness of the private acreage surrounding it.

"Welcome to the Circle K Ranch," Eric winked, turning off the main road.

"Geez, how much land does your family own?"

"About fifteen hundred acres, and that's small compared to most of the ranches around these parts. Now that we've lost the Black Angus cows, mom doesn't need all the grazing land. I think she should sell and move closer to Reno. I don't honestly see her or Karen remaining out here."

Slowly winding through tall groves of cactus, Lana finally caught a glimpse of the sprawling two-story ranch house. It was awe-inspiring, much like the wrought iron gate. Its outward appearance resembled a Spanish-style hacienda. Red tiles covered the roof while towering stucco arches framed the front of the house. Hidden from view was an extended narrow patio. The veranda was enhanced overhead with timbered logs perfectly spaced to reveal the beautiful blue skies. Tall windows exquisitely encased with decorative wrought iron frames lined the length of the structure. Dark, green Bougainvillea vines covered the stucco exterior. An abundance of hot pink flowers sprawled between the ornate window frames and upwards towards the roof.

"Wow, Eric, it's gorgeous. Were you born and raised here?"

"Yes. It was Dad's gift to mom. She loves horses, and he felt guilty for leaving her to chase his dreams. Playing on the poker circuit took him away from home for long periods. After graduating from college, I guess you could say that I left to pursue my interests. Living with two overbearing women wasn't for me, and the Marines seemed like a great option."

"Didn't you feel guilty leaving? The work required to maintain this place must have been daunting."

"Not at that time. I was young and looking for adventure. Remaining at the ranch was never an option, plus Dad hired enough ranch hands to oversee the upkeep. Jake came on board to ensure everything was kept in working order, and later, he stayed on after dad passed, giving me the freedom to chase my dreams. I'll give you the grand tour."

Parking near the entrance, a tall, burly gentleman with grey hair walked towards the car.

"Well, the prodigal son returns. It's so good to see you," Jake smiled, embracing Eric within his strong muscular arms. "Son, I'm sorry about your mother. She's a strong woman. I'm sure she'll be just fine. Who's this gorgeous young lady?" Jake questioned, watching Lana step out of the car."

"Lana, meet Jake."

"Nice to meet you, Miss Lana. Let me take those bags inside," Jake suggested as Eric sat their luggage on the gravel driveway.

"The house looks great. Some things never change," Eric smiled.

"I suppose you know your mother sold the cattle. It hasn't left me a lot to do but tend to the horses. You're both in luck. I just cooked a huge pot of my famous stew. With your mom in the hospital, I've become the chef as well. It was either cook or starve. The few ranch hands we have left certainly deserve a hearty meal, and I must say a bowl of my stew does the job quite nicely."

"Oh, you don't have to ask me twice. I'm starved," Eric grinned, looking over at Lana. "I'm sure it's amazing. Let me grab one of those bags," Eric mentioned as they walked towards the front entrance.

Noticing Lana's reluctance to comment on the menu, Eric laughed. Feeling a bit naughty, he had to play into her hesitation.

"So is it your usual elk or rabbit stew? I remember you always brought in the wild game for mom to cook, and even though she was always skeptical, she did her best to please your palate."

"She's a great cook. However, after raising Black Angus Cattle for so many years, I only use one hundred percent prime beef in my stew," Jake laughed. "Don't worry, I promise you it's delicious," he added, looking over at Lana.

"Thanks, Eric," Lana smiled, poking him hard in his forearm. "He teases me relentlessly."

"Yeah, and I have the bruises to show for it too," Eric grinned, giving her a quick kiss.

"Why don't you show this young lady around? Then, I'll put your bags upstairs and warm up the stew," Jake chuckled. Opening the oversized double doors, intricate carvings within the dark oak frames complimented the Spanish décor.

Watching as Eric took Lana upstairs, Jake could feel the connection between the young lovers. It was just what the old house needed. It sorely missed the playfulness and vibrancy of young people in love. Unfortunately, Karen had never bothered to bring anyone out to the ranch. She had grown up being somewhat independent and a loner. With Roy having passed, he had just himself, Kathie, Karen, and a few ranch hands to tend the enormous house and adjoining acreage. After Roy's death, it felt like he had taken the joy of living in such a beautiful remote location with him. Now, most days, Jake felt like the walls of the Hacienda closed in around him, suffocating the life out of him. Perhaps with a bit of luck, Eric might finally decide to move back to Carson City. He could only hope.

Lighting the burners on the vintage freestanding stove, Jake was surprised to hear the kids, as he now thought of them, hurriedly bounding back down the stairs.

"Are you guys ready to eat?"

"I'm afraid we will have to pass on the stew," Eric frantically announced. "Karen just called. She's freaking out. It appears that mom had another stroke. It seems serious. They are taking her into surgery. We've got to go, but please save it for later."

"Wait just a minute. I'll ride into town with you," Jake insisted, quickly storing the stew in the fridge.

"Why don't you drive the truck? We'll need two cars. We borrowed Karen's Suburban. Having two vehicles would give you the choice of coming home later tonight if we decide to stay at the hospital," Eric suggested.

"Okay, that makes sense. I'll lock up the house and be right behind you," Jake agreed.

Driving back into Reno, Eric appeared somber and worried.

Reaching over to rub Eric's tense shoulder lovingly, Lana smiled.

"Eric, please try not to worry. I don't understand how her condition could have changed so suddenly, but I'm sure she'll be just fine."

"We should never have left the hospital. Why did I ever listen to

Karen? If something happens to mom and I never get to speak to her again, I'll never forgive her."

"Babe, you can't blame your sister. I'm sure she thought Kathie was going to be just fine, and she didn't want you to spend your entire day at the hospital."

"You don't know Karen as well as I do. We were raised together, and she was always selfish. We came all the way from Alaska, and now she's the one with mom."

"Eric, I think you're overreacting. Karen couldn't possibly have known Kathie's condition might deteriorate in such a short time. Calm down. You'll get Jake worried. He's such a sweet older man. You need to be strong."

Arriving at the hospital, Eric quickly found two open parking spaces. Then, waiting for Jake to park the car, they hurriedly walked towards the hospital entrance.

"Eric, please don't worry. Like I told you, your mom's a strong woman. She'll pull through this, I'm sure of it," Jake assured him.

"I wish I had your confidence."

Entering the hospital, they took the elevator up to the ICU Unit. Reaching the nurse's station, Lana put her arms around Eric.

"I'm Eric Kolbeck. My mother, Kathie Kolbeck, has been taken into surgery. How is she?"

"Please take a seat across the hall in the waiting room. Someone will be out soon to speak with you."

"No, I'm not waiting. I need to know my mother's condition. Now!" Eric demanded abrasively.

Hearing Eric's voice, Karen walked out of the waiting room.

"Eric, we've got to wait. The doctors are still in surgery with mom right now."

"Karen, you told me to leave earlier. You gave me your car keys and suggested I take Lana out to the ranch."

"You're right; I did. But, I could never have predicted this would happen. Mom seemed to be doing so good at the time, and you staying here wouldn't have accomplished anything. She needed to rest."

"Well, if anything happens to her, I'll never forgive you."

"Eric, that's ridiculous. Get a grip," Karen frowned.

"Babe, Karen's right. You need to calm down and give the doctors a chance to do what they do best," Lana suggested.

"Eric, they're right," Jake added. "I'm going downstairs to the cafeteria and get everyone some coffee. I'll be right back."

"Okay," Eric reluctantly agreed. "Thanks, that sounds good. I could use a cup."

Returning in a few minutes, Jake handed out four cups of steaming coffee and sat down.

"Has there been any news?"

"No, we've heard nothing, and I'm worried," Eric replied, taking a sip of his hot beverage.

"Well, I'm sure everything will turn out just fine. I'm sorry, did anyone want anything to eat? I forgot to ask. We didn't get around to eating my fabulous stew. I bet you guys are starved. I'll go back down to the cafeteria and check out what's available."

"Oh, no thanks, we're fine for now. We ate on the plane, but I must admit, I was sure looking forward to enjoying a bowl of stew," Eric frowned.

"Well, it's in the fridge, so help yourself when you get back to the ranch."

Noticing one of the doctors from ICU walk in, Eric stood up and walked over to meet him.

"Are you the Kolbeck family?" he inquired.

"Yes. Is there any news?" Eric asked somberly.

"Please, everyone, follow me to the room across the hall."

As the doctor closed the door, every fiber of Eric's being told him to expect the worst.

"I'm Dr. Harnell," he hesitated. "I'm afraid the news isn't good. Mrs. Kolbeck had a massive bleed into the brain. I'm sorry. There was nothing we could do when we got her into surgery. Truly, this is the hardest part of my job. Do you have any questions?"

"What happened? She appeared to be doing so good earlier," Karen cried.

"I'm sorry, but I can't give you any definite details. As doctors, even we don't have all the answers. Regrettably, the damage was extensive when we got her into the operating room. We have Mrs. Kolbeck temporarily in a room downstairs. I'm sure you'll want to see her. If there is anything further I can do, please have me paged. Again, I'm truly sorry for your loss."

Attempting to stand, Karen collapsed into Eric's arms.

Calling for an attendant, Dr. Harnell rushed over to check Karen's vital signs. "Her vital signs are good. One of our nurses will be right in. She appears to have fainted," he stated, helping Eric ease her into one of the chairs.

At that moment, a nurse rushed in with smelling salts, and within minutes Karen was revived.

"Mom didn't make it, did she?" Karen pleaded, holding onto Eric.

"No, sis, I'm afraid not. Please don't cry. I'm here," Eric whispered as tears filled his eyes.

Watching Eric, her strong Marine, lovingly embrace his sister, Lana's knees almost buckled. With tears rolling down her cheeks, she took a seat next to Eric. Putting her arms around him, she felt helpless. Looking over at Jake, he appeared utterly distraught.

"Sweetheart, I think we should all go downstairs," Lana suggested, gently wiping Eric's eyes with the back of her hand.

"Give me a few minutes. I've got to regain my composure before I see Mom," Eric wept.

"Babe, I'm so sorry," Lana cried softly.

"I know. I just need a minute. I never expected this to happen. I'm not prepared to let Mom go," Eric whispered, wiping his eyes.

"Eric, what am I going to do without Mom?" Karen sobbed.

"Sis, I told you, I'm here. We'll figure that out later. But, first, we need to go downstairs and see her before she's moved to the morgue.

"I'm not sure I can even stand up," Karen questioned.

"Don't worry. I've got you."

Helping his sister up from her chair, Eric held tightly to Karen as they walked toward the elevator.

"Why don't I give you all a few minutes alone with your mom before I say my final goodbyes?" Jake said softly.

"Thanks, Jake. We won't take long."

Walking into the dimly lit room, nothing could have ever prepared them to see their mom in this state. She appeared angelic, merely asleep with her head covered in white bandages. Yet, her lips reflected the hint of a smile. Perhaps the only plausible explanation for the smile was her peace with finally being reunited with dad.

"Oh, Mom, I'm going to miss you. I love you," Eric wept, picking up her hand. "Mom, I'm so sorry for leaving you after dad died. Can you ever forgive me?" Everything seemed surreal as he wiped his eyes. He wasn't ready to let her go. Leaning over her body, he softly kissed her goodbye. "Mom, I love you. I'll always love you." Utterly distraught, Eric stepped aside. It was Karen's turn to say goodbye.

"Oh, Mom, I love you. You can't leave me. You just can't! I don't know how I'm going to live without you," Karen cried uncontrollably. "What will I do? I need you." Completely breaking down, Karen leaned over her mom's body. Holding her for the last time, she sobbed bitterly.

"Sis, it's okay. I'm here," Eric whispered with tears in his eyes as he gently lifted his sister away from the lifeless body. "Let's go home."

Walking over, Lana quickly said her goodbyes.

"I'm so sorry that I didn't get to spend more time with you. I love you, and I love your son. Please don't worry about him. I promise to take good care of him," Lana wept.

Opening the door, Jake stood patiently waiting to say his final words.

"You can go in now. We'll wait for you."

After a few minutes, Jake walked out with tears in his eyes. No one would ever know the words he spoke over Kathie that evening. However, it didn't matter. There was no doubt that he loved her. Maybe if there hadn't been such a vast age difference between them, things might have been different after Roy died. Kathie's death undoubtedly would now leave a massive hole in his heart.

"Let's go home," Jake suggested wiping his eyes.

"Why don't you take the girls out to the car? I need to make some final arrangements. It shouldn't take that long," Eric suggested.

"Okay, girls, let's go. I have a huge pot of beef stew waiting for us."

"Jake, only you could think of food at a time like this," Karen replied with the hint of a smile.

Finally, seeing Eric approach the parking lot, they were ready for the short trip home. There were hardly any words spoken in the suburban on the short drive out to the ranch. The unforgettable events of the day had taken an enormous toll on everyone.

Arriving back at the ranch, Karen clearly was already missing her mom.

"Eric, how am I supposed to walk into the house knowing Mom will not be coming home?" Karen wailed.

"Well, I'm not sure I have the answer, but hopefully, knowing that you are not alone and surrounded by family that loves you will help. Although I love you, sis, I know you are hurting. We all are."

Slowly walking up the front of the house, Jake quickly caught up with them.

Unlocking the door, he stood back to let the ladies enter.

"I'm going into the kitchen to rustle up some stew. Karen, would you like to help out in the kitchen?"

"If you don't mind, I'm going up to my room. I'm not hungry," Karen frowned.

"Okay. But if you get hungry later, I'll leave a bowl for you on the stove."

"Thanks."

Watching as Karen slowly walked up the stairs, Jake worried about her. He knew that losing Kathie would take a heavy toll on her. But, maybe with a bit of insistence, he could talk Eric and Lana into remaining at the Circle K for a few weeks. Hopefully, it would give Karen enough time to readjust to life at the ranch.

"Where's the coffee pot?" Eric inquired, walking into the kitchen. "I need something strong to drink."

"Why don't you and Lana sit down at the table? We could use something a little stronger than coffee," Jake suggested, reaching into the cupboard for glasses. Opening a bottle of Remy Martin Cognac, he poured shots into three small balloon glasses.

"Oh, I'm not sure about cognac. I think I'll pass," Lana smiled.

"Just take a sip," Eric winked. "You could use something to help you relax. Today has been hard on all of us."

"Well, okay, if you insist," Lana hesitated. Then, slowly lifting the glass to her lips, she downed the entire drink.

Watching to see her reaction, Eric and Jake winced.

"Babe, you're not supposed to guzzle it," Eric laughed.

"Not bad. It tasted like peaches and honey with a hint of nutmeg. Okay, you can pour me another."

"Wow, I think we have a little connoisseur on our hands," Jake smiled, immediately refilling her drink.

"Slowly, just sip it. It's meant to be enjoyed, not swallowed in one gulp," Eric teased.

Finishing his drink, Jake quickly poured himself another.

"I'll go warm up supper. You both enjoy your drinks," Jake mentioned leaving the bottle on the table.

Returning with bowls of piping hot beef stew and a tray of warm rolls, the aroma was overwhelming. It smelled heavenly.

"Wow. This is delicious. I couldn't care less if it were elk or rabbit," Lana laughed.

"Oh, somehow, I believe that's the cognac talking," Eric grinned.

After enjoying several bowls of stew, Jake suggested they retire to the living room, where he would build a roaring fire in the massive stone fireplace.

"Nights can get quite cold out here in the high desert even in early spring," Jake smiled. "Let's take our drinks into the living room. I'll walk out to the patio and grab a few logs."

Watching as Jake started the fire, Lana was amazed at the size of the great room. Its enormous vaulted ceilings reflected the glow from the fireplace. Other than the foreboding deer head with antlers which appeared to stare at them from above the stone fireplace, she loved its décor. Lounging back on the oversized black leather sectional, she cuddled into Eric's arms. Feeling warm and cozy, it was only moments before the cognac had Lana falling asleep on Eric's shoulder.

"Wow, she didn't last long," Jake mentioned. "I really like her. I think you've found yourself a keeper," he chuckled, taking another sip of cognac.

"Yep," Eric nodded. "But don't let her know. I'm thinking of asking her to marry me. Losing Mom has given me a reason to think seriously about getting on with my life," Eric revealed, taking a long, slow sip of his drink.

"I thought you were happy flying bush planes in Alaska?"

"Well, I am or should say I was before I met this gorgeous girl. It's not much of a life for her or a place to raise a family. She loves the excitement of Vegas. So I've given a lot of thought to joining the poker circuit like dad. There's a lot of money to be made playing poker tournaments. Mom always wanted me to follow in dad's footsteps. I think it's time to give it a try. Karen is going to need not only your help but financial help as well to keep this place afloat. Playing poker would benefit everyone," Eric stated, rubbing his eyes.

"Wow. That's a pretty hefty commitment," Jake acknowledged.

"Yeah, just keep it all under wraps for now. More than anything, I want to marry this sleepyhead," Eric smiled, gently kissing Lana on the forehead. "I think I'm going to turn in for the night. The cognac, along with the warmth of the fire, has me extremely tired."

"Of course, don't mind me. I'll probably hang downstairs and spend a little more time with this bottle. I don't relish the thought of going to bed right now. I'm sure going to miss your mom. I probably would have asked her to marry me if I'd thought there was any chance in hell that she could have fallen in love with an old buzzard like me. Guess now I'll never know," Jake grinned.

"Wow, and on that note, I'm off to bed. I don't rightly know how to reply to that," Eric laughed, picking Lana up from the sofa.

Carrying Lana upstairs to his old room, Eric smiled at the mere thought of his mother ever marrying Jake. Lying Lana on his bed, he took off her shoes putting her under the warm covers. Stripping down to his briefs, Eric slipped into bed next to her. Feeling the warmth of her body next to him, he knew he never wanted to be alone like Jake. Somethings in life couldn't wait, Eric thought to himself. Perhaps tomorrow, he would try to get away without Lana and drive to Reno to shop for an engagement ring. However, before he could pop the question to the gorgeous girl sleeping so peacefully beside him, he had the daunting task of planning his mother's funeral. With tears in his eyes, his emotions were a mixture of extreme sadness and the hope of having Lana in his life forever. Closing his eyes, one last thought of Jake marrying his mom made him smile before exhaustion from the day took its due course.

Surprisingly, as the morning sun peeped in through the curtains, Lana woke first. Lana's heart sank, staring at the strong, handsome Marine who still slept so peacefully. She knew the next few days would probably be some of the most challenging days of his life. Snuggling against his muscular body, she smothered him with kisses. Eric slowly opened his eyes, feeling the warmth of her touch.

"Babe, I'm so sorry you lost your mom," Lana whispered. "I'm so sad that I'll never get the chance to know her. What can I do to help?"

"Shush, no talking," he smiled, pulling her even closer. "I just want to know that you'll never leave me." He had only one thing on his mind this morning, and it had nothing to do with an ongoing discussion about his mother's recent death. Instead, evidently, it was his way of coping with grief.

"Eric, I love you. I would never leave you. I followed you to that dilapidated shack in Alaska, remember?" Lana whispered into his ear.

"Hush," he smiled.

Returning her kisses with passion, he'd never wanted her more. He desperately needed to feel the closeness of her body, the warmth of her skin. Knowing that life could be taken away instantly, there was no promise of a tomorrow. He loved her with every ounce of his being. Time could be elusive, and he had to make every second count. If making love to the beautiful girl in his arms made time stop, if only for a few moments, he relished in their quiet and intimate moments. Nothing else existed, just the love shared between the two of them.

Afterward, lying in his arms, Lana could still sense the worries spinning through his mind. She took his hand with tears in her eyes and held it over her heart.

"Babe, do you feel my beating heart? I promise you, I'm not going anywhere, and neither are you. We're going to die old and in each other's arms. I know today will be difficult planning your mother's services, but I'll be right by your side. We've got to be strong for Karen."

"You're right. I think it's the overwhelming regret of leaving mom and Karen alone for all those years while I selfishly chased my dreams. I had no idea she would pass so young."

"Eric, she was not as young as you remembered. Kathie was seventy-nine. However, I must admit she didn't look a day over fifty, at least to me. You have some dominant genes in your family. I think we should get dressed and head downstairs. I'm sure Karen is probably awake. I'll cook pancakes for everyone," Lana suggested giving Eric a quick kiss before heading to the bathroom.

"Hey, Gorgeous, I love you," Eric smiled.

"Love you too, now get up and get dressed."

Standing under the warm water of the shower, Lana smiled as she lathered shampoo through her long auburn curls. She had never seen this side of Eric before. It amazed her that even a Marine could be vulnerable. She loved seeing this side of her handsome man. It made her love him even more.

Walking into the kitchen, it appeared Jake had read her mind. He was flipping pancakes.

"Coffee is ready. Grab some cups. Would you guys prefer bacon or sausages this morning?"

"Actually, bacon sounds good if you're asking," Eric replied.

"Okay, bacon it is," Jake announced, reaching into the fridge.

"Where's Karen?" Eric asked, pouring Lana a cup of coffee. "Is she up?"

"Oh, yeah, she took her horse, Midnight, for an early morning run. I'm sure she'll be back before long. I think she just needed some solitude. It's her way of dealing with things this morning," Jake added.

"I can easily understand. I guess we all have our ways of dealing with grief," Lana whispered in a low, barely audible voice. Then, staring at Eric, she smiled, taking a sip of coffee.

"What did you say?" Eric questioned, leaving no doubt he'd heard every word.

"Oh, nothing. It was nothing at all," Lana teased.

"Oh, is that right?" Eric winked.

Lana laughed, knowing that Eric appeared in a better mood.

I'll serve up the pancakes if you guys are ready to eat—no need to wait for Karen. Things will be cold by then. She can eat when she returns," Jake stated as he took warm plates from the oven. "Oh, and when Karen gets back, I think we should all sit down and discuss your mom's services."

"Yes. I think that would be a good idea. Do you know if mom had prearranged anything?" Eric asked, pouring himself another cup.

"No, but I'm sure Karen would know. Lana, if you would be so kind, please take a couple of plates from the cupboard, and grab the silverware from the side drawer."

"Certainly," Lana smiled.

"I'll bring the pancakes, syrup, and bacon."

Sitting together at the table, it seemed surreal to be eating without Kathie once again. The stillness of the room was suffocating.

"Wow, these pancakes are delicious," Lana remarked, breaking the silence.

"Oh, thanks, nothing much to them. A simple recipe," Jake spoke up, taking a sip of coffee.

"Yes, they're fantastic," Eric agreed as he shoveled pancakes into his mouth.

Just as Jake was about to get up from the table to grab the coffee pot, the back door slammed shut.

"I think Karen is back," Jake announced.

"Good morning, everyone. I guess you decided to start without me," Karen grumbled, grabbing a cold plate from the cupboard.

"Well, I didn't know for certain when you would be back. I didn't want things to get cold, being, as Eric and Lana were already up."

"Oh, I was just teasing. I had a bowl of oatmeal before I left. However, those pancakes look amazing, and I'm hungry."

Pouring herself a cup of coffee, Karen sat down next to Eric. "Please pass the syrup."

Watching as she stacked several large pancakes on her plate, Eric laughed.

"Sis, looks like you've worked up an appetite."

"Geez, Eric, what a nice thing to say. I'm starving. I've already fed and watered all the horses this morning, plus took Midnight out for a ride. Might I ask what you've done so far?"

"Not much. I just got up."

"Well, I'm sure Jake has a list of things that need to be done. The fence along the back forty needs to be repaired. Maybe that's something you might help with?" Karen suggested.

"Karen, listen, I'm not here to spar with you. We have more important things to discuss. Do you know if Mom had prearranged her services? We have a funeral to plan," Eric reminded her.

"No. Mom never wanted a fancy service. She simply wants to be buried next to dad in the family cemetery. She was always adamant about this, and I, for one, will see that her wishes are carried out. Do you understand?"

"Sis, I'll do whatever she wanted. I'm not here to argue with you." Eric could feel his blood pressure rising. "Don't you think this is killing me too? Don't you think I feel guilty for leaving you and mom after Dad died?"

"Well, you sure have a funny way of showing it. You never came back, only for short periods when you were on leave from the Marines," she retorted, shoving pancakes in her mouth.

"Karen, do you even know what the word commitment means? I couldn't just walk away from the Marines. Heck, I served three tours in the Middle East."

"Bro, no one understands the word 'commitment' more than me. I stayed. I never left. Don't you think I had dreams too? Did you ever think I might have wanted to leave Carson City? I put my life on hold to stay and help Mom with the ranch? I don't want to hear your sob story."

"Listen, Karen. We need to get along. I'm sorry. I realize now that choosing the Marines rather than staying at the ranch was selfish and narrow-minded. I can't turn back the clock, but I can promise you things will be different from now on. Do you trust me?"

"Well, I guess since you've apologized, I have no other choice. After all, you are my brother, and I do love you. I don't think Mom would want us to argue and fight. She loved you, and I guess she loved you enough to let you go." Karen sighed, picking up her cup of coffee for a long sip.

"Karen, I'm proud of you for giving Eric another chance, and Eric, I know you'll do the right thing and not leave Karen with the upkeep of the ranch. I'm not getting any younger, you know. Let's finish eating breakfast before everything gets cold. We'll talk about Kathie's services afterward," Jake smiled, warming his coffee.

"Eric, I'm proud of you too, but I think we need to talk. Does this mean we're not returning to our home in Alaska?" Lana whispered.

"Sweetheart, we'll talk later tonight. Today I just want to arrange Mom's burial."

"Okay, I understand," Lana agreed, giving his hand a gentle squeeze under the table.

After everyone finished eating, Jake suggested they go into the living room, where everyone would be more comfortable.

"Why don't you all go in the living room. I'll clean up the table and kitchen. This has nothing to do with me. I'll bring in some hot coffee," Lana insisted.

"Thanks, Babe."

Following behind Jake, Karen and Eric made themselves comfy on the sectional.

"So Karen, what were Kathie's last wishes?" Jake inquired.

"Well, Mom certainly doesn't want a funeral of any kind. So no funeral. Mom never wanted a huge gathering of people from the community. She simply requested to be buried next to dad and only desired a few friends and family in attendance. She wanted to keep things simple. So I think that's exactly what we should do," Karen suggested wiping tears from her eyes.

"Sis, I totally agree," Eric smiled, getting a Kleenex for Karen.

"I agree. We'll keep things just as Kathie would have wanted," Jake acknowledged.

"Why don't we set the burial for Saturday? That will give us a little time to make all the arrangements. I want to order flowers and run an obituary in the newspaper. Also, we need to call mom's friends from church and let them know her services will be private. Karen, as far as Mom's friends, who do you think should be invited?" Eric questioned.

"Well, for sure we need to invite Ruth, Anna, and Kate. They were mom's closest friends. Of course, all the ranch hands will be invited. A few of the older guys have since retired, but I'm sure they would want to come and pay their respects. Also, there is Aunt Joan, who lives in Sacramento. However, she is much older than mom and not in good health. After talking to her on the phone last night, she might not be able to drive over. That's it. Mom's family is all deceased, and there is no one left on dad's side either. It looks like we're a dying breed," Karen moaned.

"Is that it? Are you certain?" Eric asked.

"Yes. It will be a small private burial. Just what Mom wanted. However, we should have a catered dinner at the ranch house afterward. Don't you agree?"

"Yes. Is there a particular restaurant we should call?"

"I'm thinking the Roadhouse in Carson City. They have a large catering menu with special entrees, including prime rib, seafood, and chicken. It was Mom's favorite place to eat. She loved their prime rib."

"Okay, the Roadhouse it is. I'll call and make the arrangements for Saturday. Let's have them set up an hour before the service starts at 3:00 p.m. How does that sound?'

"Great, I'll get a delivery of drinks from the local beverage store," Jake chimed in.

"Well, I think that covers it. I'll contact the mortuary and make the arrangements," Eric added. "I'll also oversee the obituary and flowers. Mom loved pink roses."

"Thanks, Eric. I'll contact Mom's friends."

"Would anyone like a cup of coffee?" Lana asked, walking into the room.

"No. I think we're all done with the arrangements. I have to drive into Carson City. Jake gave me the keys to his truck. He's going to stay with Karen to finalize some of the arrangements."

"Wait, I'll grab my sweater and ride into town with you. We need to talk."

"Okay, but can't our discussion wait until later? I'm not in the mood to continue that topic ."

"No. I need to know why you made that statement to Karen. We are together, right? I mean, we are still a couple, right?" Lana questioned. "Then, I deserve some answers."

"Sweetheart, after this morning, how could you even doubt what we have together? I love you," Eric winked. Then, pulling her into his arms, he kissed her with such intensity it left no room for doubt. "Go get your sweater. We'll talk," Eric added. "I'll wait for you outside on the patio. Hurry."

Standing in the warm morning sun, Eric cupped his hand to light a cigarette. Taking in the distant views of the snow-capped Sierra Mountains, they were undeniably breathtaking. Rubbing his day's growth of stubble, he worried. What if Lana didn't want to move to the ranch? What if she didn't like the idea of him playing poker? There were so many questions swirling around in his head. He could only hope she would agree with the changes he was about to bring into their lives. He didn't want to choose between the love of his life and his sister. Now that he and Karen had finally resolved many of their past conflicts, it appeared the death of their mom had somehow strangely brought them together. Eric cherished the thought of possibly having a close bond with Karen. However, he never wanted it to come at the expense of losing Lana. That would never be an option he could live with. Eric shrugged to himself. Either way, he would soon have his answers one way or another.

Hearing the front door close, he was pulled away from his thoughts as Lana walked over. She looked amazing. She was undeniably stunning, wearing tight, dark denim jeans, a white button-down shirt with white sneakers, and a black sweater tied around her slim waist. Her long, curly tresses were pulled back in a ponytail.

"Wow. You look gorgeous," Eric winked, putting out his smoke.

"Babe, you're sweet. I love you," she smiled, giving him a quick kiss.

Walking over to Jake's red vintage 1960 Ford truck, Lana paused. "Geez, it's unique, but does it run?" She questioned.

"Well, I guess we're about to find out," Eric laughed, opening the truck door helping her inside.

Putting the key into the ignition, instantly the engine started. The hum of the motor signified the old truck still had a lot of useful miles on it.

"She appears to be in good shape," Eric remarked. "Jake never has been the kind of man who would trade in a good truck just to keep up with the latest trends. He's a man after my own heart. However, I don't think the air conditioner is working. You might want to roll down your window."

Entering the long narrow drive leading to Highway 50, Lana rolled down her window, allowing a stiff breeze to cool the truck's interior. Looking over at Lana, she appeared to be enjoying the bumpy ride. The day was picture-perfect. Blue skies beautifully framed the snow-covered Sierras. How could Lana not love living in such grandeur? However, his impending proposal now hinged on her answers.

"So, what is this big secret that you're keeping from me? What does Karen know that I don't? I know she's your sister, and I'm happy that you've mended your relationship. Still, I'm curious why you haven't included me. What's going on?"

"First of all, it isn't a secret. I'm not trying to hide anything from you. I promise. Unexpectedly, my subconscious thoughts just came to light in a recent conversation with Karen. You know the remorse and guilt I've had for leaving mom and Karen alone when Dad died. Well," he hesitated, trying to read her facial expressions. "What if I told you that I would like us to relocate to Carson City, more specifically the Circle K Ranch? But wait, there's more," he paused. "What if I told you that I want to follow in my dad's footsteps?"

"Are you telling me that you want to play poker for a living?" Lana questioned. "What about Alaska, your business, and the plane?"

"Yes. I suppose that's exactly what I'm saying. I would simply put the plane up for sale. I'm sure Gunner knows people who would easily purchase the bush plane. Lana, I'm good at poker, like really good. I don't have to remind you that Dad made outrageous money playing cards on the poker circuits. That is before he lost it all in the stock market. Fortunately, I inherited his innate abilities at the game. Lana, we could travel. We don't have to live permanently at the ranch. Think of it more like our home base. We could purchase either a single-family home or condo in Vegas. I thought you loved living in Las Vegas?"

"Wow, you've caught me off guard this morning," Lana smiled. Then, shifting in her seat, she moved closer to Eric, caressing the nape of his neck. "Babe, are you sure you've given this a lot of thought? Do you really want to gamble with our future?" Lana questioned.

"Doll, I love your sense of humor. Does this mean you're on board?" Eric winked, kissing her on the forehead. He stopped the old truck before he turned onto Highway 50. As things appeared to be going in the right direction, Eric needed her full attention. Turning to face her, he waited pensively for her answer.

"Maybe?"

"What kind of answer is that? Sweetheart, I'm talking about the rest of our lives. I need a definite answer."

"Yes. Babe, after following you to Alaska and living in a dilapidated cabin, I think everything else is a piece of cake," Lana laughed.

"Oh, God, Sweetheart, I think you've just made me the happiest guy on earth."

Pulling her into his arms, he kissed her with such passion it left the rest of the trip in question.

"Geez, slow down, Cowboy. If you keep this up, we may never make it to Carson City," Lana teased.

"Lana, I think you've just given me everything I never knew I wanted," Eric whispered, kissing her ear.

"Okay," Lana paused. "Eric, you do realize we're parked in the middle of nowhere."

"Doll, I just want to savor the moment. How did I ever get so lucky to find you?"

"Are you crying?" Lana asked, wiping his moist eyes. "Wow, my strong, handsome Marine who wears his emotions on his sleeves. I love you," Lana winked, caressing his face with her hands. Kissing away his tears, she lovingly wiped his cheeks, feeling his growth of stubble. She'd never loved him more.

"Well, since I'm on a roll, I have just one other question," he smiled with a wink. Without hesitation, he was unable to contain his thoughts.

"Lana, will you marry me?"

"What did you say?"

"Marry me?" Eric asked again.

"Oh, my God, yes, a thousand times, yes," Lana screamed.

Holding Lana tight in his arms, tingles of excitement raced throughout her small frame. She'd always known he was going to pop the question, but his proposal had caught her off guard. Of all the places on earth, parked in the middle of nowhere would never have been her guess. However, it didn't matter; nothing mattered. Only the simple fact he'd asked, and she had said, yes without hesitation.'

"Lana, I had envisioned proposing on the shores of Lake Tahoe under the brilliance of the night sky, but it's these unexpected moments in life that sometimes make us do the unthinkable. I can't explain it, but I just felt this sense of urgency. I haven't even picked out a ring. I'm sorry."

"Eric, trust me on this. The location has nothing to do with it. I could care less if you'd proposed on the shores of Lake Tahoe or the Taj Mahal. My answer would always be yes. I love you. I'll always love you. Now you've made me the happiest girl on earth," Lana smiled, kissing him passionately.

Taking a few deep breaths, Eric tried to regain his composure.

"Well, I suppose we better get this old truck on the road. Why don't we drive to Reno and shop for a ring?"

"Sounds like a wonderful idea," Lana remarked, looking down at her ring finger.

"I might have to purchase this old truck for its memories," Eric laughed once again, pulling back onto the narrow road.

Later that night, they returned to the Circle K with a new accessory on Lana's left ring finger. She now sported a two-carat heart-shaped diamond. Having found the perfect ring in Reno, it now reflected the new life they would soon share as man and wife. Needless to say, Karen and Jake were thrilled with the news. Jake already envisioned the house coming alive again with the sounds of young children.

Saturday, Kathie was laid to rest beside her loving husband as a few close personal friends and family gathered around her gravesite. While saying their goodbyes wasn't easy, it had unexpectedly brought the family closer. Karen would no longer have the worries of running the Circle K alone. There was only one thing left to do. Eric and Lana would return to Alaska to finalize their relocation to Carson City and the ranch. They were about to begin the next step of their journey together. They were on their way back to McGrath.

Chapter Eight

"Ladies and gentlemen, welcome to McGrath. The temperature is a sweltering seventy-four degrees. The local time is 4:30. For those of you who live in McGrath, welcome home."

"Geez, I feel exhausted. The layovers make this trip extremely tiring," Lana yawned, stretching out her arms.

"I know, but we're almost home, or I should say back to the apartment. Hopefully, we're only going to be here for a week. I don't think Gunner will have a problem helping me sell the plane. It's still in good shape. He can vouch for that.

On the other hand, the cabin might be a problem. I don't think we should put any money into restoring it. It simply is what it is, a shack in the woods," Eric laughed.

"Wow. You don't want to keep it so that one day we can show the kids our first home?" Lana suggested.

"Babe, did you use the word, kids? I don't think I've ever heard you mention children before," Eric smiled. "So, how many kids do you want?"

"Well, I guess it just slipped out. I want lots of kids. Are you surprised?"

"No. Not at all. I guess it's just the fact we've never talked about a family before. Of course, I'd love to have a whole house full. Does that surprise you?" Eric teased. "In fact, I'm ready when you are," he winked.

"I think we might want to make our union legal first. I don't relish bringing a baby into the world who doesn't have a legitimate father."

"I agree," Eric kissed her quickly before reaching into the overhead bins for their carry-on bags.

"May I please have your attention before we open the cabin doors? Please check the overhead bins to ensure you have all your belongings," the flight attendant announced.

Taking the escalator downstairs to the baggage-retrieval area, Eric hurriedly retrieved their bags. Then, walking outside, he hailed a cab for the ride into McGrath.

"Wow, we're finally here," Lana beamed as the taxi came to a stop. "I wonder what's going on at Tillmans? There are a lot of cars parked out front, and it's only 5:30."

"I'm not sure, but I'm too tired to walk over this afternoon. So we'll go over in the morning. Norman isn't going to be happy with the fact he's going to lose his best employee," Eric mentioned.

"I know. I feel bad not giving Norman at least a month's notice. In fact, I can't even give him a two weeks notice. Our return tickets are booked for this weekend, and you have that meeting in Reno on Monday," Lana reminded Eric, following him upstairs.

Entering the apartment, it smelled stale and musty. Even though Eric and Lana had only been away less than two weeks, it reeked of uncirculated air. Running over, Eric opened the windows, allowing a rush of fresh air to infuse the apartment. It felt refreshing and invigorating. Immediately, it dispersed the heavy foul-smelling odor. Setting their bags in the hallway, they were both too tired to unpack.

"Geez, that's a lot better. I think I can breathe now," Lana remarked.

"Yes, that helped. Are you hungry?" Eric questioned, walking towards the fridge.

"No. I think I'm going to take a nap. Want to join me?"

"Well, actually, that sounds good. But, after looking inside the fridge, we've got to go grocery shopping, and I don't relish spending the next hour shopping for food. So, maybe after a short nap, I'll be more enthused about temporarily re-stocking the fridge."

He took Lana by the hand and led her down the narrow hallway into the main bedroom. Pulling back the duvet, they took off their shoes and slipped under the warm, cozy covers, fully clothed.

Turning to face her, Eric grinned.

"Sweetheart, remind me once again, how many kids do you want?" he smiled.

"Eric, go to sleep. You're funny," she laughed, turning away from him. Within minutes, she was out like a light bulb.

Staring at the love of his life, he envisioned the two of them as a family. He couldn't wait to start the adventure. However, she was right. They needed to be settled before committing to a family. Gently pulling back her long auburn curls, he kissed her cheeks. Snuggled against the warmth of her slender body, it was only moments before he also fell asleep.

Forgetting to set the alarm, and surprising as it might seem, they slept straight through until the following day. Then, awakened by the noise from the street below and the sun's brilliance, which filled every crevice of the bedroom, Eric opened his eyes. Sitting up in disbelief, was it possible they had somehow managed to sleep until the next morning? Glancing at the clock on the nightstand, it confirmed his suspicions. It was 6:00. Waking Lana, they were finally faced with the unwelcome task of going to the store. The fridge held nothing except a few condiments.

"Lana, it's time to wake up," Eric whispered lovingly.

"What time is it? Did you go to the store?"

"Sweetheart, I think you're going to find this hard to believe, but we slept through the entire night. We must have been completely exhausted. The stress of losing Mom and the funeral finally took its toll on us. However, we're now faced with grocery shopping. Can you believe we're out of coffee?"

"Oh, no, my strong, handsome Marine has no coffee," she teased, running her fingers through his silky brown hair. "What, no room service either?" she laughed, smothering him with kisses. "What was it you asked me before we went to sleep?"

"How many kids you wanted?"

"I want six. I want six children," she reiterated.

"Where did that come from?" Eric questioned.

"Oh, I don't know, maybe I was dreaming about the size of our family. Who knows? I only know that I want six children," Lana smiled.

"I thought you wanted to wait until we were married and settled into a house of our own? Well, doesn't a girl have the prerogative to change her mind? Who are you? You're scaring me," Eric laughed.

"Weren't you the one that said life is short and we should live in the moment?" Lana reminded him.

"Well, Sweetheart, you certainly don't have to ask me twice. I'm more than capable of making your dreams come true," he winked, pulling her into his arms.

Maybe groceries were overrated. Eric laughed to himself. Who was this girl he was about to make mad passionate love to? It didn't matter. Once again, nothing mattered. She was right. Living in the moment was the only way to live, and he'd never loved her more. Eric knew that dealing with death could make anyone hypersensitive to the world around them. The worst part was that his mother would never be at their wedding or hospital to welcome her first grandchild.

Snuggled into Eric's arms, Lana felt safe. With Blake finally out of her life, she was finally ready to embrace a future with her handsome Marine and God-willing, a house full of happy, rambunctious children.

"Okay, I'm starved," Lana giggled, quickly getting out of bed.

"Why don't we walk over to Tillmans? Maybe, if we're lucky, Norman might have a pot of chili on today's menu. Then, we can shop for groceries afterward."

"I think you could eat chili every single day. First things first," Lana smiled, running into the bathroom. Turning on the warm water, she opened the door. "Want to join me?"

"Maybe," Eric laughed, quickly getting out of bed.

Walking across the street to Tillmans, they were both famished. Entering the dimly lit bar, Norman was drying pint glasses.

"Hey guys, welcome home!" Norman shouted as they entered. "Gunner and I were wondering when you two would show up. How is your mom?"

"I'm afraid the news isn't good. Sadly, we lost Mom last week. She had another stroke while she was in the hospital, and unfortunately, she didn't make it."

"Oh, my God, I'm so sorry. Truly, you have my deepest sympathy. Sit down. I'll pour everyone a drink."

"Thanks, Norman. Is your famous chili on today's menu?" Eric inquired. "We're starved."

"Of course, that's a staple around here. Without my chili, I'd lose a lot of customers," Norman chuckled, reaching for three shot glasses. Then, opening a bottle of Crown Royal, he began pouring their drinks.

"Oh, I think I'll pass on the drink. Too early in the day for me," Lana smiled. "But I won't pass up a bowl of chili. I'm becoming a connoisseur. It's all this guy eats these days," she laughed playfully, punching Eric in his forearm.

"Hey, you love it, and you know it," Eric winked, kissing her on the cheek.

"Wait just a minute," Norman paused, pouring the shots. "When did this happen?" he grinned, reaching for her hand to inspect the dazzling diamond. "Wow, I guess congratulations are in order. Have you set a date?"

"No. Not yet. But you and Gunner will definitely receive an invitation," Lana beamed.

"Gunner is going to be thrilled. I swear he's been here every day asking if you were back."

"Let's toast to the future Mrs. Kolbeck," Norman suggested ensuring everyone had a drink.

"Here's to Lana, the prettiest girl in McGrath, and a long, happy life for you both," Norman toasted. "Wow. I feel like a proud papa."

"Well, we're back, but not for long," Eric mentioned, downing his drink.

"What?" Norman quizzed, pouring them another round.

"Yes. I'm sorry with Mom having passed, my sister, Karen, needs help with the ranch. After years of leaving them alone with all the upkeep, I finally promised to move back. It's more than she can manage, and our ranch hand Jake is getting up there in age. So it's time," Eric stated, throwing back another shot.

"Geez. Gunner is going to be so disappointed."

Norman grabbed two bowls, filling them to the brim with chili. Then, topping them with grated cheese, he returned to the stove, adding a platter of hot french fries.

"Wow. This smells delicious," Eric grinned, shoveling spoonfuls of the warm chili into his mouth. "I swear I could eat this stuff every single day."

"Eric, you're silly, but I do believe you could eat it every day. Although I'll have to admit, it's good," Lana admitted covering her fries with ketchup.

"Norman, I'm going to sell the Aviat Husky. Do you think Gunner would know anyone interested in purchasing the plane?" Eric paused, looking up between spoonfuls of chili.

"What? Are you selling the bush plane? You're not going to keep it. I mean, fly it down to Carson City?" Norman questioned his decision to sell his investment. "Gunner would be your man when it comes to aircraft," Norman answered, scratching his head in unbelief. "Wow. So you're really going to do this. Move to Carson City?"

"Yes, and I won't be taking the plane. Instead, I'm starting a new career."

"Oh, really, and what would that be?" Norman inquired, topping off their bowls.

"I'm finally going to follow in my father's footsteps. I'm going to join the poker circuit."

"Say that again? I'm not sure I heard you correctly." Norman was mystified. "Is it really possible to earn a living simply playing cards? I know your father was a legend and that you won money in Vegas recently, but are you sure you're not taking a huge risk?" Norman was more than confused about how Eric would give up his love of flying and living in the rugged outbacks.

"Yes. That's exactly what he said," Lana frowned. "I'm afraid he's going to gamble with our future."

"Have you given this a lot of thought? I think you could use another drink," Norman questioned, rubbing his forehead as he opened the bottle of whiskey. He had significant worries for the young couple.

"Norman, there is huge money playing in the tournaments. My dad wasn't only famous, he was wealthy. However, he gambled most of it away in the stock market before he died. Of course, I would never do that. Trust me. I learned a lot from him. Lucky for me, I inherited his exceptional gaming skills. "

"Gunner and I are going to miss you, and I'm certainly going to miss the best employee I ever hired," Norman grimaced.

"Hey, guys! I didn't know you were back!" Gunner shouted, walking into Tillmans with a huge grin.

"Well, speak of the devil," Norman laughed. "Gunner isn't going to take lightly to the news that you're leaving. Best let you break it to him," Norman whispered.

"So when did you guys get back?" Gunner questioned, slapping Eric on the back. "Norman, serve up a couple of Duck Farts."

"Oh, thanks, but I've just had several shots of whiskey. It's too early in the day to get wasted. However, you're just the man I wanted to see," Eric replied.

"Hey, Gorgeous, you've been sorely missed in this old bar," Gunner smiled, giving Lana a huge, overbearing hug. "Now, I reckon things will finally get back to normal. The stockroom has turned into a disaster since you left. Oh, I'm sorry, I completely forgot my manners. Eric, how is your mom? I hope she's a lot better."

"Gunner, she didn't make it. We lost her last week."

"Oh, my God, Eric, I really hate to hear that. That's just God-awful. Man, I'm so sorry. I really am. I know you must miss her," Gunner sympathized.

"Yes. She was a great woman and the best mom in the world."

Taking a seat at the bar next to Eric, Norman served up Gunner's usual Duck Fart.

"I sure hate that you lost your mom, but it's so good to have you back in McGrath. I kept a close eye on that bush plane of yours. I must say she's holding up nicely considering the fact she's still setting outside in this damn weather," Gunner scowled, tossing back his drink. "I think we're going to have an open spot in the hanger soon. You should think seriously about getting her moved inside."

"Well, actually, I wanted to talk with you about the plane. It looks like I'm going to be putting her up for sale."

"What? Why in the hell would you even think of selling her? She's a great aircraft. Trust me, I know a lot about bush planes," Gunner questioned with a puzzled expression.

"Gunner, Lana, and I are going to be moving to Carson City. I'm going to help my sister, Karen, with the ranch. It's long overdue."

"Oh, hell no! You guys can't leave McGrath," Gunner stuttered. "Norman, you better pour me another Duck Fart. Oh, hell, keep them coming. I thought once I took care of that fellow who came up here looking for Lana that you would make McGrath your permanent home." Gunner appeared utterly bewildered. "Really, you're leaving?" He was taken entirely by surprise with the unexpected news.

"Gunner, I'm afraid so, but you're always welcome at the Circle K. In fact, both you and Norman are always welcome to come down and stay as long as you want. If you guys ever get tired of running this bar and working on aircraft, I'm sure I could always use a couple of good ranch hands."

"Thanks, but I can tell you now that will never happen. This old bar isn't much, but it's my life. Gunner can speak for himself, but he's the main guy keeping these old bush planes in the air. Someone's got to contribute to keeping the tourist dollars pouring into our small community. Our economy depends on keeping the tourists happy. But, of course, that doesn't mean we might not show up for a visit on the rare occasion."

"Hold the horses," Gunner grinned, finally noticing the shimmering diamond on Lana's left hand. "Are you guys engaged?"

"Yes," Lana beamed. "I'm one lucky girl. I can't wait to marry this hunk, and you're definitely invited to the wedding whenever we set the date."

"Congratulations. I'm happy for you guys. Eric, you were the lucky one finding this pretty young thing in Vegas."

"Oh, you don't have to remind me. I won a lot more than money on that short jaunt to Ceasars. She's the love of my life," Eric winked, giving Lana another quick kiss.

"So, I guess you're serious about selling the Husky?" Gunner frowned, tossing back his drink.

"Yes, and I hope you can help. But we're only here until the end of this week."

"Well, that's not very much time to sell a plane, but I might just have a buyer. One of the guys I talked to last week is looking for a plane. He's adding another aircraft to his fleet. She's in good condition, and you shouldn't have a problem selling her. It's a damn shame I don't have a little reserve cash. I would certainly take her off your hands. Norman, give me a bowl of that chili," Gunner added, changing the subject.

"What will you do with the cabin and the Jeep?" Norman questioned, sitting a steaming bowl filled to the brim on the bar.

"I'll make you a good offer on both?" Eric laughed.

"Thanks, but I'm afraid I'll have to pass. That cabin needs a lot of repairs. Are you going to sell it like it is?"

"Yes. I don't have the time or money to do all the work."

"Why don't you leave them in my hands," Norman suggested pouring another Duck Fart. "I'm sure I can find you the right buyer given a little time. Guys are always coming into the bar looking for transportation. But, of course, the cabin is a different story. That might take longer. However, you never know, it is located by the river, and we have a lot of fishermen who frequent the bar. It's certainly dilapidated, but some of the old guys who live around here might not be bothered by the fact it needs extensive repairs."

"Geez, thanks, Norman. Are you sure?"

"Yes. That's the least I can do to help. You guys only have a week, and I'm afraid it'll certainly take a lot longer than that to unload the cabin. Have you given your notice regarding the apartment?"

"No, not yet, but that's on my list of things to do after grocery shopping."

"Well, apartments go pretty fast around here, not a lot of them. Gunner and I can put the word out about the vacancy."

"Yeah, and don't worry about the cabin. It might need repairs, but the location is good," Gunner agreed, wiping chili from his mouth.

"Speaking of groceries," Lana smiled. "Babe, I think we better be going, or else someone is going to bed hungry again tonight."

"Yes. You're right. Norman, what do I owe you for the chili and drinks?" Eric asked.

"Not a thing. It's on the house."

The remaining week seemed too short. Leaving McGrath was hard. However, the worst part was saying goodbye to Norman and Gunner. At this point, they were family.

The plane and Jeep sold quickly. Leaving the cabin in Norman's capable hands, Eric had no worries he would eventually find the right buyer.

Boarding the plane out of McGrath, Eric turned around, taking in his last views of the remote town. Even though he had lived there only a short time, it was a place he would always hold dear to his heart.

"Welcome aboard," the young flight attendant announced. "Our flying time down to Seattle this morning will be approximately 3 hours and forty-nine minutes with one stop in Anchorage."

With her head pressed against the window, Lana found herself becoming somewhat emotional. Trying to hide the tears welling in her eyes, she inconspicuously reached into her purse for a Kleenex.

"Sweetheart, are you crying?" Eric questioned.

"Yes. I'm going to miss those two. But, unbelievably, Gunner never did tell me how he got rid of Blake," Lana sighed.

"No worries. Somehow I think you'll get your answers one day," Eric winked, kissing her moist cheeks.

As the plane lifted into the skies above McGrath, they were on their way home to Carson City and their new life.

Chapter Nine

Arriving in Reno, Jake met Eric and Lana at the airport.

"Hey, guys, welcome home. I borrowed Karen's Suburban. How was your flight?"

"Great," Eric remarked, retrieving their bags from the luggage carousel.

"Your flight came in sooner than I expected," Jake mentioned picking up one of the larger suitcases. "Karen said you called and took an earlier flight out of Seattle. She asked if I would take her car and drive up to meet you. She was in the middle of preparing a huge pan of lasagna. Let's hope it taste as good as it looks," Jake teased.

"I'm sure it will be delicious. I'm starved," Lana smiled, giving Jake a warm hug.

"I guess we'll find out. Karen was never known for her culinary skills," Eric laughed, walking out of the airport.

"Oh, I'm parked in short-term parking. Over here," Jake pointed. "It's so exciting to have you back at the ranch permanently. Things were a bit depressing when you left."

"Well, it's good to be home, but I have to drive back up to a meeting tomorrow. Then depending on the outcome, I might have to fly down to Vegas. However, Lana will be staying at the ranch," Eric mentioned tossing the luggage into the back of the suburban

"Eric, I'm coming with you," Lana whispered, giving him a stern look.

"I thought you might like to stay at the ranch. I'm meeting with Dad's old friend, Harvey Goldstein.

"No, I'm going with you," Lana insisted, jabbing him in his upper arm.

"Okay, Doll, no need for violence," Eric teased.

Arriving at Circle K, Jake and Eric unloaded the luggage. Then, walking in through the ornate double doors, the smell of lasagna infused the air.

"Hey, Sis, we're home," Eric announced, walking into the kitchen.

Wiping her hands on her flour-covered apron, Karen looked up with a huge smile.

"Hey, Bro. I hope you brought your appetite. Lana, it's good to have you back," Karen smiled, greeting them with a huge hug. "I thought we would celebrate your return with a nice dinner. I've even prepared a loaf of homemade bread."

"It smells heavenly, and what girl doesn't love warm bread?" Lana complimented.

"Well, I'll reserve my comments until I've tasted it," Eric teased.

"Sorry, I wasn't able to meet you guys at the airport, but I was in the middle of putting the lasagna together when you called about getting an earlier flight."

"No problem," Lana smiled. "Trust me; I'm glad you stayed behind. I'm starved."

"Lana, if you don't mind getting the china from the cabinet and setting the table, I believe everything is finally ready."

"Certainly."

"Oh, there's just going to be the four of us tonight," Karen added, slicing up the warm loaf of French bread.

"It looks amazing," Lana smiled as Karen removed the large pan from the oven.

"Eric, if you don't mind, maybe you could go down to the wine cellar and retrieve us a bottle of Merlot. I'll have Jake take the suitcases upstairs to the main suite."

"Karen, are you sure? That was mom's room."

"Yes. I do not need a room of that size. It has an ensuite. I'm sure you'll both find it comfortable."

"Thanks, Sis," Eric smiled, heading down to the cellar.

Spending the next hour leisurely eating dinner, which was as delicious as the aroma it exuded, Karen suggested they end the evening enjoying wine in the living room.

"I asked Jake to throw some logs on the fire pit. I thought it would be a great way to end the evening," Karen suggested curling up on the leather sectional with a glass of Merlot.

"Sounds wonderful," Lana smiled, removing her shoes as she snuggled into Eric's muscular arms.

"So, you mentioned the fact you're meeting with Harvey tomorrow. Is there a good chance you'll be able to get a seat on the World Poker Circuit?" Jake questioned.

"I certainly hope so. It's kind of the reason we're back. I mean, I want to help out around the ranch as much as I can, but it will provide us with a home base when I'm not on the road," Eric explained, taking a slow sip of his drink.

"Well, whatever your reason, it's good to have you home."

"Do you ride?" Karen questioned, glancing at Lana. "I mean, do you ride horses?"

"No. I've never exactly been around horses before, but it sounds like fun. So if you're up to teaching me, I would love it."

"Alright, I know just the horse," Karen suggested downing her entire drink.

Karen, I don't think that's the least bit funny," Eric snapped back. "I was raised with you. But, unfortunately, your idea of practical jokes can be taken too far."

"Eric, don't be silly. I'd never do anything to hurt Lana. I want to show her the Circle K, and taking the horses out for a ride is the best way."

"Okay, I'm trusting you," Eric grinned, popping the cork on another bottle of wine.

Conversation flowed freely as the four of them reunited as a family. Reminiscing about childhood memories shared with their mom was cathartic. However, it was finally time to leave the past behind and look forward to creating new memories.

"Let's take our glasses outside. It's getting dark, so I'll start the fire," Jake suggested standing up to stretch his legs. "Eric, you grab the wine."

"Sounds good."

"I have everything ready to make s'mores," Karen mentioned walking towards the kitchen.

"Do you need help?" Lana offered.

"No. I've got this. I'll be out in a few minutes."

Walking outside, Lana put her arms around Eric, attempting to stay warm in the chilly evening air.

"Wow. It's gorgeous. I don't think I've ever seen so many stars," Lana remarked, gazing upward at the evening sky.

"Sweetheart, it is spectacular, but it doesn't compare to the Aurora Borealis."

"You're right. I do miss Alaska. It was our first home," Lana agreed, sitting down on the circular stone bench surrounding the fire pit.

"Geez, Karen thought of everything," Eric laughed, reaching for one of the folded blankets. "I have to give her credit, she didn't miss a thing."

"I'm looking forward to the s'mores," Lana giggled. "As a child, I spent many evenings on the beach with my family, sitting around a roaring fire and enjoying smores. I'm craving chocolate."

"Well, you don't have to wait much longer," Eric grinned as Karen walked over with everything needed to make the tasty delicacy.

"Okay, the fire is hot. Who wants to go first?" Jake announced, handing out the long skewers.

"That's easy. It's Lana. She's craving chocolate," Eric suggested.

Watching as she stuffed the oozing marshmallow covered in dripping chocolate into her mouth, Eric laughed.

"Geez, Sweetheart! You didn't put it on the graham cracker. Let me make you a proper s'more," he smirked.

"Eric, who cares about the technical process?" Lana frowned. She was enjoying the yummy treat her way, entirely smothered in chocolate.

Wiping chocolate from her mouth, Eric gave her a quick kiss. He adored her childlike fascination.

"These are phenomenal," Lana laughed, continuing to pop the melted marshmallows into her mouth

"Babe, I think you should slow down on those. I foresee someone getting a stomach ache later tonight."

"Oh, Eric, don't be silly."

"Okay. Don't say I didn't warn you," he grinned.

As the evening got later, the embers slowly began to cool.

"I think I'm going to call it a night," Jake smiled. "Do you want me to add a few logs before I retire?"

"No. I think we'll be following you inside in a few minutes," Eric answered.

"Well, I'm turning in for the evening too," Karen smiled. "I've got a warm bed upstairs calling my name. I'm happy you're home."

"Sis, thanks for dinner and the amazing s'mores. Surprisingly, it was all delicious."

"Thanks, Eric. You make it sound as if I don't know what I'm doing in the kitchen."

"Guess time will tell," Eric grinned.

"That it will," Karen smiled, giving them each a hug.

Lana appeared extremely relaxed as she rested her head on Eric's shoulder. "Are you ready for bed, or would you like to sit outside while the flames go out?" Eric questioned.

"I'm fine. I don't think I can move. I over-indulged. I ate way too many," Lana sighed, gently rubbing her stomach.

"Yeah, I believe someone warned you as you continuously stuffed them in your mouth," Eric laughed

"Lana, since we're alone, I wanted to talk with you about the meeting tomorrow. But, first, I want to make sure that you're fully on board with me joining the World Series of Poker Tournaments."

"Yes. Why wouldn't I be?"

"Sweetheart, our lives will change dramatically if I secure a position. Traveling will become a huge part of our lives. With any luck, our future is going to look a lot brighter. Are you willing to stay at the ranch while I'm away? I get the feeling you might not be happy here with me leaving. What are your thoughts?"

"Eric, I love you, and I love your family. Karen and Jake couldn't possibly have treated me nicer," Lana paused, staring into the depth of his blue eyes. "But," she hesitated. "I'm not staying here without you. I didn't accept your proposal to be away from you. Do you understand? I don't care if I have to live in a motel. I'm coming too. This is our dream," Lana explained, wiping tears from her eyes.

"Okay, Doll, don't freak out. I'm not trying to make you emotional. We've had a wonderful evening, and I love you even with your face covered in chocolate," he winked, pulling her closer into his arms. "My parents took a different path regarding my dad being away from home. My mom stayed behind at the ranch. She, for the most part, raised us here in Carson City. We did travel with him in the summer and on the school holidays. I wanted to make sure that we were on the same page. You're right. This is our dream."

He was relieved to hear they shared the same thoughts regarding the amount of traveling their new venture would entail. Kissing Lana passionately, he loved her even more. Knowing that she didn't want to spend not even a moment apart, he knew she was one in a million. How did he ever get so lucky? They would make it work, no matter the logistics.

"I've given this some thought. Maybe we could purchase a single-family home in Vegas. Of course, we can always stay in a hotel suite, to begin with, at least until we have kids. Afterward, we would definitely need a house of our own. The Circle K will sort of be our home base. We can stay here when I'm not on the circuit, and I can help Karen and Jake with the upkeep. How does this sound?"

"Great, I especially love the part about us having kids," Lana hinted with a smile.

"So, you're completely alright with me joining the WSOP? You're not worried about me gambling with our future?" Eric grinned.

"No, not as long as your winning," she smiled.

"Sweetheart, I swear, you're one of a kind. You're my kind of girl."

Smothering her with kisses, he felt like the luckiest guy on earth.

"Wow. Did you see that?" Lana yelled enthusiastically, pulling away from him.

"See what?"

"A shooting star! I swear, I just saw a shooting star."

"Geez. The way you screamed, I thought you saw a mountain lion. Let's hope it's lucky," Eric added, quickly kissing her.

"Did you make a wish?"

"Of course."

However, he knew in his heart after tonight he didn't need a shooting star for luck. He was holding all the luck he would ever need in his arms. Winning Lana at Ceasars Palace had brought him enough success to last a lifetime.

"Let's go inside. It's getting cooler."

Picking up the love of his life, he carried her inside and upstairs to their main suite. Pulling back the enormous duvet, they undressed, turning out the lights, they slipped under the warm covers. Knowing the importance of his meeting the next day with Harvey, sleep didn't come easy. Lying awake, he stared at Lana sleeping peacefully next to him. He had to make their new venture a success. Failure wasn't an option. He could only imagine the worries and stress his dad must have had, especially before each tournament. However, he knew he was an exceptional card player. The old saying, 'the apple doesn't fall far from the tree,' kept playing over and over in his mind. Eric knew he'd inherited his dad's unique abilities. Snuggling close to sleeping beauty, he waited for the sun to rise. Feeling the warmth of her body next to him, he knew he had everything he needed to become successful. Roy Kolbeck was known worldwide. Now, it was time to add another name to this year's list of tournament winners.

Eric sat up, watching the morning sun wash over the room with a soft glow. He'd not slept at all, not a great way to start the day. Hopefully, several cups of coffee would suffice. Then, deciding a hot shower was in order, he gently slipped out of bed, trying not to wake the gorgeous girl still sleeping beside him.

Walking into the bathroom, he turned on the hot water in the shower. Standing under the invigorating warm water, he tried to remove any lingering worries about the day ahead. Lathering shampoo through his hair, he unexpectedly felt Lana's petite hands massaging his back.

"My God, Babe, I thought you were asleep. I didn't want to disturb you," Eric smiled, turning around to face her.

"Eric, I knew when you got out of bed. You can't get away from me that easily," she whispered, kissing his muscular chest.

Sweeping back her long wet curls with his fingers, he caressed her face with his hands pulling her close.

"Well, Sweetheart, I guess we should take advantage of the moment," he whispered, kissing the nape of her neck. "Here's the shampoo," he winked wickedly.

"Really, Eric, shampoo?" Lana smiled, gently tossing the plastic bottle in the corner. "This is how you repay a girl who follows you into the shower?"

"No, Doll, this is how I repay a girl who follows me into the shower," he whispered, pulling her into his arms. Kissing her passionately, the shower quickly became a steamy, romantic rendezvous.

The worries of the day quickly escaped them.

The smell of fried bacon wafted upstairs.

"Wow. I smell bacon. I think Karen is cooking breakfast," Eric smiled.

"I certainly hope so. I'm famished."

Lana wanted Eric to look his best by picking out a gray dress shirt with a darker matching tie and black trousers.

"You look amazing," Lana commented. "They would have to be crazy not to give you a place in the tournaments, regardless of the fact that you're the son of Roy Kolbeck."

"Awe, thanks, Babe. That's sweet. You look ravishing."

Lana thought their attire matched, wearing her long auburn hair swept back with a pearl hair comb, a stylish black halter sundress matched with black heels.

"Okay. Let's go downstairs and see what Karen made for breakfast."

Entering the kitchen, Karen whistled, noticing Eric walk in.

"Wow. Eric, you clean up nicely, and Lana, your dress is amazing. I may have to borrow it."

"Not a problem," Lana agreed.

"I've got tons of fried bacon on the stove, along with hash browns and scrambled eggs. The biscuits are almost done," Karen stated, reaching for a potholder. "Grab some cups. I made a whole pot of coffee."

"Thanks, Sis."

"I must warn you, don't expect this every morning. You got lucky today. Most mornings, I don't cook, and you'll be on your own. But, of course, we always have tons of oatmeal and cereal in the pantry," Karen added. "What time is your appointment with Harvey?"

"Oh, it's not until 1:00 p.m., but I thought I'd introduce Lana to some of my old high school buddies at the hotel before the meeting."

"So, where are you meeting Harvey? I don't think I've seen him since Dad passed."

"Oh, at Harrah's. We're just going to get lunch and mix in a little business. You're welcome to tag along."

"Thanks, but I've got some work to do in the horse stalls. Afterward, I'm going to take Midnight for a ride."

Hearing the timer on the stove, Karen removed the hot biscuits from the oven.

"Everything is ready. Why don't we just help ourselves this morning? Then, we can take our food and coffee to the dining room."

"Sounds good," Eric grinned.

Taking a plate, he filled it to overflowing with bacon, hash browns, and scrambled eggs. Next, piling hot biscuits on top, he handed it to Lana.

"Here you go, Babe. After this morning, I think you've earned it," he laughed.

"Geez, Eric. Why don't you just advertise our private life to the whole family?" Lana sternly whispered.

"What was that?" Karen questioned.

"Oh, nothing. Your brother is just being silly this morning."

"You'll get used to that," Karen laughed.

"Hey, guys. I thought I smelled the aroma of bacon," Jake grinned, walking into the kitchen.

"Serve yourself and join us in the dining room," Karen suggested. "Oh, there's plenty of hot coffee."

"Thanks."

Filling his plate with more than enough food to feed two people, Jake poured himself a cup of coffee and joined the others in the dining room.

"Wow. You two look nice," Jake complimented. "I bet you're excited to be honing your skills finally. Your father would be proud. I'm sure he's looking down from heaven this morning with a huge smile on his face," Jake smiled, stuffing several pieces of crisp bacon into his mouth.

"Awe, thanks, Jake. It's been a long time coming, but yes, I'm excited. The tournaments start at the end of this month. So I'm going to get in at the beginning. I've got a small reserve from the sale of my plane. I plan on winning as many of the tournament bracelets as I can. So I say go big or go home," Eric bragged, taking a huge sip of coffee.

"You're beginning to remind me of your dad. That's a good sign," Jake mentioned.

"Karen, you didn't inherit that gene?" Lana questioned.

"Oh, no, for heaven's sake. There's nothing even remotely appealing to me about sitting around a table in a dim, smoke-filled room with a bunch of hustlers. Give me the sunshine and outdoor activities any day of the week. I've always been drawn to horses. Would anyone like a coffee refill?"

"Yes. Would you make another pot of coffee? I'm going to need some extra caffeine this morning," Eric asked.

"Hand me your cup. I'll refill it now and then make another pot."

"Thanks, Sis."

"Not a problem," Karen smiled, returning to the kitchen.

Lingering at the table, deep in conversation, they quickly managed to finish the entire pot of coffee. Finally, Eric glanced down at his watch.

"Geez. It's getting late. Let's get on the road."

"Eric, I'll just help Karen with the kitchen duty. Do I have time to help with the dishes? It won't take long."

"Sorry. There's not enough time. Just put everything in the sink for now."

"You two get out of here. I'll clean up the kitchen," Jake insisted. "You might get your dress dirty washing dishes."

"Thanks, Jake," Lana smiled

"Oh, Sis, I almost forgot, I'm going to need the Suburban. I hope you don't have plans today."

"No. You're lucky. I'll grab my keys."

"Thanks, Sis. I forgot to mention last night that I would need to borrow your car."

Quickly returning with the keys, Karen handed them to Eric.

"You better drive safe. That car is my only transportation."

"Don't worry. I'll take good care of her."

"Okay. Get out of here before I change my mind," Karen teased. "Oh, good luck with your appointment."

"See you later this evening," Eric grinned, pulling Lana towards the front door.

"Well, we're finally on our way. Are you nervous?" Lana questioned, putting her arm around him.

"Heck no, I'm just meeting with Harvey to get advice. I'm not playing poker."

Arriving in Reno a short time later, Eric parked at Harrah's.

"It's a little early, but let's go inside, and I'll introduce you to Mike and the boys. They've been dealing cards at Harrah's for many years. I want the guys to see how lucky I got," Eric winked.

Taking Lana's hand, he led her inside the casino.

"You better not do anything silly or embarrass me in front of your friends."

"Doll, I would never do that. You trust me, right?" he smiled, giving her a quick kiss.

Lana felt at home hearing the loud sounds emitting from the slot machines.

"Geez, Babe, I miss working at Caesars. Maybe I could get my old job back," she questioned.

"Sweetheart, hopefully with our winnings, you're certainly not going to need your old job," he laughed.

Walking toward the card tables, Eric stopped for a moment. Then, catching sight of Mike dealing Black Jack, he had an idea.

"I'm going take a seat at the table and see if Mike notices."

However, before he even sat down, Mike looked up.

"Oh, my God, Eric, where did you come from?"

Motioning for a dealer to replace him, Mike appeared genuinely thrilled to see his old friend. Mike was tall, thin with jet black hair, and exemplified an athlete's physique. Yet, his handsome profile appeared unchanged, not looking a day older than the last time they met.

"What the hell brings you back home?" Mike questioned, totally surprised.

"Well, Mom recently passed, and I decided to come back and help Karen with the ranch. Geez, you must work out a lot. I swear you never appear to age."

"Oh, I try. I'm still an avid cyclist. Eric, I was so sorry to hear about your mom. I read Kathie's obituary in the paper. She was a wonderful woman, and I know you and Karen miss her. Do the guys know that you're back?"

"No. Not yet. Mike, I'd like you to meet Lana, my fiance."

"Wow," Mike paused, staring at Lana. "How in the world did this gorgeous thing get involved with the likes of you?" he teased. "It's about time. The guys and I were beginning to think you'd never get married."

"I met this beautiful girl in Vegas at Caesars Palace."

Extending her hand, Lana smiled. "Hi, Mike; it's nice to meet you."

"It's nice to meet you too. Geez, Eric, you were fortunate to find this gorgeous girl. I've got a break coming. Why don't we walk over to the bar, and I'll buy you both a drink? I'll give the guys a call."

"Sounds good."

"I must say you were the last person I ever expected to see today. However, I better warn the other dealers that Roy Kolbek's son has entered the building," Mike laughed. "Lana, I'm sure you're aware that Eric's dad made quite a name for himself playing poker."

"Yes, seems like Eric's mentioned that fact once or twice," Lana laughed.

"So, what brings you guys into Harrah's?" Mike questioned, pulling back a seat at the bar for Lana.

"Well, believe it or not, I'm finally going to enter the World Series of Poker, and I came up to meet with Harvey. You remember Harvey Goldstein, an old friend of Dad's?"

"Of course, I know Harvey; everyone knows Harvey. He's in here all the time. His reputation still precedes him, not to mention his notorious addiction to Cuban cigars. He's still on the circuits, but he never had your dad's abilities. However, with that being said, all the dealers still take notice when he walks in. Harvey's still considered a high roller around these parts. What are you drinking these days? It's on me."

"Well, not Duck Farts, that's for sure." Eric laughed.

"What the hell is a Duck Fart?"

"Oh, we just moved down from Alaska, and a friend of ours always drank a shot of Crown Royal, layered with Kahlua and Bailey's Irish Cream. It's called a Duck Fart."

"Trust me, they're nasty," Lana smirked.

"I'll have a Jack with Coke. Lana, would you like a glass of wine?" Eric questioned.

"Thanks, maybe a glass of White Zin."

"I'll call Randy and Alex," Mike mentioned ordering their drinks.

"Awe, that's too bad. He's not answering his phone," Mike frowned. "Let me try to get in touch with Alex." After a few minutes, Mike turned around, thoroughly disappointed. "Geez, he's busy training some new dealers at the moment and can't get away. He said to give him a call later. Here's his phone number," Mike added, writing it down on a paper napkin.

"Here's to old friends," Mike toasted as the bartender sat their drinks on the counter. "How long will you be in town? Perhaps, we could have dinner later when my shift ends."

"Oh, we're headed back to the ranch after I meet with Harvey. I'll call you later, and we'll set a date to get together. How does a barbeque sound?"

"Sounds great to me. Sorry, I have to go. It's jam-packed in here today. Mike grinned, giving Lana a quick hug. "It was awesome seeing you both. I look forward to the barbeque. Oh, here's my card. Call me."

"Thanks for the drinks. It was nice seeing you too. We'll be in touch," Eric grinned, standing to give his old friend a quick hug.

"Good luck with that meeting."

"Thanks."

"We have a few minutes before we meet Harvey for lunch. Do you want to try your luck with the slots?" Eric smiled.

"Of course, hand me your wallet," Lana laughed, pointing to a row of dollar slots. "Let's try this one. It looks lucky."

"So, you always know the lucky ones, do you?" Eric teased.

Quickly shoving a twenty into the end slot, Lana pulled the lever and held her breath as she watched the machine slowly come to a stop. Disappointed that she hadn't won, she decided to try her luck again. She pulled the lever and begged the device to stop on a winning line. Once more, the slot didn't align with a payout. Sitting back in the chair, she scowled.

"This machine doesn't like me," she pouted, looking up at Eric.

"Let me try," Eric grinned.

Pulling the lever, it only took moments for the slot to hit a winning line.

"I won a hundred dollars," Eric yelled as the sounds emitting from the slot became deafening.

"That's not fair," Lana frowned.

"Sweetheart, you're with me, right? It's our winnings. Take the ticket and try another machine."

"Thanks, Babe," Lana laughed, pulling the ticket from the slot as she led him toward a row of quarter slots.

Lana decided her luck might change and found an open seat at a Wheel of Fortune machine.

Suddenly smelling the pungent aroma of a Cuban cigar, Eric turned around.

"Oh, my God, Harvey, it's so good to see you," Eric grinned, noticing a stout middle-aged man with gray hair walking toward him. Wearing a pair of baggy brown trousers matched with a tan shirt and tie, it was apparent at first glance Harvey's sense of fashion was of little significance. Eric knew that Harvey had more money than God, and his image wasn't a concern.

"Hey, son, it's been a while. I ran into Mike, and he mentioned that you were already here. Hell, it's been too long since I've seen you." Harvey grinned, giving him a huge bear hug. "The last I heard, you had just retired from the Marines. What brings you home?"

"Oh, I was in Alaska flying bush planes, and Karen called to let me know that Mom had been taken to the hospital. So sadly, we lost her."

"I know. I'm so sorry—what a tremendous loss. I know Roy was thrilled to be reunited with her, but you and Karen must be devastated.

"Yes. It was totally unexpected."

"Why don't we walk across the street to the Black Angus? I'm craving a rare cut of Filet Mignon.

"That sounds delicious. Harvey, this is Lana, my fiancé."

"Wow. Congratulations. Darling, you're just about the prettiest young thing this old guy has ever seen," Harvey exclaimed. "We were beginning to think Eric would never get married. Let's walk over to the Black Angus. I want to know everything," Harvey grinned, taking a long draw on his cigar.

Entering the dimly lit restaurant, Harvey was immediately recognized. The aroma of sizzling, prime beef, and warm bread infused the air.

"Good afternoon, Mr. Goldstein. Follow me," the maitre d' stated, ushering them immediately to a private table.

"Welcome to the Black Angus. My name is Tony, and I'll be your waiter this evening. Can I get you started with drinks?" a tall young man with flaming red hair and facial piercings inquired.

"Yes, we'll start with a bottle of your finest Merlot while we glance through the menu," Harvey replied, putting out his cigar.

"Great," Tony replied, handing them menus. "I'll be right back with the Merlot."

"I've got this. Just take your time and order whatever appeals to you."

"Oh, I'm going to have the Filet Mignon, rare, covered in sauteed mushrooms and onions with steak fries," Eric grinned, glancing at his menu.

"Darling, what can Uncle Harvey order for you?"

"I'll have the same as Eric, but well-done with garlic mashed potatoes."

"Excellent choices," Harvey suggested.

Harvey informed Tony of the order as he returned to the table with glasses of water.

"May I have your choice of salad dressings?" the waiter inquired.

"Oh, I'll have the blue cheese," Eric spoke up.

"I'll have the ranch dressing," Lana smiled.

"Make that two ranch,' Harvey mentioned.

"Thanks, I'll be right back with the wine and your salads," Tony smiled, collecting the menus.

Returning with a bottle of 2006 Mandolin Merlot, the waiter uncorked the bottle pouring a small sample for Harvey. "It's not our most expensive, but it is our most preferred."

Swishing the Merlot inside his mouth, Harvey agreed.

"It tastes of spice and vanilla, with a hint of bing cherry and chocolate mint. Great choice," he added as the waiter continued to pour the wine.

"Sounds good to me. I heard the word chocolate," Lana agreed.

Returning with their salads and the main course, Tony served piping hot plates of Filet Mignon cooked just to their standards. With their preference for vegetables and a loaf of warm garlic bread, it smelled heavenly. Silence overtook the table as they each enjoyed their delicious meal with wine. Later, Harvey inquired about dessert.

"If anyone is interested, they make one hell of a cheesecake."

"Thank you. But I think I'll pass on dessert," Lana answered.

"That goes for me as well. I'm stuffed," Eric agreed. "Thank you for dinner it was delicious."

"Yes, thank you, it was wonderful," Lana added.

"My pleasure. You know I've always felt like your uncle. Roy and I were as close as brothers. I still miss him terribly even today. So tell me, how did you two meet?" Harvey questioned, leaning back in his chair as he lit a cigar. "Do you mind if I smoke? One of my few vices," he grinned.

"No. Not at all," Eric spoke up. "Well, there's not much to tell. It's not like we have known each other for a long time. I needed some extra cash to fund my business in Alaska, so I flew down to Vegas. I won this gorgeous girl at Caesars Palace," Eric teased.

"Eric, you're silly," Lana laughed. "You won a poker game. I simply found and returned your wallet. Let's keep the story straight. I was working as a cocktail waitress at Caesars."

"Yes. She literally saved my business. I had my entire life savings in that wallet, and she was honest enough to return it. How could I ever let this stunning girl go after that? I bought her dinner and later begged her to go with me to Alaska. It's pretty much that simple," Eric smiled, leaning over to give Lana a quick kiss.

"Yes. Eric drives a pretty hard bargain. However, he forgot to mention the fact that I had just relocated to Vegas to escape a previous abusive relationship. It just so happened that my former boyfriend Blake showed up that night to try and force me back to our beach house in Oregon. So, knowing that, Alaska began to look like a great alternative."

"Geez, Doll, you make it sound as if you were just using me," Eric laughed.

"Eric, you know I love you. I would never have let you get away that easily. I actually fell in love with this guy at first sight," Lana smiled, reaching over to hold Eric's hand.

"Well, I must say how pleased I am that you two found each other. I know Roy and Kathie are looking down with a huge smile on their face. So, now, getting down to business. What did you want to discuss?" Harvey questioned, exhaling a ring of smoke.

"Harvey, I wanted to get some information about signing on with the World Series of Poker next month in Vegas."

"My, God, it's about time! Hell son, what took you so long? Now, I know Roy is looking down with a huge grin. What do you want to know?" Harvey grinned, taking a drag on his smelly cigar.

"Well, I've got some cash coming in from the sale of my bush plane. Should I buy directly into the tournament at a high level or work my way up to a seat through satellite events a week or two before the game?

"Son, to be honest, I know you're Roy's son, and I know you've no doubt inherited his abilities," Harvey began explaining. "But, you're still a little naïve, simply because you haven't polished your skills. Now trust me, your name alone will offer you a lot of opportunities. However, that doesn't mean you should be too quick to accept any of them. If I could get somewhat personal, and I'm not trying to pry, it'll just help me, help you, if you catch my drift," Harvey continued. "What are your goals? I mean, are you doing this just for a quick infusion of cash? Do you and this little lady have a backup plan? If God forbid, this doesn't work out, or are you in this for the long haul like your Dad?" Harvey quizzed intently, staring at Eric as he took another long draw on his cigar.

"To be honest, I'm looking to make it a career, just like Dad. But, I guess you could say that I'm in it for the long haul."

"Wonderful, that was what I was hoping you would say. Your dad always wanted you to join us for the World Series of Poker Events." Harvey paused, sitting up as he gave Eric his undivided attention. "I guess I'm having a hard time trying to understand what took you so long?"

"I guess you might say the timing wasn't right. I spent twenty years in the Marines flying helicopters, and I think my love for flying kept me in the air. After Mom passed, I realized that Karen needed help with the ranch. So I sold my bush plane and relocated back to Carson City. I had never given up the idea of playing on the circuits one day, but I think it had more to do with getting my priorities straight. Looking back, even though I desperately wanted to join the Marines, I missed a once-in-a-lifetime opportunity to play on the poker circuits with

Dad. I know that's what he really wanted. It's truly one of my worst regrets in life."

"Well, I'd be happy to show you the ropes and teach you everything I know. It's never too late, and there's no doubt in my mind that you've inherited Roy's talents. So, let's get you signed up. Here are my thoughts. I wouldn't jump right in with a $10,000 main event buy-in. I don't know what you received for the sale of your aircraft, but I would hold on to that and other savings you might have. It might be needed to keep the ranch going. It's the middle of May. Your time is running out to find online WSOP event qualifiers. However, I know the Rio Hotel is holding those events this year. Hopefully, you can win your way up through the Main Event Satellites for a spot in the WSOP Main Event and a chance to win the tournament bracelet. That would only cost you about $200.00 or less. What are your thoughts?" Harvey asked, rubbing out his cigar.

"Sounds good to me. I trust your judgment."

"Time is of the essence. If you're serious, and it seems to me after our discussion that you are, I lease a private jet at the local airport, and I plan to fly down on Friday. Why don't you arrange to fly down with me? We can book a couple of rooms at Caesars, which has always been my home while in Vegas. I usually spend my summers there, and I'd seriously suggest you do the same. I'm sure you remember your father being away from the ranch for long periods. I'm afraid that's some of the dues we pay for being in the business. But, again, I'm not trying to pry but is this pretty young thing, I mean Lana, coming with you?"

"Yes," Eric smiled, squeezing Lana's hand.

"That's good to hear. Being away from my wife, Helen, cost me my marriage. However, your parents were a rare statistic. They never allowed distance to separate them. There's more I'd like to go over with you, but we can do that later. I've got to run, things I need to take care of before leaving. So I'll send a car down to the Circle K to pick you up Friday morning, say about 9:00 a.m. Does that time work for you both?" Harvey inquired, pushing back his chair from the table.

"We'll be ready. Thanks, Harvey, for dinner and the information. We'll see you Friday morning.

"Alright, Son, it's so good to have you join me on the circuit finally. It's an awesome life. You've made the right decision. See you Friday," Harvey stated, covering the cost of dinner with a generous tip.

Returning to Circle K, neither expected to leave so soon. But, once again, they had just flown down from Alaska and still had unpacked bags, which at this point were probably a blessing in disguise.

"Eric, how are you going to break the news to Karen that we're leaving on Friday? She might not understand," Lana asked as they drove up to the Circle K.

"Well, for starters, there's not a darn thing any of us can do. I can't afford to miss out on the opportunity of qualifying, and as Harvey said, I don't have much time. Karen knows how much I want to enter the WSOP Tournament this year."

"You're right. I'm sure Karen will understand you leaving, but what about the fact that I'm going with you. I hate to leave her alone."

"Lana, for heaven's sake, she needs to grow up. She's a grown woman, and besides, she has Jake and the ranch hands to help with maintenance."

"Sorry, Babe, I didn't mean to touch a nerve. I forgot you and Karen don't always see things in the same light."

They didn't have to wait long for Karen's reaction as she opened the door.

"Hey, Bro, how was your meeting with Harvey?" Karen quizzed. "I was on my way outside to water the Bougainvillea."

"Sis, you're just the person I needed to see. That can wait, come inside and sit down. I have some unexpected news. "I'm afraid I will be leaving for Vegas on Friday."

"Geez, Eric, that's short notice. Here you go again, always chasing your dreams. I knew you would get a seat on the WSOP, but you're leaving so soon. I thought you were going to help repair the fences and the horse barn before you left," Karen seethed, collecting her thoughts. "Damn, Eric, you're always dumping your responsibilities on me. You'll never change," she added, reaching for a bottle of bourbon. "Well, I suppose Lana will be here to help with the housework and cook for the ranch hands."

Pouring a stiff drink, Karen began pacing the floor. "You expect Jake and the few ranch hands to get everything done before winter sets in again. He's getting old, and you know he doesn't hold up as easily."

"That's not a problem. I'll simply hire additional help. So why are you making such a huge deal out of us leaving on Friday?"

"Did you say, us? Is Lana going too?"

"Yes."

"That's just great. Now, I'll be here all alone. I'm still trying to adjust to Mom no longer being here."

"Karen, Eric has to be at the Rio on Friday. Harvey suggested that he enter the online satellite competitions and hopefully win a seat at the WSOP. He needs the practice, which will also save us a lot of money. If Eric is successful, it will benefit everyone. I have faith in him, and I know that you do too. I'm going with him because I plan on asking for my old job back at Caesars, at least temporarily through the summer," Lana explained.

"You're what?" Eric exclaimed. "There was no discussion about you going back to work. Sis, hand me the bottle," Eric vented, reaching for a glass.

"I was going to tell you later," Lana explained. "You can't expect me to sit in a hotel room all summer with nothing to do."

"Geez, women, you're all impossible," Eric murmured under his breath. Tossing back his drink, he poured another shot. "Sweetheart, remember, I told you there was no need for you to go back to work. The sale of the bush plane will give us an extra cushion of cash, not to mention we still have most of the money I won in Vegas. So we'll have more than enough savings to see us through the summer. Plus, you're losing sight of our dreams. I don't plan on losing money. I thought you believed in me, have a little faith."

"Eric, I do have faith in you. It has nothing to do with that. It's just the fact I don't like being alone in a hotel room for hours on end with nothing to do except watch movies."

"You can read," Eric suggested.

"We'll discuss this later," Lana fumed.

"Now, you know how I feel," Karen frowned. "It's not fun being alone."

"I'm going for a walk. I've got to get out of here. No wonder Dad traveled alone," Eric scolded, making his way out to the patio. Hearing the back door slam, Lana knew he was visibly shaken.

"He's a bit dramatic, but you better go after him," Karen suggested. "I didn't mean to get him upset. I'm sorry."

"Oh, I think he's unhappy with me too," Lana added, running after him.

Sprinting outside to catch up with him, Lana saw him standing next to the fire pit, lighting a cigarette. Slowly putting her arms around him, Lana pulled him close.

"Hey, Babe, I'm sorry. I planned on telling you," Lana smiled, reaching up to give him a quick kiss. " I really want my job back. You're going to be busy, hopefully winning, and we'll have our evenings together."

"Okay," Eric paused, returning her kiss. "Did Karen calm down? I swear my sister drives me over the edge," Eric grimaced, taking a drag on his cigarette.

"Eric, I think you should cut your sister a little slack. She was extremely close to your mom. It's got to be hard on her, and I know she loves you. I'm sure she was counting on me to keep her company when you left. This is a big house, and I'm sure she gets lonely. She was simply shocked to hear that I was leaving with you. She'll come around. Just give her some time."

"Well, she doesn't have much time. We leave in two days," Eric mentioned tossing his cigarette butt into the fire pit.

"I have an idea. Weren't you going to take me to Lake Tahoe? Why don't we ask Karen to tag along? The weather is beautiful, and I think she needs to get out of the house."

"Babe, I'd planned that as a special day away just for the two of us."

"Eric, I love the fact that you were thinking of us, but I'm going to have you all to myself for the entire summer. I think you need to spend some quality time with your sister."

"Alright, if you think it would help. Let's go inside and see if Karen is agreeable."

Later that evening, under a brilliant canopy of stars, Eric, Lana, and Karen enjoyed an unforgettable dinner cruise on the lake. It appeared the perfect way to rekindle their relationship.

Leaving the Circle K in Karen's capable hands, along with forty-thousand dollars in a joint account, it was finally time to take the next step toward winning the WSOP. They were on their way back to Vegas.

Chapter Ten

Staring out the window of the limo as it wound its way through fields of cactus toward the highway, Lana felt somewhat remorseful for leaving Karen. However, she knew staying behind without Eric was never an option.

Arriving at the airport, Lana felt an overwhelming sense of excitement as the sleek Lear Jet came into view.

"Eric, this is our ride to Vegas," Lana questioned in disbelief.

"Yes, Harvey only travels first class," Eric mentioned as the car slowly drove up to the aircraft. Stopping at the bottom steps, Jeffry, the chauffeur, opened their door. Retrieving their luggage, he hurriedly carried it onboard.

"Have a safe flight," he stated.

Ascending the steps to the jet, Harvey met them at the aircraft door.

"Welcome to the WSOP," he grinned as a cigar dangled from his lips. "Are you ready for the ride of your life?" he chuckled.

Lana was more than impressed with its degree of opulence entering the plane. Its cutting-edge interior contained eight rows of double club seats covered in the most beautiful tan, Italian leather, each having its television screen. State-of-the-art under-mount lighting reflecting off the gorgeous high-gloss Walnut cabinetry bathed the aircraft in a warm glow.

"Geez, Eric, this must cost him a small fortune."

"Babe, money to Harvey is simply an upgrade at this point in his life. He can afford just about anything he wants."

Taking a seat mid-way through the aircraft, Eric ensured Lana was buckled into the seat.

"Welcome aboard, I'm Cindy, and I'll be taking care of you this morning on our flight to Las Vegas. Would you like a glass of champagne?"

"Yes. Thanks," Eric smiled.

"I'll be right back with your drinks."

"Kids, enjoy the ride. I'm going to be sitting in the back this morning. I've got to crunch some numbers on a real estate deal. We should be on the ground in Las Vegas in approximately an hour. In the meantime, Cindy will take great care of you," Harvey grinned, making his way to the back of the aircraft.

Returning with two fluted glasses of sparkling Dom Perignon, Cindy provided them with a small platter of Brie, along with Carr's Table Water Crackers and sweet grapes.

"Would either of you like a warm blanket before we depart?"

"No, thanks, I think we're good at the moment," Eric replied.

"If you should need anything further, please let me know."

"Babe, is this for real?" Lana questioned, taking a sip of champagne. "I feel like a fish out of water."

"Sweetheart, relax, enjoy yourself. You're flying Harvey Air today," Eric laughed. "Of course, this could all be in our future if things go the way I plan. Dad and Harvey always traveled on private jets."

"So, why in the heck did you wind up in Alaska flying bush planes?"

"Lana, I never wanted a career in poker. Becoming a pilot in the Marines offered me the opportunities I had always wanted. I had childhood dreams of becoming a pilot, not a poker player," Eric explained. "Losing Mom and realizing Karen's financial dilemma with the ranch, things changed. Doll, we're engaged, and I want to offer you a better life," Eric winked, leaning in to give her a quick, passionate kiss. "Of course, we could always move back to our little shack in Alaska."

"No way," Lana frowned. "I could easily get accustomed to this lifestyle. You better win," Lana smiled, snuggling into his arms as the jet lifted skyward.

Arriving in Vegas, a limo awaited their arrival.

"Did you kids enjoy the ride?" Harvey grinned, approaching their seats. "The car will take us to Caesars. After we check-in, I'll buy lunch, and then we better head over to the Rio. Lana, you're welcome to tag along or just enjoy some downtime in your suite this afternoon. I'd be happy to reserve you an appointment at the spa if you'd like. It's up to you," Harvey smiled.

"Thanks, Harvey. I think I'll just hang back in the room today. Then, I'll probably catch up with John, my former boss, and check on the possibilities of getting my job back."

"Suit yourself. If you should change your mind about the spa, just mention my name. That should open a few doors for you," Harvey ginned, lighting his cigar as he descended the steps of the aircraft.

Checking into Caesars, Harvey was instantly recognized. It appeared he was well respected as a 'high roller.'

"Good evening Mr. Goldstein. It's so nice to see you. I've reserved the penthouse for you and a suite for your guests. Here are your room keys. I believe your guests are in room 1104, and you're in the same tower. However, you're in the penthouse. It's a pleasure to have you back with us. If there is anything we can do to make your stay more enjoyable, please let us know," the hotel receptionist smiled. "I'll have your luggage sent up immediately."

"Thanks, Carl," Harvey replied as he was given the room keys.

Walking toward the elevator, Lana once again felt awkward. Having worked as a cocktail waitress in Caesars, she now felt like a celebrity checking in with Harvey.

"Oh, here is your room key. I almost forgot," Harvey mentioned handing it to Eric as they stepped into the elevator.

Looking down at the suite number, Eric gasped. It was the same suite that they had shared previously in Vegas. The odds of that happening were astronomical. However, Eric took it as a good sign.

Stopping on the 11th floor, Harvey stepped aside, allowing Lana to exit first.

"Well, kids, this your stop. Uncle Harvey will come down in an hour and take you to lunch. Afterward, Eric and I will head over to the Rio. See you in a bit," Harvey grinned, taking a puff on his cigar.

"Geez, Eric, this whole thing feels surreal," Lana beamed.

"Well, I assure you it isn't. You've just entered the world of Harvey Goldstein," Eric laughed, opening their door.

"Wow," Lana exclaimed, entering the luxurious suite. "Eric, this suite looks the same as the one we stayed in before!"

"It's the same suite. Can you believe it? What are the odds?"

"Oh, my gosh, that's unbelievable," Lana questioned, taking off her shoes.

The glass-enclosed balcony revealed the full view of the bottom floor as it led upward to the main suite. Walking over to draw back the elegant sheer drapes, it exposed magnificent strip views.

"Hey, Doll, want a drink?" Eric inquired, immediately walking over to the bar. "We've got a bottle of white zin."

"Okay, but just a small glass. I can't afford to get tipsy. I'll be meeting with John, my former boss, later."

Walking over to the extended leather sectional, Lana lounged back.

"Eric, can you believe we're back in Vegas? I'm so excited. I've got to call Megan."

"Call her tomorrow. We just arrived here. Drink this; it'll help you unwind," Eric smiled, handing her a glass of wine.

Relaxing next to her, Eric pulled her close, kissing the nape of her neck.

"Eric, we've only got an hour. After that, Harvey's going to take us out for lunch, remember?" Lana mentioned trying to avoid his loving gestures.

"Doll, you can do a lot in an hour," he teased.

"I love you, but you're acting silly. I need to unpack my clothes."

"Alright, but tonight my future Mrs. Kolbeck, you're not getting away from me so easily," Eric laughed. "I'll take the luggage upstairs."

"Do you remember the outdoor spa?"

"Are you kidding? Of course."

"Then follow me upstairs, and we'll check it out," Eric suggested.

"Okay, but no funny business. We've got lunch plans, and I'm meeting with John afterward."

Following Eric upstairs, thoughts of their last time together in this same suite flooded her mind with memories. How did she ever get so lucky? However, she knew staring at her handsome, muscular Marine carrying their luggage up the stairs. Evidently, the wish she'd made tossing her coin into the fountains at the Bellagio had come true.

"Doll, you know there is one major change since we previously stayed in this suite."

"Oh, really, what?"

"Clothes, I swear, you've got way too many clothes," he laughed, dropping the suitcases inside the bedroom.

"You're right."

Playfully taking her hand, he led her toward the massive kingsize bed, pulling her down next to him.

"Do you see yourself living here during the summers?" Eric whispered, smothering her with kisses.

"Yes. That is until we have kids. After that, I think we're going to need a house. A large house," Lana added.

"So, remind me, how many kids did you want?" he asked, pulling her closer.

"Six," she laughed, giving him a hard pinch to his upper arm.

"Do that once more, and I swear you're not getting out of here today," Eric teased, kissing her passionately.

"Oh, you wouldn't," Lana laughed. "I'd like to see you explain that one to Harvey."

"Oh, Babe, somehow I think Harvey might just understand," Eric winked mischievously. "Doll, you might not know men as well as you think," he smiled, placing his watch on the nightstand.

Unable to resist his wit and passion, Lana gave in to his desires.

She loved him with her whole being. If only they had the entire day to linger in bed. It didn't matter; she knew they had their entire life ahead of them.

Hearing the alarm on Eric's watch, they had just enough time to shower and dress before Harvey stopped by to take them to lunch.

Later, a knock at the door announced Harvey's arrival.

"Hey guys, are you ready to find some chow around here?" he grinned, puffing away on his smelly habit, Cuban cigars. "How does Mexican food sound? I know the best little restaurant in Vegas. Your father and I used to hang out there. I've arranged for a limo to pick us up. Afterward, I'll have the car drop this gorgeous girl back at Caesars. Then, you and I can head over to the Rio. How does that sound?"

"Sounds great," Eric agreed.

Following Harvey over to the elevator, he pushed the button to the main floor. Walking through the casino, it was a microcosm of people and machines. The loud noise emitting from the numerous rows of slots had both young and old attempting to beat the odds at winning. Finally, reaching the outside entrance, they stepped inside the limo for the short drive over to Mama Rosa's Restaurant.

After enjoying a delectable meal of slow-cooked enchiladas, refried beans, and rice, they quickly gave up the idea of dessert. Instead, looking down at his watch, Harvey noted the time.

"Well, son, as nice as this has been, I think we need to get down to business. So let's drop this pretty lady back at Caesars and head over to the Rio. Are you ready to take on the world of poker?" Harvey questioned.

"I think I've been ready my entire life. I just never knew it until now," Eric grinned.

"That's my boy, let's go."

Motioning for the waiter, Harvey covered the cost of lunch, plus a generous tip.

Arriving back at Caesars, they dropped Lana at the hotel before continuing to the Rio.

Quickly kissing Eric, Lana stepped out of the car.

"Harvey, thanks for dinner. Good luck, Babe. Karen and I are counting on you."

"Oh, somehow, I don't think luck will have anything to do with it. It's called DNA. He inherited his skills from Roy," Harvey laughed, exhaling a large puff of smoke.

"Okay, let's get down to business."

As the limo slowly drove into the entrance of the Rio Hotel, the doorman opened the car door, "Good afternoon, Mr. Goldstein, welcome to the Rio."

Eric followed Harvey as they made their way through the casino floor and to an area reserved for high-stakes poker.

"Son, I'm going to put you in the game starting at a thousand dollars. I've got faith in you, but after this, you're on your own," Harvey stated, puffing away on his cigar. "I see no need starting with a Steps Tournament just to get a cheaper buy-in with your skills. You've easily got this."

"Harvey, I can cover the costs, but thanks."

"No need to thank me, consider it a gift. I'll be keeping my eye on you, don't disappoint me."

"Thanks."

Buying in at the high level of a thousand dollars, Eric sat down with ten other players. It was time to bring his innate abilities to the table. His hands were sweating as the dealer placed two cards face down in front of each player. Eric checked, holding his own. Then as the dealer dealt the flop, surprisingly to his advantage, he placed his first bet. After the turn, his hand showed even more promise. Upping his chance, he could only hope and pray the river held the cards he needed. Unbelievable, he was holding four of a kind. Sitting back in his chair, he smiled.

"Thanks, Dad," he whispered.

After an hour, Eric remained along with seven others. However, they were slowly eliminated as Eric's abilities saw him through to being one of the final two players remaining at the table. Wiping his forehead, he felt confident he could pull off a winning hand. He couldn't disappoint Harvey after he'd covered the thousand-dollar entry fee. He had to win the tournament. Whispering a prayer, it was undoubtedly heard as Eric was declared the winner, holding a royal flush.

At last, he had won a seat at the WSOP. After rounds of congratulatory comments from his opposing players, he walked away with a huge smile. It appeared no one at the table had made the connection between his last name and his famous father.

Walking over to the bar, he needed a stiff drink. He ordered a single shot of Blanton's Bourbon and savored the flavor as he took his first sip. Then, as the calming effects of the smooth bourbon hit him, he downed his entire drink. Ordering a second shot, Harvey walked up behind him, slapping him on the back.

"Congratulations, I knew you could do it! Son, I'm so proud of you. I know your dad is looking down with a huge smile. So, what are we drinking? Shots of Blanton's?" Harvey questioned with a grin. "Your dad's favorite sipping bourbon."

Starting a tab, Harvey informed the bartender to keep pouring. For the next hour and a half, as only an uncle and nephew could, they sat at the bar reminiscing about Roy.

"Eric, I know I'm not your biological father, but Son, tonight I couldn't be prouder of you than if I were. I love you, and I'll always be there for you, Lana, and Karen. But, I want you to know that whatever you or the girls need, you come to Uncle Harvey. Do you understand?" he asked with tears welling in his eyes. It was apparent they were both beginning to feel pretty good at this point of the evening.

"Yes. Thanks, Harvey. I love you," Eric grinned, hugging him. "Thanks for putting up the thousand dollars, without so much as a hint of my repaying you."

"Son, it's the least I can do. But, as I said, it's a gift. If it hadn't been for your father, I wouldn't be where I'm today. I owe that man a lot. At least, I can help his son," Harvey smiled, tossing back his entire drink.

Looking down at his watch, Harvey noted the time.

"Well, I guess I better get you back to the hotel. It's getting late. Lana, might not appreciate the fact that I'm bringing you back so late, especially after having a little too much to drink. I hope she isn't too mad or disappointed with me. But, hell, Son, we had to celebrate. We're both going to have seats at the WSOP. That's quite an accomplishment," Harvey stated. "I'll call for the limo."

After ensuring the limo would pick them up, they downed one last round of Blanton's.

"Son," Harvey paused, blurring his words. "Here's to one of us winning that bracelet, and you know what, I would be just as happy if it turns out to be you. How much money does one old geezer need anyway?" Harvey smiled, downing his last shot of bourbon.

Slowing making their way to the front of the hotel and outside to the entrance, the doorman noting Harvey's condition, helped him inside the limo. "Let's go home, Son. I've got a warm bed waiting for me."

Entering the limo, Eric thought of Lana for the first time this evening. He had been so distracted by the importance of the game he felt guilty for leaving her. Eric also felt terrible that Harvey only had a warm bed to look forward to. He had the best thing that ever happened to him waiting in their hotel suite. Hopefully, she would cut him a little slack for his inebriated condition.

After a short drive, the limo drove up to the grand entrance at Caesars Palace.

"Welcome back, Mr. Goldstein," the doorman greeted.

"Thanks," Harvey mumbled.

Observing Harvey's condition, Eric lovingly took him by his arm, aiding him through the casino and over to the elevator. Eric knew he would need to see that Harvey made it up to his penthouse.

"Sir, would you like some help with Mr. Goldstein?" the concierge inquired, noticing Eric's dilemma as he held onto Harvey's arm.

"No. Thanks. I'll help my uncle up to his penthouse."

Getting him inside the elevator, Eric reached into Harvey's pocket for his room key. Pushing the button to the top floor, he managed without help to get Harvey inside the penthouse. After realizing the main suite was upstairs, Eric managed to get Harvey over to the large leather sectional. Gently laying him on the couch, Eric ran upstairs to grab a pillow and blanket. Removing his shoes, Eric lovingly rested Harvey's head on the pillow and covered him with a blanket. "Good night, Harvey," Eric whispered. Closing the door, he couldn't wait to see Lana.

Taking the elevator down to the eleventh floor, he worried that Lana might be upset about him staying out late. Unlocking the door, Lana was nowhere in sight. Bounding up the stairs, he almost tripped. Opening the bedroom door, she was sleeping peacefully. Quietly, he walked into the bathroom, closing the door. Taking a warm shower, he shaved and brushed his teeth using plenty of mouthwash to mask the scent of bourbon. Finally, splashing on a small amount of cologne, he opened the door. Slipping into bed, he gently put his arms around her warm body.

"So, did we win?" she whispered.

"We did."

Early the next morning, sunlight permeated the entire room with a soft glow. Eric slowly opened his eyes. He was surprised to find Lana awake.

"So, we won," she smiled, smothering him with kisses. "I'm so proud of you. I imagine Harvey must have felt extremely proud. Does this mean you earned a seat at the big event?"

"Yes. Can you believe it?" he winked, pulling her close. Then, returning her kisses with passion, he smiled. Apparently, she had not been aware of his drunken state when he came in. Holding her in his arms, there was no better way to start the day than showing the future Mrs. Kolbeck how much he loved her.

"Doll, I remember something about your wanting all those kids. Maybe we'll get lucky," he whispered.

"Maybe, I love you," she whispered.

Later that morning, after calling for room service to order breakfast, Eric called Harvey's room. He had to make sure that Harvey was okay after the previous night.

"Hey Harvey, how are you feeling?

"Great. It seems coffee, orange juice, and aspirin can work miracles. I feel fine. How are you this morning?"

"I'm fine."

"Thanks for helping an old man out last night. I really appreciate it."

"Not a problem. It was the least I could do after you put up the entry money."

"Son, that was nothing. I knew you were going to win. How did the little lady take you coming in late and a bit hungover?"

"Oh, she never knew. She was sleeping when I came in."

"Well, you two have a lovely day. You have a lot to celebrate. I'm going boating with some old buddies on Lake Mead later today. I'll give you a call sometime tomorrow. Thanks again for getting me home. Talk to you later."

"Okay, Harvey, have a great time. See you tomorrow."

Hanging up the phone, Eric turned around. To his surprise, it appeared Lana had overheard their conversation.

"Okay. What was it that I never knew?" Lana inquired.

"Nothing, sweetheart. Trust me. It was nothing," he babbled.

"Oh, are you referring to the fact that you were drunk last night when you came in?" she vented, trying to keep a straight face.

"Doll, there's no way possible you could have even suspected it after all the time I spent in the bathroom," he laughed.

"Eric, I know you too well. I could smell the bourbon on your breath."

"But, you never said anything?"

"I knew you were under a lot of stress, and the fact you won, I decided not to mention it," she smiled. "Of course, if it happens again, you might not get off so easy."

"Babe, I love you. How did I get so lucky to find you?" Eric winked, pulling her into his arms giving her a quick kiss. "What would you like to do today? It seems we have the day to ourselves. Harvey is going boating."

"Why don't we look at houses? I think we should check out the market."

"Sounds like a great idea. I'll go online and find an agent," Eric suggested. He was happy to have escaped the possible wrath of Lana having scolded him for bad behavior. At this point, he would have certainly done anything she requested.

Hearing a knock on the door, it announced the arrival of breakfast.

"Good morning, sir," the young man smiled, pushing a cart laden with food inside the room. The strong aroma of coffee, along with bacon and pancakes, infused the air. Then, tipping the room service attendant, he was on his way.

Lana removed the silver lids from the chafing dishes, revealing crispy fried bacon, blueberry pancakes, and a side order of scrambled eggs.

"Wow. This looks delicious. I was going to jump in the shower, but after seeing what you ordered, I'll wait until after breakfast."

Heaping tons of butter and warm maple syrup on top of her pancakes, Lana added a few pieces of bacon to her plate.

"Why don't we take our food over to the sofa? Then, I'll pour the coffee," Eric suggested.

"Nothing like room service," Lana laughed, taking a huge bite of her pancakes.

"You're right," Eric grinned, handing her a steaming cup of coffee. "However, if we buy a house, someone will have to cook."

"Or," Lana paused. "We could always hire a housekeeper," she teased.

"Really. You would prefer to have a maid?" Eric questioned.

"Never. I was joking. Trust me, Babe, I'm completely capable of running my own ship," she laughed. "My mom was a maid the whole time I was growing up, and she worked hard."

"You never mention your family. Don't you miss them?" Sipping his coffee, he wondered why Lana never brought up her family in their conversations.

"I've told you my story. You know that I came from a large family, and we were never close, that my dad was always out with his boats for long periods of time, and mom was always at work. When they were home, they argued a lot. It used to drive me crazy as a kid."

"Sweetheart, I'm sorry. How in the world did they have all those kids if they were never together?" Eric paused as he was shoveling pancakes into his mouth.

"Don't ask me. You're silly."

"Oh, I almost forgot about your meeting with John? Did you get your old job back?"

"Yes. I forgot to mention it. I start next week. I have a few days before I go back to work, so I called Megan. We arranged to get together tomorrow. She can't wait to meet you," Lana smiled, walking over to sample the scrambled eggs. "Yum, these are delicious. You should try them."

"Why don't you take your shower and get dressed? Then, I'll find us an agent to show us a few houses," Eric mentioned after breakfast.

The real estate agent agreed to pick them up at the hotel within the hour.

"Good morning, I'm Barbara Brown with Gold Star Realty. We spoke on the phone earlier," she smiled, extending her hand. Introducing herself as Eric opened the door, she appeared professional. Wearing a black pantsuit, her blonde hair was meticulously coiffured in the latest style, short sporting the tasseled unkept look. By her appearance, Eric assumed she was probably in her mid-sixties. However, she was attractive and curvaceous.

"Thanks for coming on such short notice. My fiancé, Lana, will be right down. Why don't we go into the living room? Would you like coffee?" Eric asked, showing her over to the long sectional.

"No. Thanks for asking. Why don't we go over what you're looking for in a new home? Do you have a certain location in mind? What size home are you currently looking for, you know, square footage, number of bedrooms, single or two-story?" Barbara inquired.

"Well, I'll need to run this past Lana, but the location needs to be close to the strip. It doesn't matter if it's single or two-story if we like the floor plan. However, I would definitely like a four-bedroom with a large two-car garage. Also, we're looking for a new home. We're not in the market to purchase an older property which might need a lot of work."

"Thanks. That really helps. I've got quite a few houses in our inventory that would easily meet your criteria."

Watching as Lana descended the stairs wearing her long auburn curls pulled back in a ponytail enhanced her gorgeous sculpted facial features. Sporting black cropped jeans with an oversized gray tunic and sneakers, Eric thought she looked ravishing. Taking another quick look, her face appeared to have an unusual radiance. Eric swore under his breath if they were alone, he would have instantly scooped her up in his arms and carried her back up the stairs.

"Barbara, this is Lana, my fiancé," Eric smiled.

"It's nice to meet you. Eric has given me some specifics as to what you're both looking for, and as I told him, I have several properties to show you today. If you're ready, I have a car downstairs waiting to give you a tour?"

"Sounds great," Eric replied, taking Lana's hand.

After viewing almost a dozen properties, they realized that the day had flown by rather quickly. As Barbara brought them back to the hotel, the sun began to set over the mountains.

"Here's my card. Don't hesitate to call if you have any questions or would like to revisit one of the homes."

"Thanks. We'll be in touch," Eric grinned.

Walking into the foyer of the hotel, Lana was exhausted.

"Geez, Eric, I've never seen so many beautiful houses in all my life. I think I'm more confused than ever. How do we ever narrow down the list?"

"Well, for starters, we don't have to make any quick decisions. We've got plenty of time. I just wanted to get an idea of what's available," Eric mentioned as they stepped into the elevator. Pushing the button to the eleventh floor, it was clear that they were both exhausted.

Unlocking the door, Lana ran over to crash on the couch. Throwing off her sneakers, she lounged back, taking a deep breath. "Man, I'm pooped."

"I'll call room service and order dinner. What sounds appetizing?"

"Anything at this point. I'm starved."

"How does steak and garlic mashed potatoes sound? I'll add a salad to the order. Would you like cheesecake for dessert?" Eric inquired, quickly removing his shoes.

"Sounds yummy."

After calling room service and asking if they could expedite dinner, Eric sat down to relax on the sofa next to Lana.

"So, Doll, which house was your favorite?"

"Well, that's a difficult question," Lana answered, snuggling against Eric's broad shoulders. "I liked the Tuscany-inspired house. Remember the one with the gated courtyard in the front and a fountain? I loved the open layout of that particular house. It had a huge living room, with oversized windows to the back of the house that you could slide open, bringing the outside into the living area. It had an awesome kitchen, and I loved the granite countertops with stainless appliances. It had a huge kitchen island that overlooked the family room and four spacious bedrooms with an office that could be used as a fifth bedroom. I loved everything about it, including the location. Which was your favorite?"

"I'm more traditional. I liked the two-story colonial. I liked how each room was separated when you walked inside. The staircase at the entry was gorgeous. I loved the dark mahogany stairs with the impressive white banister. I also liked that the living room was separate from the kitchen and dining room. It also had four bedrooms and a two-car garage, but the location wasn't ideal. It was farther away from the strip."

"Eric, it didn't have the open concept which I wanted. Trust me. When you're watching children, you need to be able to see what they're doing."

"Lana, we're not in a rush to buy right now. Maybe other homes will come on the market before we're ready to make a purchase. There's also the possibility of having a custom home built."

"I never thought about that! We could design it to fit our specifications. You better win that tournament," Lana insisted. "Mama needs a new house."

"Geez, Doll, is there something you're not telling me?" Eric questioned with a smile, giving Lana a tender kiss on the forehead.

"Oh, no, just a figure of speech, but it could happen. You know we're no longer using birth control. You do know that, right?"

"Sweetheart, of course. And trust me, I will be ecstatic when the time comes. I can't wait to be a dad," he winked, giving her another quick kiss before he got up to answer the door. "I think dinner has arrived. I'm famished."

Once again, the downstairs was infused with a delectable aroma of warm bread, grilled steak smothered in onions, and garlic potatoes.

"Wow. It smells heavenly," Lana remarked, loading her plate with steak and potatoes. "Let's take our food and eat in the living room. It's more comfortable sitting on the sofa."

Piling his plate to overflowing, Eric followed Lana over to the sofa.

"Babe, this is delicious," Eric winked, cutting into his rare steak sitting in red, undercooked juices

"Yuck, how can you eat your meat raw?" Lana detested. "That's disgusting."

"Sweetheart, it's the only way to eat steak. Here try it," he laughed, attempting to shove his fork loaded with the raw meat into her mouth.

"Eric. Don't you dare! I'll throw up, I swear."

"Come on. Be a good sport! How do you know that you might not actually love it?" Eric teased playfully.

"No way! You take your fork away from my mouth this instant. Do you hear me, Mr. Kolbeck?" Lana yelled.

"Oh, Mr. Kolbeck, is it?" he laughed. "Okay, but you don't know what you're missing."

"Trust me. I do," she reiterated.

After finishing dinner and avoiding Eric's impulsive demand to sample his steak, he had an idea.

"It's been a long day. Why don't we open a bottle of wine and relax in the spa?"

"Actually, that sounds like a great idea. My feet ache from all the walking we did earlier."

Scooping Lana up in his arms, he playfully carried her upstairs.

"Geez, Babe, I'm not helpless. I can walk."

"Oh, I know, but you said your feet were aching, so I thought I would offer my services," he winked.

"Eric, no wonder I fell in love with you. You're the best," Lana smiled, kissing him on the cheek as he carried her up the stairs.

Turning on the warm water, Eric ran downstairs to retrieve a bottle of wine and two glasses.

"Would you like to wear one of my flannel shirts like before?" Eric laughed, running down the stairs.

"No thanks, I'll pass. Remember, I have clothes," Lana answered.

Sitting in the warm, swirling water felt heavenly. The glow radiating from the enormous neon signs along the strip infused the balcony with a soft ambiance. Relaxing in the spa, Lana's thoughts were on the luxurious houses they had toured earlier and their outrageous asking prices.

"Eric, what happens if you don't win the tournament?" Lana asked, taking a sip of wine.

"Where did that come from? I thought you had faith in me."

"I do have faith in you. I guess I just worry."

"Sweetheart," Eric paused, pulling her close. "You do trust me, right? Then why are you so worried?"

Kissing her on the forehead, he could easily understand her concerns. He had worries too, but he never wanted to dump his concerns on her. For a moment, he wondered how his mother had survived all those years being married to a gambler. It was a risky lifestyle, probably not for the faint of heart. However, he knew deep within his spirit he had the inherent abilities and the determination to make his new career choice work. He just had to make Lana believe in him without spending a lifetime worrying.

"Because financially, speaking, you're gambling with our entire future."

"Lana, I love you. You have to trust that I would never do anything to jeopardize what we have together. But, Doll, I need to know without a doubt that you're on board with this lifestyle. Otherwise, I'm telling you right now that I will pull out of the tournament tomorrow rather than chance losing you. I can always fly charters for a living." Taking a sip of wine, he waited pensively to hear her response.

"Eric, I know that you would never risk our future, and I do trust you. I guess it was just that we looked at houses today, and with thoughts of starting a family, that's a huge financial obligation. Don't worry. I love you, and I will support you in your dreams."

"Wow, Doll, you had me nervous for a moment. I don't want you to worry," Eric winked, refilling Lana's glass.

After relaxing in the spa for almost an hour, Eric noticed Lana rubbing her eyes. Apparently, the effects of the warm water and the wine were beginning to make her drowsy.

"Maybe we should call it an evening. I think you're about to fall asleep."

"Yes, I feel drowsy," Lana smiled, reaching for a towel.

Later in bed, Lana snuggled close to Eric.

"Babe, all this talk about houses and babies has me excited. I can't wait for us to welcome our first child. I know I will do a better job at raising a family than my parents," Lana whispered.

"Sweetheart, of that, I have no doubts," Eric mentioned kissing her passionately. He knew her desire to start their family was as strong as his desire to win the tournament. They were now in Vegas, and he was determined to succeed at both.

Reaching over to turn out the light, he pulled her closer.

Chapter Eleven

The next six weeks found Lana busy resuming her job as a cocktail waitress. It quickly filled the late hours while Eric continued to practice his skills at poker. Harvey was leaving nothing to chance. He was determined to push Eric straight to the top. It was time for Eric to step into his father's shoes and the Kolbecks to take home a new championship title, earning the respect of his peers. Everything seemed to be going according to plan. Maybe even more than Eric realized, as Lana began experiencing the early bouts of morning sickness. Coming in from work that evening, she appeared exhausted.

"Sweetheart, you look tired," Eric commented.

"Yes. Today was grueling. We were short on help," Lana smiled, walking over to give Eric a quick kiss.

Even though Lana had not confirmed her suspicions, she, like most women, did not doubt that she was expecting their first child. Perhaps it was time to make Eric aware of the changes in her body. Walking over to her purse, she removed one of the two pregnancy test kits she had purchased after leaving work that evening. Then, pensively, she waited for his reaction.

"Babe, I have some news to share with you," Lana smiled. "I thought we should do this together," she beamed.

"Oh, my God, Sweetheart, are those what I think they are?" Eric questioned with a huge grin. Pulling her into his arms, he held her close, giving her a quick, passionate kiss. "Are you pregnant? How long have you known?"

"Well, I'm not sure, but we're about to find out. I've had bouts of nausea and overwhelming tiredness this past week. It's made me highly suspicious."

"Why didn't you say something?"

"I knew you're under a lot of stress, and I wanted to wait until I was sure it wasn't just a case of nerves from the move."

Taking the test kits, Lana walked into the bathroom. It was only minutes before Eric heard a scream.

"Are you alright?" Eric yelled. Evidently, it indicated the results.

Lana emerged from the bathroom with a huge smile. Running toward him with the results in her hand, Eric knew instantly.

"Eric, we're pregnant?" Lana announced. "Can you believe it?"

"Sweetheart, are you sure?" he questioned, already knowing her answer.

"Yes. Yes! See for yourself," Lana smiled, showing him the test strip.

"Babe, this is the best news ever!" Eric grinned, scooping her into his arms. Then, holding her tight, he twirled her around the room with excitement.

"We're going to be parents. Do you even know how much this means to me?" she whispered, smothering him with kisses.

He knew Lana's desire to start a family was paramount, and he was ecstatic. Wiping his moist eyes, he only wished his mother had lived long enough to welcome her first grandchild.

"Eric, are you crying?" Lana teased playfully, kissing away his tears.

"It's just the fact we lost Mom, and she will never have the chance to know her first grandbaby."

"Oh, I'm not so sure about that. I somehow believe Kathie is watching. Eric, if we have a girl, I think we should name her after your mom."

"Sweetheart, I totally agree. I think that's a wonderful idea. What if we have a little boy?" he laughed.

"Well, I guess we'll just have to cross that bridge when we come to it," Lana beamed. "However, someone does come to mind, your father, of course."

"Sweetheart, are you serious?"

"Yes. However, ask me again in nine months," Lana smiled.

"Do you even know how much I love you?" Eric grinned, pulling her once more into his arms.

"I hope so! I'm carrying your child."

Wiping her eyes, it quickly appeared she was now the one becoming emotional. Her dream of becoming a mother was a reality. She vowed to do a better job than her parents. Their child would never lack parents who adored them and always had their best interests at heart.

"Now look who's crying," Eric smiled, kissing away her tears as he led her over to the sofa. "I think we should take a moment and let the results sink in. Is there anyone you want to call? Perhaps your mother, Megan, or one of your sisters?"

"No. I don't want any contact with my family. I just want to enjoy this moment with you, just the two of us. So I'm in no hurry to make any announcements. I want to wait a few weeks," Lana smiled, snuggling against his broad shoulders.

"Sweetheart, whatever you want. I won't even breathe a word to Harvey."

"Awe, thanks, Babe, but you can tell Harvey. He's living so close to us now. It would be almost impossible to keep this a secret for much longer. So you might as well enjoy a Cuban cigar with him. Harvey feels like the father I never had. He's one of the reasons we're here in Vegas."

"Are you hungry?" Eric questioned, changing the subject.

"Are you kidding? I'm starved."

"Do you feel like eating out tonight, or would you rather order room service?"

"I feel exhausted. I would much prefer to order in tonight if that's alright with you?"

"Your wish is my command," Eric smiled, reaching for the phone.

After ordering Lana's favorite steak and lobster meal, along with an extra glass of milk, he removed her shoes, making sure she was comfortable.

"Did I hear you ask for a glass of milk?" she shuddered. "I hate milk."

Well, young lady, I think you better get used to it, at least for the next nine months," he smiled, kissing her affectionately on the forehead. "So," he smiled hesitantly. "What's the next step on our journey to becoming parents? You were one of ten children. I'm sure you easily know the routine," Eric anxiously inquired. "Shouldn't we schedule a doctor's appointment? What are those doctors called anyway? I think we should call tomorrow. Maybe you should quit working and get more rest."

Looking into Eric's eyes, Lana laughed. This tall, muscular Marine was entirely in unfamiliar territory, and she found it genuinely amusing. "They are called obstetricians, and I think you need to calm down."

Lana knew the reality of the moment was making him nervous, even though he was entirely excited at the prospects of becoming a new father. Lana could hear the sound of worry and fear of the unknown in his voice. Knowing that Eric was a few years older and had no prior experience with young children or babies, she laughed. This regimented ex-Marine was about to become a father. She readily sympathized with his worries.

Taking his hand, she gently laid it across her belly.

Babe, this little girl or dude as you called him is going to be okay. We're all going to be fine. So relax. We still have about eight months to go and a lifetime after that," she laughed. "You're right. I was raised in a house filled with children and babies. You're silly. It's as natural as rain." Cuddling in his arms, she found his worries hilarious.

"What if we're having twins?" he gasped.

"Sweetheart, there are no twins in my family, and I'm pretty sure there are none in your family as well," Lana smiled. "Relax, I'm pretty sure that I'll be doing most of the work," she laughed. "I just need you to be my confident captain."

Hearing a soft knock at the door indicated the arrival of room service. Not a moment too soon, Lana thought as Eric needed a distraction from his worries.

The intoxicating aroma of steak and seafood infused the air, and she was starved. Eric quickly piled her plate to overflowing and brought it over to the sofa along with the tall glass of milk.

"Isn't that a bit much?" she laughed, seeing the enormous portions of food.

"Well, you are eating for two."

"Yes. But this little guy is probably no bigger than two of those peas you just put on my plate. So he doesn't require that much food, at least not at this point."

"Sweetheart, you just referred to the baby as a little guy," Eric grinned. "Do you think it's a boy?"

"Eric, don't read too much into anything I say. I don't have any feelings, whether it's a boy or a sweet baby girl. I just want a healthy baby," she suggested, quickly shoveling morsels of steak into her mouth.

"I totally agree. It doesn't matter. Now drink your milk," Eric suggested.

"Hey, I somehow managed to eat almost everything on my plate. However, if it will make you happy and ease your worried mind, I'll try."

Unbelievably, she somehow managed to drink the entire glass.

"That's my girl," he grinned, putting away the empty glass.

Pushing the empty food cart out into the hallway, Eric unexpectedly noticed Harvey stepping out of the elevator.

"Hey, Son, I stopped by to see if I could take you both to dinner this evening, but it appears you've beaten me to the punch."

"Thanks for the invitation, but Lana came in exhausted from work this evening, and we decided to order room service. Why don't you come in for a quick drink?"

"Thanks, Son, but I have a huge rack of barbequed ribs downstairs waiting for me. How about a rain check?" Harvey grinned, hurrying to catch the elevator door before it closed.

"Sure. Not a problem."

Tomorrow Eric and Lana would give Harvey their exciting news.

Opening the door, it appeared the new expectant mommy was falling asleep.

Lovingly, he picked Lana up. Carrying her up the flight of stairs, he could never have loved her more. Gently laying her on the bed, Lana opened her eyes.

"Awe, thanks, Babe, guess I was tired," Lana yawned.

Eric pulled back the blue damask duvet while Lana changed into her nightgown. Then, kissing her as she snuggled under the warm covers, he decided to take a quick shower and shave before going to bed.

Returning from the bathroom, the love of his life was out like a light bulb and snoring like a purring kitten. He laughed, snuggling next to her warm body. Watching as she slept, he smiled, knowing that Lana's dream of becoming a mother was finally coming true. Lovingly, he pulled her long curls away from her face kissing her goodnight. Now, only one part of their dream was still missing, and he was more determined than ever to ensure it happened. Winning the poker tournament took on a new significance. It was paramount.

Waking the following day, he rolled over, surprised to discover Lana was already up. He gasped, rushing into the bathroom, finding Lana once again nauseous.

"My God, Babe, why didn't you wake me?" he demanded.

"Eric, I feel horrible."

"What can I do?"

"Maybe you could warm one of the small hand towels. I don't think I can move right now."

Hurriedly turning on the tap in the sink, he ran the hot water. Then, grabbing a washcloth, he ran it under the warm water. This was all new to him. He had no idea what to do. Searching for a hair tie in the bathroom cabinet, he quickly pulled back Lana's hair. Gently wiping her flushed face with the warm towel, Lana looked up.

"Thanks, Babe, you're a lifesaver," she smiled.

"Let me get you a cup of water."

"Eric, if there is any Ginger Ale downstairs in the fridge, that would be awesome. Maybe a few saltine crackers," she added.

"Sweetheart, I'm not sure we have any crackers, but I'll check. Hang on. I'll be right back."

Running downstairs, he found a couple of cans of 7-Up. However, seeing no crackers, he decided to make toast. Finding the toaster, he popped two slices of bread inside and reached into the cabinet for a small plate. Finally, grabbing the warm toast and cold soda, he headed upstairs. Entering the bedroom, he found Lana sitting up in bed.

"Are you feeling better?"

"Somewhat, at least my nausea seems to have passed."

"Take a few slow sips. There wasn't any Ginger Ale, but I found 7-Up. And, I brought you some toast. We're all out of crackers. I'll make sure we're stocked up today."

"Eric, what would I do without you?" Lana smiled, slowly sipping the carbonated beverage.

Gently taking a seat on the bed, he softly kissed her forehead.

"Lana, I think you should call in sick today. There's no way you can go to work like this."

"I think you're right. I'll give work a call."

"Sweetheart, I planned to meet up with Harvey this morning. It's important to get familiar with the poker players who've also advanced to the next round. We had planned to go to the Bellagio to play poker. Do you think you could possibly do without me this morning? I'll check on you around noon."

"Eric, I'm pregnant, not dying," Lana smiled. "I'll be fine. If it makes you feel any better, I'll just lounge around today and take it easy. We're here for you to win the tournament, remember."

"Thanks. I've got to get dressed. Would you like me to order room service before I leave? I think you should try and eat something. How do soft scrambled eggs and toast sound?"

"Babe, I think I'm more than capable of ordering room service. Now get out of here. You're beginning to drive me crazy."

"Okay. I love you," Eric smiled, kissing her on the forehead before running to take a quick shower. "Oh, would it be alright to tell Harvey our good news?" he yelled from the bathroom.

"Sure, why not? Harvey is like family, but have him keep it under wraps for now. I want to wait a while before giving your sister and Jake the news."

"Okay. No problem."

Stepping into the elevator, Eric was running a little late. However, he knew Harvey would definitely understand, especially when given the reason. Eric smiled as thoughts of becoming a dad once again consumed him. Entering the casino, he hurriedly made his way through the maze of slots. Finally, reaching the outside entrance, Eric walked down to the Bellagio. He couldn't wait to give Harvey the unbelievable news.

Arriving at the Bellagio, Eric knew precisely where he could find Harvey, the lounge at the Baccarat Bar. It was known for its specialty drinks and its selection of fine cigars. And no one enjoyed a fine cigar more than Harvey. Walking in, Eric saw Harvey sitting at one of the tables. As was typical, he had a drink in one hand and a cigar in his other hand.

"Hey, Son, take a seat. I thought you had forgotten about me," he chuckled, looking down at his watch.

"No, never. Lana wasn't feeling her best this morning."

"Oh, hopefully, it's nothing serious," Harvey inquired, taking a long slow draw on his cigar.

"Well, since you've asked, she's fine. Just a little morning sickness," Eric grinned.

"My God, Son, did you say what I think you said?" Harvey questioned with a smile.

"Yes. Lana is pregnant," Eric instantly blurted out, unable to contain his excitement.

"Congratulations. Wow, a baby," he paused, waiting for the news to sink in. Then, finally, he stood up, giving Eric a huge hug. "This is turning out to be a great summer. I think this calls for a drink and a fine cigar," Harvey grinned, motioning for the waiter. "We'd like two shots of bourbon and a couple of your finest cigars. This young man is going to be a father," he eagerly announced, slapping Eric on the back.

"Congratulations, sir. I'll be right back with your drinks and cigars."

"Wow, Son, that's fantastic news! So when is this little bundle of joy expected?"

"Oh, we just found out last night. I must say we are both thrilled. Lana would love to have a houseful of kids. She comes from a large family. Keep it under wraps for now; I promised Lana we would tell Karen and Jake later after she's further along."

"You've got my word. I'm overjoyed. It's a damn shame that Kathie or Roy didn't live long enough to see this little one come into the world. But don't you worry. Grandpa Harvey will see to it that this little guy lacks for nothing."

"Harvey, you just referred to the baby as a little guy. You know there's a fifty percent chance it could be a girl," Eric laughed.

"Oh, trust me, Grandpa Harvey loves little girls too."

"Sir, your drinks and Cuban cigars," the waiter announced.

Quickly cutting the end of the cigars, Harvey extinguished his present cigar, exchanging it for a new smoke. He proudly smiled, passing one over to Eric, watching Eric light up. Then, taking his drink in hand, Harvey offered up a toast.

"Son, congratulations! You've made this old man mighty happy this morning. Now let's win this tournament and buy this baby a new pair of shoes," Harvey beamed.

"Thanks, Harvey," Eric smiled, lifting his glass. There's no doubt you'll take on the role of a loving grandfather. This little one couldn't be luckier to have you in their life."

"Thanks, Son, now what can I get you for lunch? They make a great Reuben sandwich."

"Sounds good to me."

After finishing lunch, Eric called to check on Lana.

"Hey, Babe, how are you feeling?"

"I'm fine. I was sleeping," Lana answered after a few rings.

"Sorry, I didn't mean to wake you. I just had to make sure that you were okay. I just finished lunch with Harvey."

"Eric, don't worry. The nausea has finally passed. I'm just a little tired. I suppose you told Harvey."

"Of course. He's ecstatic at the possibilities of playing the role of grandfather. Lana, please order some food. I think you need to eat something. We're getting ready to play a few games of poker, so it might be a few hours before I can check on you again."

"Babe, go play poker and let me sleep. I'm fine. I love you."

"Okay, see you later this evening. Love you."

Before Eric sat down at the poker table, he ordered six eloquent vases of large fragrant red roses to be delivered to Lana.

That evening when Eric arrived at the hotel, he opened the door to find the suite filled with roses.

"Hey, Babe, I'm home," Eric yelled, running up the elegant, glass-enclosed staircase.

Walking into the bedroom, he found Lana peacefully dozing next to a platter of half-eaten scrambled eggs and toast. Leaning over her petite body, he gently pushed her long curls away from her face and began smothering her with kisses.

"Eric, you're back," Lana smiled, slowly opening her eyes.

"I see the flowers came."

"Sweetheart, thank you, but why so many? The downstairs is literally covered in roses."

"Lana, I simply ordered one vase for each child that we're going to have. I do remember you wanting six babies. Isn't that right?" he smiled.

"Oh, Eric, no wonder I fell in love with you. So you remembered," Lana laughed, pulling him down next to her. "You silly goof! I think we better work on getting our first one here safe and sound," she whispered, returning his kisses with passion.

Pulling her into his arms, he silently prayed for a healthy baby. It didn't matter whether it was a boy or girl. The only thing that mattered to him was the health of Lana and their newborn.

"I'm starved," Eric mentioned, quickly devouring the remaining eggs and toast. "Do you feel like eating out this evening, or would you rather order room service?"

"If it's okay with you, why don't we eat in tonight? I haven't gotten dressed today. I've spent the entire day in my pajamas."

"Sounds good, perhaps I'll join you," Eric answered, getting out of bed to change into a pair of sweatpants and a T-shirt. "How does Italian food sound?" Eric inquired loudly from the closet.

"Actually, I think it sounds delicious. I feel fine. It only bothers me in the mornings when I wake up," Lana answered, sitting up in bed.

Later that evening, after enjoying a wonderful meal of Lasagna, along with a tossed salad and warm bread, they ended their dinner with slices of chocolate cake. Retiring upstairs, it was the end of a perfect day. Holding Lana in his arms, Eric thought back to the wish he'd made that evening at the fountains of the Bellagio. His world now seemed perfect.

"Eric, do you even know how much I love you?" Lana whispered as she began to fall asleep. "You have no idea how much having this baby means to me. You've made me the happiest girl on earth," she smiled, snuggling next to him.

"Well, Sweetheart, I don't think I can take all the credit. I love you more," Eric lovingly whispered. Closing his eyes, he knew how much this baby meant to Lana. He was more than ever determined to win the poker tournament and take her home to the ranch, where they would await the birth of their first child. But, unknowingly, fate was about to step in and raise its ugly head.

Chapter Twelve

The next three months found both Lana and Eric extremely busy. Finally, Lana felt well enough to return to work. Between her job, Eric's numerous hours spent playing poker with Harvey, and a few doctor's appointments, it seemed they hardly saw each other. The tournament now was only a few weeks away.

After Lana's next doctor's visit, she decided it was finally time to announce the baby's arrival to family and friends. Megan would be a great place to start. Inviting her for dinner the following evening seemed the perfect way to share their great news. Making the call, Megan eagerly agreed to stop by their hotel after her shift ended at the Luxor. Lana decided it would be more fun and relaxing to order food the following evening. She arranged for an array of hot and cold meats, along with potato salad and fresh vegetables, to be brought to their suite. Not forgetting dessert, Lana decided it would be fun to order a few chocolate cupcakes topped with either pink or blue booties. It would be her unique way of sharing the news with Megan. Finally, at last, everything was ready.

Getting in from work early the next afternoon, Lana hurriedly ran around the large living area downstairs, lighting candles and fluffing pillows.

"Geez, Babe, do you think you have enough food?" Eric teased, viewing the entrees as he walked in after hours of playing poker.

"Well, I wanted a choice of cold cuts. But, don't worry, I'm sure you'll have no problem consuming what's left. Check out the cupcakes," Lana laughed.

"Wow. Are you trying to give Megan a hint? They all have pink or blue booties," Eric teased, quickly shoving one of the delicious chocolate cupcakes into his mouth.

"Stay out of those, and don't say a word. It's my way of telling her about the baby. I'm serving those after dinner. We'll see how long it takes her to make the connection."

Hearing a knock at the door, Lana temporarily hid the cupcakes and ran over to answer the door.

"Hey Megan, come in. How was your day?"

"It was busy as usual. First, I went back to the apartment after work to change clothes, and then I decided to stop by the florist. I know you love flowers," Megan smiled, handing her a beautiful bouquet of pink roses. "Geez, it looks like a florist shop in here. What's going on?"

"Oh, nothing. Eric just won his first round and advanced. He was simply being silly. Thanks, Megan, they're exquisite. Come in and have a seat while I put these in water." Then, taking the gorgeous arrangement of pink roses, Lana searched for a vase.

"Something smells delicious," Megan commented as she took a seat on the leather sectional. "Hey Eric, are you ready to take on the best poker players in Vegas?" Megan asked curiously.

"As ready as I'll ever be," Eric answered without hesitation.

"Everything is ready to eat. Why don't we serve ourselves?" Lana suggested, quickly returning with the vase. "Bring your plates over to the table, and I'll get the drinks. How does iced tea sound?"

"Great. Everything looks yummy," Megan smiled, placing a slice of roast beef on her plate. "Wow. Potato salad. It's my favorite."

"I know," Lana smiled. "Of course, I didn't make it, but it looks good."

"Oh, I'm sure it's awesome."

The next hour seemed to fly by as everyone sat around the table, enjoying the variety of cold cuts and salads the delectable buffet offered.

"Why don't we go into the living room?" Lana suggested after everyone finished eating. "I'll make coffee and bring out dessert."

The bright neon lights radiating from the hotels and the lit candles bathed the living room with a soft, colorful ambiance.

"Sweetheart, you and Megan, take a break. I'll make coffee. I'm sure you girls have a lot of catching up to do."

"Thanks, Babe, but I think I'll pass on the coffee. Perhaps you could make a cup for Megan."

"Oh, just a little cream would be wonderful," Megan smiled.

"So, I guess you stay busy working at Ceasars. How long will you and Eric be in Vegas?"

"Oh, we're here until the tournament is over. So, yes, I do tend to stay busy. But, you know how it is working in a casino with all the tourists," Lana added.

"How did you like living in Alaska?"

"Different, it was different. The people are amicable. We left some great friends in McGrath, Norman, and Gunner. If you remember, Gunner was the guy who finally got Blake to leave town. I'm still waiting to hear the details of that story. However, it doesn't matter. I will always owe him for stepping in to take care of Blake. McGrath was a small, isolated place, and there wasn't a lot to do."

"Coffee," Eric smiled, handing a cup to Megan.

"Babe, sit down. I'll get dessert," Lana smiled.

Quickly returning with a small, two-tiered stand containing six chocolate cupcakes topped with pink and blue booties," Lana couldn't contain her laughter. "Would you like a cupcake?"

"Oh my God," Megan gasped, knowing Lana's quirky sense of humor. "Do those mean what I think they mean? Are you pregnant?" Megan screamed. She could hardly contain her excitement, giving Lana and Eric a huge hug.

"Yes. Can you even believe it?" Lana announced excitedly.

"So, how long have you known?"

"Not long, about three months."

"Congratulations, I'm happy for you both. Does this mean I can be referred to as Aunt Megan?"

"Yes," Lana laughed.

"Oh, we have to go shopping. Do you know if it's a boy or girl?"

"No, it's too early, but yes, we will go shopping."

"Does your mom know?"

"Not yet. You're only the second person we've told."

"Geez, Eric, you're going to be a dad. Are you excited?"

"Yes, we're thrilled. Now I really have to win that tournament."

"Oh, I somehow think you've got that in the bag. Lana has told me about your dad. I don't think those seated at your table stand a chance," Megan smiled.

After devouring the tasty cupcakes and talking about babies, Megan thanked them for dinner and once again congratulated the new parents to be.

"I'm afraid I have to call it a night. I have to be at work early in the morning. However, I do get off a few hours early tomorrow. Why don't we go shopping for the baby? Have you looked at cribs or things for the nursery?" Megan smiled curiously.

"No. Not yet. But tomorrow sounds wonderful. It would be a lot of fun," Lana eagerly answered.

"Well, why don't I stop by tomorrow after work around 2:00 p.m. We can go to the mall and check out Babies 'R' Us."

"Sounds like a date. I'll leave work early tomorrow. I can't wait to start shopping for the baby. I'm sure there are many new things for the little ones. I'll see you at two."

"Great. Thanks for dinner and for letting me know about the baby. That was such a cute idea using the cupcakes to break the news. Leave it up to you to think of something so creative! Love you. See you tomorrow," Megan smiled, giving Lana and Eric a final hug goodbye.

Closing the door, Eric pulled Lana close. "Sweetheart, why don't we call Karen and Jake and let them in on our little secret?"

"Okay. Why don't you make the call, and I'll speak with them," Lana agreed, removing her shoes. "I feel so exhausted," she sighed, making her way to the living room. Curling up on the sofa, it was apparent she was beginning to feel drowsy.

"Babe, don't fall asleep until I get Karen and Jake on the phone."

"Okay, I'll try."

After giving Jake and Karen the exciting news about the baby, Eric scooped Lana in his arms and carried her up the stairs. He pulled back the floral duvet while Lana quickly changed into her nightgown.

"Geez, I'm always so tired," Lana smiled, slipping under the warm covers.

Slipping into bed next to the love of his life, Eric pulled her close, whispering into her ear.

"Sweetheart, about tomorrow, did I mention our budget? Try not to go too crazy. I know you're excited to shop for the baby, but I haven't won the tournament yet."

Looking over at Lana, his words had fallen on deaf ears. She was already out like a light. Kissing her goodnight, it didn't matter. He knew how much this baby meant to her, and he could easily understand her wanting only the best for their child.

The following afternoon Lana left work early. Racing upstairs to change clothes, she was anxious to get to the mall. Lana had barely finished dressing when there was a knock at the door. Running downstairs, she answered the door.

"Hey Megan, come in. I'm almost ready. Let me grab my purse."

"I forgot to mention last night that Eric was welcome to tag along," Megan mentioned.

"Oh, he doesn't have much spare time. He's with Harvey, an old friend of his dad's. Harvey happens to be a retired poker player, and he is making sure that Eric is at the top of his game."

"That's great. I'm parked in the hotel garage," Megan stated as they entered the elevator.

Arriving at the mall a short time later, the girls were anxious to check every store for available baby items.

Entering Macy's, they headed immediately to the infant department.

"Oh my gosh, check out this newborn onesie! It's covered in Giraffes," Lana laughed. "Okay. I've got to get this one."

"Look at these gorgeous baby blankets," Megan smiled. "Don't you just love the white crochet blanket? It's gorgeous."

"Yes. But I'm not sure how practical white would be with a newborn," Lana explained. "Do they have other colors?"

"Yes, why don't you get the blue one?"

"Okay."

Over the next hour, Lana and Megan purchased seven brightly printed onesies, a blanket, booties, bibs, and pacifiers. The girls meticulously scouted each area of the baby section as if they were on the hunt for lost treasure. Then, excited over their purchases, they were on to the next store.

Giggling like young school girls, they made their way through the mall to Babies 'R' Us.

"Wow. Just look at this place," Lana laughed.

"Yeah. It's amazing. Where do you want to start?" Megan questioned.

"Well, how about car seats? I'm going to need a car seat to bring the baby home from the hospital."

"Okay. But how are we going to get it to the car? Those boxes are huge," Megan laughed.

"Alright, perhaps we should go over to the baby clothes," Lana suggested.

Searching through racks and shelves of infant clothing, it wasn't long before they filled their shopping carts. Lana had no self-control. She purchased nightgowns, undershirts, bibs, and pastel crib sheets in the cutest animal prints. After checking out, they decided to grab a bite to eat.

Walking into Red Robin, they were quickly ushered over to their seats. Ordering burgers and fries gave them a chance to take a short break.

"Geez. Doesn't this look yummy?" Lana mentioned as the waiter set the tasty Whiskey BBQ Burger and fries on the table along with Megan's Guacamole Bacon Burger and chips.

"Lana, I think we went a bit crazy," Megan laughed, taking a glance at their numerous shopping bags.

"No. The baby can definitely use these things. I still have to make a list of all the necessary items. I still need a diaper bag and changing pads," Lana added, taking a sip of tea. "Could we possibly make one more stop before we call it an evening? I would like to purchase a new nightgown, perhaps some perfume, and cosmetics."

"Really?" Megan roared. "Don't you think you're a little beyond needing those at this point?"

"You're silly. I want these for myself, not necessarily for Eric's pleasure. It's hard to explain, but when you're not feeling your best, it never hurts to be pampered."

"Well, if you say so," Megan laughed.

After devouring their burgers and fries, they were at last ready to finish their evening of shopping. Deciding to make one last stop at Macy's before leaving the mall, Lana found an elegant, black lace nightgown. Spotting her favorite fragrance along with a tube of red lipstick, Lana finally made her last purchase.

"Wow. I understand the purchases for the baby. But Lana, honestly, a sexy nightgown and perfume, not to mention the red lipstick, seems a bit odd," Megan teased as they walked out to the parking lot. "I'm sorry, I don't get it."

"Everyone is different, and for me, when I'm not feeling well, I love having something new to wear, perfume, along with makeup to make me feel pampered. I can't explain it. Trust me. If Eric likes it, that's just a bonus," Lana smiled. "Geez, suddenly, I'm feeling drained," Lana yawned, throwing all the bags into the back seat of the car.

"Lana, I think I better get you home before you fall asleep. I've had a wonderful afternoon."

"Yes. Me too, we'll go shopping again before I leave Vegas."

"I'm going to hold you to that. I'm certainly going to miss you."

"Well, you'll have to drive up to the ranch in Carson City."

"I may just take you up on that."

Exiting the parking garage at the mall, it was only a short drive back to the hotel. Helping Lana get the bags up to the room, Megan was soon on her way.

"Get some rest. I'll call you later," Megan smiled, giving Lana a quick hug.

Throwing all the shopping bags on the floor, Lana removed her shoes and curled up on the sofa. It was only moments before sleep invaded her petite body.

An hour later, Eric came home. He smiled, noting all the shopping bags on the floor and Lana dead asleep on the sofa. Then, quietly walking over, he softly began kissing her awake.

"Hey, Gorgeous, did you buy out the stores?" Eric lovingly whispered, pulling her hair away from her face.

"Awe, Babe, is that you?" Lana softly questioned without opening her eyes. Then, inhaling the scent of his cologne, she smiled.

"Well, if it isn't, you might be in a whole heap of trouble."

"You won't believe all the cute things Megan and I found today," Lana smiled quickly, sitting up as she came out of her stupor. "Let me show you."

"Geez, babies apparently need a lot of stuff," he joked.

"Oh, you have no idea," Lana agreed, pulling out the onesies. "Isn't this giraffe onesie just the cutest thing you've ever seen?"

He loved her attention to detail as she carefully removed each item from the shopping bags. It was easy to see that Lana would be a wonderful, loving mother. Accidentally pulling out the sexy lace negligée, Lana laughed.

"Wow. Sweetheart, I think that's my favorite piece. However, I'm not sure the baby will appreciate it as much as I will," Eric winked wickedly.

"Well, mommies need things too," she blushed.

"I totally agree," Eric grinned, scooping her into his arms. "I think the baby clothes can wait until tomorrow. However, grab that sexy, lace gown," he grinned seductively.

Picking her up, he carried her up the stairs.

Sitting Lana on the bed, he lovingly removed her clothes first, then his before putting her under the warm covers.

"Wait, Babe, what about the sexy nightgown?" Lana smiled.

"Oh, I think we've moved way past that for tonight," Eric grinned with a wink.

Needless to say, loving Lana was easy. She was more than he ever dreamed was possible, and now she was carrying his child.

The following day, Lana panicked as she woke Eric.

"Eric, something is wrong. You've got to wake up. Wake up," she yelled, shaking him frantically.

"Babe, what's wrong?" Opening his eyes, the fear and panic reflected on her face sent chills down his spine.

"Lana, what's wrong?"

"Eric, I've got horrible cramps. Something feels wrong. What if I'm having a miscarriage. I can't lose this baby. Do you hear me?" Lana cried hysterically. "I don't want to live if I lose this baby. I can't do this. Eric, call for an ambulance," she screamed insistently.

"Lana, calm down. You're acting hysterical. I'm sure it's nothing. Just try to relax. I'm sure the cramps will stop, but if not, I will call a cab and get you to the emergency room. So, let's try not to worry."

"After three hours, Lana realized something was drastically wrong as the pains increased in intensity. Eric, I don't think I can walk, and I'm in a lot of pain. Please, I think we should go to the emergency room," Lana demanded.

At this point, Eric honestly didn't know if it was safer to take a taxi to the emergency room or call for an ambulance. However, Harvey wasn't answering the phone in his room, so he decided to call for a cab. It seemed the most logical idea.

"Oh, my God, Babe, hold on. Try not to move. You're going to be okay. I'll carry you."

The words just flew out of his mouth. However, he knew things did not look good for the baby at this point. What was happening? Lana had been perfectly fine the night before. How could things have changed this fast?

"Babe, I feel like I'm going to pass out," Lana cried.

"Lana, stay with me. Don't you dare pass out? Babe, you've got to hold on," he demanded with tears in his eyes, helping Lana inside the cab.

"Is she alright," the cab driver inquired.

"We're not sure. Please just drive us to the nearest emergency room."

"Certainly. I'll get you there as fast as I can."

"Sir, what is your emergency?" the nurse asked as Eric ran through the doors of the hospital with Lana in his arms.

"It's my girlfriend. She's three months pregnant, and she's been experiencing excruciating cramps for the past three hours."

The emergency room nurse hurriedly put Lana into the nearest cubicle, where she was instantly surrounded by medical personnel.

"Her blood pressure is low but not life-threatening. How far along did you say she is," the nurse questioned. "Her vital signs are good," she added.

"Three months," Eric answered.

"How bad is your pain? On a scale of one being the least to ten being the highest, what number would you say represents your pain level?"

"A ten, it's a ten," Lana cried. "Am I losing the baby?" Lana questioned hysterically.

"I'm sorry. I can't make that determination. Dr. Warren should be in soon."

"Sweetheart, just hold on. You're going to be fine, and so is the baby. So please don't worry," Eric pleaded, grasping Lana's hand.

"Am I going to lose the baby?" Lana reiterated, visibly shaken.

"As I said, I'm afraid I can't answer that. Please don't worry. These little ones can be very resilient. I will get a stethoscope and listen to the baby's heartbeat as soon as I finish the IV. Why are you shaking? Are you cold?"

"Just nervous," Lana answered with tears streaming down her face.

"We've called Dr. Warren, so he's aware that you're here in the emergency room. Is this your first baby?"

"Yes." Hinting a faint smile, Lana looked up at Eric.

"Okay, let me listen for this little guy's heartbeat."

Searching Eric's face, it clearly reflected his fears and worries. She knew he wanted this baby as much as she did. How could this possibly have happened so unexpectedly? Anxiously, Lana waited for the nurse to hear their baby's heartbeat.

Putting the stethoscope on Lana's abdomen, the nurse slowly moved it over her belly. Finally, stopping to listen, the nurse smiled.

"Great, our little guy is still there. Everything sounds good. However, Dr. Warren will be in soon, and he can talk with you both.

"Oh, my God, thank you," Eric grinned. "Babe, did you hear that our little guy is still with us?" He leaned over, giving Lana a quick kiss.

Watching as a tall, thin guy with blonde hair pulled back the curtains, Eric wondered if he was possibly the doctor.

"Good morning, I'm Dr. Warren. I believe I just saw you a few weeks ago in my office. What's going on?"

"When I woke up this morning, I was having painful cramping. The pain feels like period cramps," Lana explained. "I'm freaking out that I'm having a miscarriage."

Noting the fear on his young patient's face, Dr. Warren offered her some reassurance. "The nurse picked up the baby's heartbeat, and your vital signs are good. Miscarriages usually happen before the second trimester. However, your blood pressure was low when you were brought in. The IV should help to bring that up. I'm going to have one of the technicians come in and do a sonogram. We're going to give you something to stop the cramping, so I'll be admitting you overnight. I'll be back after we get the sonogram."

Within minutes a young woman rolled in the sonogram equipment. It only took a few minutes before the baby appeared on the monitor.

"The baby looks great, no problems that I can detect. The doctor will be back to talk to you shortly.

Eric and Lana were captivated at the sight of their seemingly healthy baby.

"Great news, everything looks fine," Dr. Warren smiled, revealing the sonogram results. However, we will move you upstairs to a room and hook up the fetal monitors. Hopefully, once the cramping is stopped, you'll feel better. This should resolve itself with bed rest and medications, and you can go home. As I said before, most miscarriages happen before the first three months. You're further along, and right now, everything looks good. I want to keep it that way. So, it's bed rest and medications for now. Do you have any questions?" Dr. Warren asked sympathetically.

"None that I can think of at the moment," Lana smiled.

"Great. I'll see you this evening when I make rounds," Dr. Warren commented, leaving the cubicle.

"Thanks, Dr. Warren," Eric grinned.

Once the doctor was out of sight. Lana again began to panic.

"Eric, I can't lose this baby. I can't. I wouldn't be able to handle it. I want this baby more than anything. Do you understand?"

"Sweetheart, you heard what the doctor said. Everything seems to be fine, but I completely understand your worries. However, worrying will not help. Don't you think I've been concerned too? We need to give this little guy every possible chance, so no more worries. Agreed?"

"Alright. I'll try. But I'm not making any promises," Lana reluctantly agreed.

Soon the nurse returned to move Lana upstairs.

"We're going to move you upstairs to room 2012 on the second floor."

After Lana was settled into a private room upstairs, the medication was administered through her IV, and she was hooked up to the monitors. Eric collapsed into a worn-out chair sitting next to Lana's bed.

"Babe, you look exhausted. Why don't you go down to the cafeteria and get yourself a cup of coffee?" Lana suggested.

"I could use a hot cup of coffee. But, I need you to relax and try to get some sleep while I'm gone."

"Eric, I don't think I'll be popping out of bed anytime soon. I'm hooked up to all these monitors."

"Okay. I'll be right back. Do you want any magazines or something to munch on?"

"No. I'm fine. Maybe when you get back, we can call Megan."

"Sounds good. I'll be right back."

Looking around the room, it gave the impression of a nursery. The walls were painted in pastel pink, and a border of teddy bears trimmed the upper walls near the ceiling. A rocking chair sat next to the bed.

Hopefully, she wouldn't have to stay long. The room's décor appeared dated and unappealing.

Looking up at the clock on the wall, Eric was gone longer than she had expected. Then, finally, he walked in with a cup of coffee, a large vase of red roses, and a teddy bear.

"Awe, Babe, that's so sweet of you. The roses are gorgeous. But a teddy bear?" she laughed. "Look up at the border. It's teddy bears too."

"Sorry. I just wanted you to feel better."

"As long as you're here, I'll be okay."

Taking a seat next to Lana's hospital bed, Eric settled in with his cup of coffee.

"Oh, I called Megan and Harvey while I was downstairs. They're both worried sick about you and the baby. I'm sure Harvey will be stopping by this afternoon, and Megan said she'll be over tonight after her shift ends at the Luxor. Lana, depending on what the doctor says, I was hoping you could give some thought about letting Harvey fly you back to the ranch. I have to stay here for another two weeks. I'm going to win this tournament, I can promise you that, but I can't take care of you and play poker at the same time. I want only the best for you and the baby. What do you think about the idea?"

"Well, let's just wait and see what the doctor says. I'm not leaving you in Vegas.

"Just think about it, okay," Eric suggested.

Later that afternoon, Harvey came to the hospital. He was carrying an enormous bouquet of mixed flowers.

"How's my girl?" Harvey questioned as he walked into the room. "Hope you like the flowers," he smiled, gently leaning over the bed to give her a quick kiss.

"Oh, Harvey, those are exquisite. I'm okay."

"I would have come sooner when Eric called, but I was held up at a meeting at the Bellagio. Is everything alright?" he questioned.

"Yes. Dr. Warren put me on bed rest and gave me something for the pain."

"Oh, thank God," Harvey exclaimed. "Is there anything I can do for either of you?"

"No. But thanks for asking," Lana smiled. "It means so much that you came."

"Lana, when I heard that you were in the hospital, believe me, wild horses couldn't have kept me away. But, hey, Son, how are you holding up? You look beat up. Are you alright?"

"Yes. I've just been freaked out about Lana and the baby. They did a sonogram, and the baby is fine."

"Oh, thank God. Vegas has some great hospitals."

"Harvey, take this seat. I'll take the rocking chair."

"I can't stay long," Harvey mentioned sitting down in the chair. "I promised some old buddies of mine to play poker later tonight. In fact, these guys were also friends of your dad."

"Sounds like a fun evening," Eric grinned.

"Son, have you had dinner? I'll be more than happy to run out and pick up some food at one of the restaurants."

"Awe, thanks, Harvey, that's really nice of you to offer, but I'll just go down to the cafeteria later."

"Looks like our sweet girl has fallen asleep. I'm sure she's been stressed out about the baby."

"Yes. Lana hasn't taken any of this very well. She's been upset and worried. Megan took her shopping yesterday. It was the first time she bought anything for the baby. She was ecstatic, showing me all the items she purchased, and then this morning, she woke up really sick. My heart is breaking for her. Harvey, please keep her and the baby in your prayers. I'm afraid if we lose the baby, she's going to take it really hard. This baby means everything to her and me as well."

"Son, please try not to worry. Lana and the baby are going to be just fine. You just wait and see. This precious baby isn't going anywhere. Grandpa Harvey wouldn't allow it. "

"Awe, thanks, Harvey. I don't know what we would do without you."

"Well, you guys mean the world to me. The three of you are the family this old man never had. With Roy and Kathie having passed, I promised Roy many years ago that I would always have his back. So, I'm afraid you're stuck with me."

"Trust me, Harvey, we feel the same. This baby is lucky to have you as their grandpa."

"I hate to run, but it's getting late," Harvey stated, looking down at his watch. I promised to meet the guys around six. Please let Lana know that Grandpa will stop by tomorrow. Are you going to stay with her tonight?"

"Yes. Knowing Lana, she wouldn't allow me to leave," Eric smiled.

"Try to get some sleep. Son, if you need me at any time, just give me a call."

"Thanks, Harvey. Have a good evening."

"See ya'll tomorrow."

It appeared the turmoil from the morning had taken its toll on Lana. She slept the entire afternoon. Megan stopped by not long after Harvey left. Regrettably, Lana was still sleeping, so Megan decided not to stay. Instead, she just dropped off some magazines and a small floral bouquet.

Later that evening, Dr. Warren walked into Lana's room.

"Good evening, I'm Dr. Warren. I believe we met earlier this morning in the emergency room," he smiled.

"Yes," Eric acknowledged.

"It appears the medication has somewhat slowed the contractions. However, I'm afraid they're still significant. I'm increasing the meds, and we'll keep a close watch on Miss Harris through the night. She is fifteen weeks pregnant, and unfortunately, if her body continues to abort the fetus, minor surgery will be required. I wish I had better news. I'm glad to hear that she slept most of the day. Oh, I'm going to be in the hospital tonight. I have two scheduled Cesareans this evening. If you need anything, call for the nurse or walk out to the nurse's station," Dr. Warren explained before leaving. "Hopefully, she will begin to respond to the medications. At this time, it's waiting. I'm sorry."

Eric was relieved that Lana had slept through Dr. Warren's visit. He was sure that if she had been awake, it would only have been cause for more worry. Lana definitely didn't need more stress. It was going to be a long, tense night. Deciding to ask for a blanket and pillow, Eric went to the nurse's station. Walking back to Lana's room with both items, Eric was happy to see that Lana was finally awake.

"Hey, Babe, I was scared you might have decided to go back to the hotel," Lana questioned.

"Lana, give a guy a little credit. There's no way that I'm leaving you tonight. I just went out to the nurse's station to get something to make me more comfortable tonight. I'm afraid this chair isn't very comfortable," Eric laughed.

Especially after hearing what the doctor had to say, there was no way in hell he was leaving.

"Eric, have you had dinner?" she questioned.

"Sweetheart, please don't worry about me. I'm fine. How do you feel?"

"Well," she hesitated. "I've still got those cramps. I thought the medication was supposed to stop those. They're still really painful."

"Dr. Warren came by to check on you while you were sleeping. He said they were going to increase the medications."

"Did he say anything else?"

"No. Only the fact that he's going to be in the hospital tonight. He's got a couple of C-Sections scheduled."

"Did he mention anything about the baby?"

"No. Sweetheart, nothing has changed. Harvey and Megan stopped by to visit. They brought you those gorgeous flowers. Megan also gave you some magazines. They'll stop by tomorrow," Eric quickly mentioned trying to change the subject.

"I remember Harvey being here, but I must have fallen asleep before Megan came to visit."

"Trust me. They completely understood. You needed your rest."

"Babe, why don't you go down to the cafeteria and get something to eat? It's getting late, and I'm sure you haven't had anything to eat today."

"Actually, coffee does sound good. Can I bring you anything?"

"No. I'm not hungry."

"Okay. I won't be gone long. I'll probably just grab a burger and coffee. I love you," Eric smiled, giving her a quick kiss.

He was only gone for about an hour. However, things had drastically changed when he walked in from the cafeteria. Lana was writhing in pain, and the alarms on the monitors were beeping.

"Oh my God, Lana, what's wrong?" Eric panicked.

"Eric, I've got the worst cramps ever. They're taking my breath away."

Suddenly, the room was filled with medical personnel.

"Sir, I'm sorry. We're going to have to ask you to leave. There's a waiting room at the end of the hall. Someone will be down to speak with you."

"I'm not leaving. I'm Eric Kolbeck, the baby's father," he demanded.

"Mr. Kolbeck, I'm truly sorry, but you must leave. There is nothing you can do. The waiting room is at the end of the hall," the nurse reiterated.

"Her blood pressure is plummeting," one of the nurses stated loudly.

Standing outside the door, Eric overheard the nurse.

"Oh, my God, please tell me what is happening," Eric asked again in disbelief. Please," Eric begged with tears in his eyes.

However, he knew without being informed they were losing their first child. I'm sorry, we need to get her into surgery. Someone will be down to speak with you."

Watching as Lana was transferred to a gurney and rushed out of the room and down the dim hallway, Eric felt as if his knees were going to give way. "How could something happen so fast?" he uttered to himself.

"Sir, there is a chapel on the first floor. It's very private and might offer you some comfort," the nurse suggested putting her arms around him.

"Thanks."

Not fully understanding the process of what was happening with Lana, Eric was overwhelmed. The fact they were losing their first child was devastating.

"Immediately, Eric took the elevator downstairs. Finding the chapel, he walked up to the altar and dropped to his knees.

"Oh God, you know it's been a while since we've talked, but I'm begging you, please don't let anything happen to Lana. God, she's all I have. She's

all I've ever wanted. Please, I'm pleading, don't take them both. I can't live without her. You just took my mom. Please don't take Lana," Eric bitterly sobbed.

Getting up, he collapsed into the front pew. Bowing his head, he honestly didn't care if he lived or died. He merely had to know that Lana would be alright. Finding a box of Kleenex under the pew, he pulled one of the tissues from the box and wiped his eyes. Taking a moment to regain his composure, Eric sat in silence. There was nothing more he could do. At this point, it was up to a higher power. After a few minutes of meditating and prayer, he finally decided to take the elevator back to the waiting room on the second floor and wait for Lana to return.

The waiting room seemed like the loneliest place on earth as he took a seat in one of the chairs. He had never felt more abandoned or alone. Looking up at the clock on the wall, it was only 7:30 p.m. This time last night, they were looking at baby clothes. Lana was happy, and their world was perfect. How could things have changed so drastically and so fast? Nothing could have ever prepared him for such heartbreak.

After what seemed like an eternity, Dr. Warren walked into the waiting room.

"Mr. Kolbeck, I'm sorry for your loss. There was nothing further that could have been done to prevent the miscarriage. Often they are spontaneous. Miss Harris is young, and even though it might not seem comforting at this time, there is nothing to stop her from having children in the future. We were able to stop the bleeding with minimal loss of blood. She's asleep now, but she'll be fine, and I expect a full recovery. We'll keep her overnight. She could go home as soon as tomorrow. I'll check on her in the morning. Right now, Miss Harris is still in the recovery room. As soon as she comes out of the anesthesia, she'll be brought back to her room. Again, you have my condolences."

Deciding to make the dreaded phone calls to family and friends, Eric thought it best to get them out of the way while Lana was still in the recovery room. There was no need to involve her.

Calling Harvey first, it appeared he took the news really hard. Becoming a grandpa was evidently a role he was anxious to play. Eric could hear Harvey's heart literally breaking over the phone.

Next, he called Megan. He hated giving her the news over the phone. He knew she would be alone, and there would be no one to console her. Completely breaking down, Megan was speechless. There was no sound other than her muffled cries. Eric cried with her. Asking her to be strong for Lana, Eric had one final request. He would make arrangements with the hotel concierge to allow Megan entry to their hotel suite. Eric needed Megan to stop by the hotel and return all the purchases for the baby. Thankfully, she promised to go over early the following day before Lana came home.

Finally, he called Karen and Jake, the most challenging call. They were both truly devastated. After recently losing Kathie, it was like reopening an old wound. However, they both promised to be there for Lana, helping in every possible way to heal, recover, and move forward. Eric knew if Lana chose not to stay in Vegas, the ranch would be a quiet, safe place for her to recuperate.

After the calls were made, Eric was anxious to return to Lana's room. He wanted to be there when she was brought back from the recovery room. Eric's heart was breaking into a million pieces as he slowly walked down the dim, narrow hallway. However, he vowed to be strong. He had to get Lana through the worst heartbreak of her life.

Walking into Lana's room, he saw that she hadn't yet been brought down from recovery. The room was dimly lit, and a feeling of dread and sadness overtook him. Tears gently rolled down his face as he sat down in the chair by the window. He would never understand why they lost their precious baby, but he had to be strong enough for both of them.

Finally, Lana was brought in. She appeared to be sleeping. Walking over to her bedside, she sensed his presence and slowly opened her eyes.

"Eric, we lost our precious baby," Lana cried softly. "I'll never get to see our sweet baby's face. I'll never get to hold our baby or touch his soft skin. We'll never see his precious smile or watch him grow up," she sobbed relentlessly. "I'll never know if he resembled you."

Eric leaned over the bed with tears flooding down his face. Pulling Lana into his arms, they mourned the loss of their first child. There were no words. Sadness and tragedy consumed them. They wept as an unforeseeable tragedy rocked their world. Eric held Lana in his arms.

Life could never prepare a person for this depth of loss, this depth of grief, or true despair. Today their lives were forever changed and not in a way one would hope to remember. At this moment, thoughts of every birthday, every holiday, every milestone, every moment they would never have with their sweet baby devastated them.

The following morning Lana was released from the hospital. Her emotions were all over the place. She appeared to be coming apart at the seams on their drive back to the hotel.

"Eric, I'm leaving. I can't stay here."

"Sweetheart, what are you saying? Are you leaving me or Vegas or both?" he panicked. "Lana, I'm just as depressed as you. Trust me. You are not in this by yourself. For heaven's sake, that was my baby too."

"Eric, I love you, but I'm not sure about anything right now. I need some time to be alone. I'm leaving Vegas. I'm sorry."

"Lana, I love you more than life itself. Babe, I'm totally committed to this tournament. I've got two more weeks in Vegas. Winning this tournament is paramount to our financial future. I can win this. I can't explain it, but I'm confident. I can't leave with you. I'm sorry. I have to know that you understand, that you're on board. Babe, please don't do this. Don't do this to us. We just lost our baby. I can't lose you too. Lana, you have no idea how much I need you," Eric pleaded. "Sweetheart, I have an idea. Why don't you go back to the ranch? Karen and Jake would love nothing more than having you back with them. You can stay at the ranch until the tournament is over. I can't think of a better place for you to recuperate. The fresh air will be good for you. Trust me. They loved this baby. Don't you think they are hurting too? Would you do this for me? I promise I'll fly home as soon as the tournament is over. I'll leave that same night."

Eric was desperate. He was at the end of his rope, and the ranch seemed to offer the best chance of them staying together. Tragedies often end relationships. There was no way he would ever give up on her or what they had together. He was determined to do whatever was within his power to keep her in his life. Throwing in the chance of winning the poker tournament and eight million dollars was almost inconceivable. It would be a hard pill to swallow. However, unbeknownst to Lana, in his heart, he knew that he would do anything to keep her in his life, even dropping out of the tournament. He whispered a prayer that she would never ask that of him. It was like a game of cards. Although he loved her and would do anything, he wasn't willing at this point to let her see his hand. The only chance of having everything they ever wanted in life depended upon her answer. Biting his nails, he waited pensively for her reply. The next few seconds were the longest of his life.

"Eric, you know how much I love you," Lana began with tears in her eyes. "The day we met in the casino and the evening I made the wish at the fountains, everything led me to you. Following you to Alaska, your stupid shack, every moment we've shared, I've fallen more and more in love with you. I'm not about to let you go. I love you, and if you feel that going to the ranch would be the best thing for me to do, I'll go. Babe, I love you enough to let you stay behind. However, eight million dollars is a lot of money. You better win," she smiled.

"Damn, Babe, you had me biting my nails. I thought you were leaving me," Eric grinned. "Come over here and kiss me."

"Eric, you're driving."

Immediately, pulling over at the next exit, Eric stopped the car. Pulling her into his arms, he kissed her with every ounce of his being. They were oblivious to their surroundings. He'd just been given a second chance at having everything he ever wanted in life. The first time was the evening Lana walked on board his return flight to Alaska. They had been through the worst tragedy two people could face. Now more than ever, he needed to change their future by winning the tournament.

Chapter Thirteen

Entering their hotel suite at Caesars Palace, there were no traces of the shopping bags containing the purchases for the baby. Instead, Megan had taken care of making all the returns.

"Eric, I feel completely exhausted. I just want to sleep the day away," Lana frowned as she headed upstairs to the bedroom.

"Sweetheart, you sleep. I'll join you in a few minutes. I have a few phone calls to make.

Calling Harvey, arrangements were made to fly Lana back to Reno on his private Lear Jet the following morning. Staying at the Circle K would offer her the peace and tranquility she so desperately needed. No one could possibly take better care of her than Karen and Jake. She needed time to heal both mentally and physically.

Next, Eric called Karen.

Leaving a message after no answer, Eric had no doubts this plan was for the best.

"Hey, sis. Harvey is flying Lana home in the morning. I know that you will take great care of her. She's depressed, and it's just going to take time for her to heal and recover. Harvey has arranged a limo to pick her up at the airport and drive her out to the Circle K. There will be no need for either you or Jake to meet the plane. Sis, please give me a call in the morning when she arrives. Talk with you soon."

After making all the arrangements, Eric ran upstairs. Walking into the bedroom, he heard muffled sounds. Lana was crying softly with her head buried in a pillow. Pushing back the covers, Eric quickly slipped into bed next to her. Pulling her into his arms, he lovingly kissed her forehead. Words of comfort didn't come easy. He was hurting, and there were no words that would ever bring back their precious child.

"Babe, please don't cry. I know how hard this is for you. Trust me. I'm hurting as well. But, together, we're going to get through this. I promise," he whispered, pulling back strands of her damp hair. Holding her tight against his chest, he felt helpless. "Lana, Harvey has made arrangements with his flight crew to fly you home in the morning. Once you arrive, a limo will take you out to the ranch. Karen and Jake are expecting you, and I will call you every day."

Looking down at the love of his life, she had fallen asleep. It was for the best. There was nothing he could do. But, there was no way he was leaving her alone. Turning out the lights, he tenderly held her in his arms.

The following day, Eric and Harvey rode with Lana out to the airport. As much as Eric hated the thoughts of her leaving, he knew there was no other choice. Lana had made it very clear she no longer wanted to remain in Vegas. It held too much pain for her.

"Sweetheart, I love you. Please call me as soon as you arrive. I promise to check on you every day. God, I'm going to miss you," Eric smiled, kissing her passionately before she ascended the steps to the Lear Jet.

"Babe, I love you too. I'll call you soon. You better win."

"Lana, no worries," Harvey grinned. "I'll take great care of Eric. He's going to win the tournament. Of that, I have no doubt."

Watching as the jet rolled to the end of the runway and lifted skyward, it carried within it the love of his life. He was more determined than ever not to disappoint her. He had a tournament to win.

Harvey kept Eric busy and away from his thoughts of losing the baby, which still haunted him. He knew that Roy's DNA pulsed through Eric's veins. Eric had everything he needed to win the poker championship easily.

The following morning, Harvey stopped by Eric's room, bringing with him the pungent odor of his Cuban cigars.

"Hey, Son, are you ready. There's a poker table reserved for us at the Golden Nugget, my favorite hangout on Freemont Street. I've called in a few favors with some of my old buddies. They are the best in the world of poker, and I simply need you to sharpen your skills. Now, please don't misunderstand me. I know your skills and abilities, and you can easily hold your own against the entire lot of them. Still, it never hurts to get familiar with their unique strategies. These old buzzards are sharp, but I'm looking forward to the shock on their faces as they are forced to fold their cards," Harvey grinned, taking a long draw on his cigar. "If you're ready, I think we have just enough time to get breakfast. How do steak and eggs sound? I need a cup of coffee," he smiled, walking toward the door.

Stepping inside the limo, they were soon on their way to the Peppermill Restaurant for a hearty breakfast before arriving at the Golden Nugget on Freemont Street.

Walking in, everyone recognized Harvey. He was almost a permanent fixture. Escorting him to his favorite booth, the waitress smiled.

"Good morning Harvey. Do you need a menu, or is it your usual steak and eggs?" she asked, showing them to a booth near the back

"Good morning Shirley. The usual, but my friend will probably need a menu."

"Okay. I'll be right back with your coffee," Shirley replied, handing Eric a menu.

"Geez, Harvey, do you know everyone in Vegas?" Eric laughed.

"Well, certainly not these days, but years ago when your father and I were on the circuit, Vegas was a much different place. I have to say. I miss those days. You young folks will never know the Vegas I fell in love with. But, I digress, so what looks good?" Harvey questioned as Shirley returned with their coffee. "The blueberry pancakes are phenomenal."

"Suppose I'll have the blueberry pancakes with sausage and a side order of scrambled eggs. I'm sure they have to be good if you recommend them," Eric smiled.

Enjoying breakfast, Harvey inquired about Lana.

"So, how's my girl doing? Son, I don't have to tell you how sorry I am. Hell, that had to be hard. How's Lana coping with being back at the Circle K?"

"Okay, I suppose. Life certainly threw us a curveball. You know some marriages don't make it when going through such difficult times," Eric sadly mentioned. "But we're doing good, and Lana seems to be adjusting to life at the ranch. Jake has been a big help and Karen."

"Well, I'm certainly glad to hear that. But, don't you worry, you'll have a house full of kids before you know it. I can't wait to take on the role of grandpa."

"Harvey, you'll be the best. Of that, I have no doubt," Eric smiled, taking a sip of coffee.

After enjoying breakfast, they were finally on their way to the Golden Nugget.

"Geez, this place is almost as old as you," Eric teased as they walked inside the casino. Making their way through the labyrinth of slots, Harvey led him to a table near the back after stopping by the teller cage to purchase a rack of chips.

Approaching the table, four older gentlemen who appeared to be about the same age as Harvey looked up from the table.

"Hey, gents, this is Eric. He's a friend of mine. I thought you guys might teach him a thing or two about the game of poker," Harvey grinned.

He had deliberately not mentioned Eric's last name, not wishing to divulge Eric's connection to Roy. Everyone seated at the table had known and played poker with Roy Kolbeck. Harvey smiled, knowing they didn't stand a chance to beat Eric at a game of poker. Nevertheless, he found it amusing, lighting up his cigar. Harvey knew these guys possessed the best skills at challenging Eric's abilities.

"Eric, this is James, don't worry about him. He's not the one to stress over," Harvey laughed.

"Thanks, Harvey. I'll let the young man figure that one out. You do know he's known for lying," James laughed.

This is Al. I must say he's a pretty good poker player. I taught him everything he knows."

"Right. Nice to meet you," Al grinned.

Next is Jerry. He's brilliant. We toured together on the WSOP."

"Thanks. Any friend of Harvey's is a friend of mine. Take a seat," Jerry smiled.

And last, next to Jerry, is Wilford. But, again, don't let the cowboy hat and boots fool you. He's a rancher from Elko, Nevada, but trust me, even though he spends almost every day with his cattle, he eats and breaths poker," Harvey laughed.

"Okay, Harvey, did you bring the kid here to chat or to play poker, Wilford roared, lighting up a cigarette. Are you going to join us?"

"Well, I hadn't planned on getting in the game, but on second thought, why not?" Harvey laughed. "Eric, don't mind me. My skills are no longer that of a WSOP poker player."

"Right. Remember, I told you, Harvey lies," James grinned, taking a sip of bourbon.

Finally, after all the introductions and mindless banter, the men placed their chips in the center of the table as the dealer opened a pack of cards, dealing them out clockwise around the table.

Eric knew the guys seated around the table brought years of valuable skills to the game despite Harvey's introductions. However, he looked forward to eliminating them one by one, including Harvey.

The first round of cards that Eric was dealt held nothing significant, not even a pair. His disappointment was visible as he lit a cigar.

After an hour, two men were eliminated and left the game. Eric's stack of chips grew larger as his luck changed.

Finally, Eric smiled, watching as Harvey was eliminated, leaving only himself, Wilford, and James. After James exited the game, Eric faced Wilford, his last challenge. He wiped the sweat from his brow and held his breath, picking up his cards. Astonishingly, he was dealt a royal flush, the Ace, King, Queen, Jack, and Ten of hearts. "Thanks, Dad," he whispered silently under his breath. He had managed to eliminate the men seated at the table over a few hours. Harvey smiled, knowing without a doubt that Eric could easily win the WSOP. Eric's innate abilities inherited from his dad would easily see him through the tournament and be announced as the winner.

"Son, I must say, you made me proud," Harvey grinned.

"Great game," Wilford remarked.

"Well, I think this calls for a celebration. So let's cash in those chips and grab us a steak and some bourbon."

Cashing in the chips, Eric picked up an extra ten thousand. Then, handing his winnings over to Harvey, who had bankrolled the little endeavor, he politely declined.

"Son, I think you more than earned it. Consider it a financial contribution toward those kids you'll soon be raising."

"Thanks, Harvey."

"Now, let's get out of here. I know a great steak house."

Harvey was an epicurean. It appeared the two most important things on his mind after poker were cigars and food.

In the following weeks, Eric entered numerous poker games. Missing Lana wasn't easy, and playing poker kept his focus on the game and away from his worries. Winning his way up through the tournaments, he had won the ten thousand dollars for the buy-in and a seat at the final WSOP final tournament.

"Well, Son, are you ready?" Harvey questioned as they made their way down to the casino floor and outside.

Entering the limo, they were on their way to breakfast at the Peppermill. Again, it appeared Harvey was a creature of habit. Afterward, they would continue to the Rio Hotel, where the WSOP final tournament would be held.

Enjoying his usual steak and eggs at the Peppermill Restaurant, Harvey knew the stress Eric would soon face.

"Are you nervous?" Harvey questioned.

"A bit, but not much. I've worked really hard to get here, and as I see it, I've earned a seat at the table," Eric answered, sipping his coffee.

"You've got this, son. Trust me. I'm sure Roy is up there cheering for you, and you'll make him proud. Heck, you'll make us both proud," Harvey grinned, finishing his steak.

"Well, if you're ready, we should head over to the Rio," Harvey mentioned.

"As ready as I'll ever be, I suppose," Eric smiled.

Arriving at the Rio, it was a sea of people. Reporters, news crews, spectators, participants who had bought in, and hotel guests. The casino exuded excitement.

"Son, I see a few old friends. I wish you the best of luck. I'll be watching," Harvey said, walking toward a group of men and their wives. "No worries, kid. You've got this. It'll be the most exciting one hundred twenty minutes of your life," he added.

"Thanks, Harvey. I'm going to sign in and get my table assignment. I'll meet up with you afterward. This is it," Eric grinned.

Walking away, Harvey knew Eric had everything within himself to win. Roy's genes, abilities, and strategies. He also knew Eric needed to be in the game mentally. He could only pray that Roy might give him some heavenly guidance from above.

Harvey took a seat in the spectator's area and watched on pins and needles as Eric slowly won his way into the lead. With every minute that passed, Harvey clutched his chest, thinking he would have a heart attack as he watched Eric come closer to winning. Finally, after two long hours filled with tension, Harvey held his breath as Eric easily eliminated the last player from the table. Eric Kolbeck had won the WSOP just like his father before him. His name would always be synonymous with the other winners. But most importantly, Eric Kolbeck had just won eight million dollars.

Finally, after endless photos and interviews with reporters, Eric was ready to leave the Rio Hotel. There was only one thing on his mind.

"Congratulations, Son. So, what's next?" Harvey grinned.

"Harvey, could we possibly fly back to Reno this evening? I need to see Lana. I want to tell her in person."

"Say no more. I'll call and have the jet ready."

Entering the limo, they were soon on their way to the airport after checking out of the hotel.

As the plane touched down on the runway in Reno, Eric knew his life, Lana's, Jake's, Karen's, and the entire Circle K was about to change forever. No more would they have the worries of upkeep, including ranch hands.

Karen had made provisions for Lana to stay in Eric's former bedroom. She knew it would offer a place of comfort for her to rest. Staying at the Circle K had been cathartic, and life had finally reappeared in Lana's smiles. She had even started to make peace with the idea that if Eric lost the tournament for some horrific reason, it would not bring their world crashing down around them. The love they shared was strong enough to get them through anything, even the loss of their first child. Lana was finally at peace, not only with herself but with the world around her. Turning in for the night late one evening, Lana had no idea how suddenly her life was about to change in the wee early hours of the morning.

Unlocking the front door, Eric quietly ran up the stairs hoping no one heard him enter the house. There was only one person he wanted to see, and she was sleeping peacefully upstairs. Silently, Eric slipped into bed, pulling Lana into his arms. Gently kissing her awake, he whispered with a smile.

"Sweetheart, we won."

Prologue

On a warm summer afternoon the following year, as the wind blew briskly through her hair, Lana and Eric stood together hand in hand on a cliff above the Grand Canyon. Looking only at each other, unaware of the breathtaking scenery surrounding them, they took vows to love each other until they drew their last breath.

As Harvey, Gunner, Norman, and Megan witnessed their union, there was never a doubt they were meant to be together forever.

Wearing a gorgeous Alencon lace wedding gown, it clearly revealed her very pregnant profile. As the breeze lifted her long flowing veil, they were pronounced, *man and wife*.

"Babe, I think my water just broke," Lana whispered.

"Oh my God. We've got to get you to the hospital," Eric panicked.

Helping Lana inside one of the two sleek silver helicopters sitting on the precipice, they were on their way back to Las Vegas to welcome their new baby girl. Apparently, she was ready to make her appearance on their wedding day.

Reaching the Women's Hospital, where only a few months previous their lives had been rocked by tragedy, it would now welcome their second child, a beautiful baby girl.

"Okay. Just one more push," Dr. Warren urged with a smile.

Within moments, the unforgettable cries of a newborn filled the room. Placing the precious baby on Lana's chest, tears of happiness flooded her face. The memories of this day would never be forgotten.

"Sweetheart, she looks like you," Lana beamed proudly.

Kissing his daughter, Eric whispered.

"Welcome to the world, Kaitlyn Kolbeck."